Gid and the Arborinium Prophecy

Andy Gee

To Izzie. Really hope you enjoy this. Andy Gee

instant
ap▢stle

First published in Great Britain in 2013

Instant Apostle
The Hub
3-5 Rickmansworth Road
Watford
Herts
WD18 OGX

British Library Cataloguing-in-Publication Data

A catalogue record for this book is available from the British Library

This book and all other Instant Apostle books are available from Instant Apostle:

Website: www.instantapostle.com
E-mail: info@instantapostle.com

ISBN 978-1-909728-11-0

Printed in Great Britain

Contents

Chapter 1: Watching

Two pairs of tired but vigilant eyes peered out. Their owners crouched and waited patiently, hidden from view in the dense bushes that lay at the foot of the hill. It had been the same every night for the last year. Every night they would sit and wait, no matter what the weather. It had to be this way: they had been chosen to keep watch on the hill, and they knew he would arrive this year. The prophecy had spoken of the year, the time and the place. The warrior would appear before the year was out, in the night, on this hill – and every night they waited faithfully for his arrival.

Gideon, or Gid as his friends called him, was a normal kid. His dark brown hair was always neat when he left for school and wild by the time he arrived, and more often than not he had a cut or a bruise on one of his knees and dirt under his fingernails. He was what teachers referred to as 'a pleasant lad', but his school report was always full of comments like 'could do better' or 'must try harder' and 'often daydreams when he should be working'.

This was all true, and Gid knew it, only he didn't want to change. He was happy knowing that if he needed to, if he really wanted to, he could probably achieve anything. He didn't see himself as lazy but rather as having potential. Gid always felt that he would probably do something amazing one day, something that would mean people would recognise him in the street and ask for his autograph, but right now he was happy just being a kid. For now he would climb trees, play war games, make dens, swing on ropes – and daydream. Everything else could wait until he was older.

So far Gid's day had been pretty much like any other. His mum had woken him from his dreams at 7:30, given him the usual chocolate-coated cereal and two slices of toast (nearly burnt, with plenty of butter), made sure he had washed (even though he was 11), and bustled him out of the house. He had met his friends at the bus stop and talked about the normal stuff and then jumped on the school bus which, as usual, was on time. In science, his first lesson of the day, he had learnt about the body and how it changes and found out that his eyes were still brown, he was still skinny and in height he was still a little shorter than average. Maths and English had gone by in a boring blur, and a cross-country run in PE had finished off the school day in soggy style. The only odd thing had been the dream that his mum had roused him from this morning.

Every night for the last year he had dreamed the same dream. He would fall from the night sky and smash into the ground near the top of a grass-covered hill because he didn't know how to use his wings. Where the wings came from he didn't know, but they were always there. After recovering from the crash he would struggle to his feet, readjust his leathery wings and make his way towards the summit, and then he would wake up back in his room with his mum telling him that his breakfast was ready. Every night the same thing. Until last night, that is. Everything had been the same up to the point where he would walk towards the summit of the hill, but this time, for some reason, before he set off he had turned around and suddenly felt afraid. He wasn't alone. Somebody or something was watching him from somewhere near the foot of the hill – he was sure of it – but before he could decide what to do next his mum was once again in his room, shaking him awake.

What would happen tonight? It bothered him – would he have the same old dream or would he find out who or what was lurking out of sight at the bottom of the hill before he awoke? It had been on his mind all day and hadn't gone unnoticed by his teachers or his friends. He was always easily distracted, but today he had been more vacant than usual.

That evening, his mind wasn't on his homework or the television – he hadn't even bothered with his computer games and had barely touched his favourite meal of spaghetti bolognese. His mum had sensed that something was wrong and had said she would book him an appointment with the doctor if he was still out of sorts in the morning. For the first time in his life Gid was afraid to fall asleep. He loved his dreams because they were a way to escape from his normal life and live in a world where anything was possible. Sometimes his dreams were so real he wasn't sure if he had really been to sleep at all! Tonight was different, though: he didn't want to fall asleep; he didn't want to know what had been watching him. He decided there and then that he would stay awake all night. If he was tired tomorrow his mum would probably take him to the doctor and he would at least have a day off school. Then by tomorrow night this would probably all have passed; he would fall asleep and dream that he was a ninja or that he was flying (always a good dream!). But not tonight. Tonight, sleep would just have to wait. It wouldn't be that hard to stay awake, he thought. After all, he had a computer, he could watch TV and he could maybe even finish his homework if he got really desperate.

Gid sat with his mum and watched a disturbing wildlife programme about the battle for life between crocodiles and zebras. It ended with the zebra finally losing to the stronger croc and having its neck noisily broken before being devoured. The news followed, with updates on the recent war and the story of a teenager from America called Brett Johnson, who went to sleep at the age of ten and slipped into a coma. He was now 18 and the doctors were no clearer about why it had happened. TV at night was always a sure-fire way to keep any kid awake, and he was now satisfied that falling asleep would be almost impossible.

Gid said goodnight to his mum, had a kind of a wash and went to his room. He loaded a game on the computer where he was in command of a Roman army that was currently conquering Britain, but he had reached a part that seemed almost impossible to beat. The Romans were in a fort and were being bombarded by local tribes; all he had to do was keep the invaders out and defend his general, but this was proving to be very difficult. Gid decided to lie down on his bed, just for a minute, to come up with a plan. He wouldn't fall asleep – he just needed to rest his eyes and think about how to win.

—

Chapter 2: The dream

From above the clouds the moon seemed far bigger and brighter than when it had to contend with street lights and pollution from the towns and cities. Even its colour seemed more vivid, and its ice-blue glow lit up the clouds below like a vast calm ocean. For a moment, Gid felt as though he could almost touch Heaven.

'Hang on a minute, why is the moon blue? And more to the point, how on earth am I floating above the clouds?'

Reality slammed into him like a bull in a frenzied charge. 'Not again. I must have fallen asleep,' he muttered angrily to himself. Suddenly his stomach started to dance to a tune that his body couldn't keep up with. The clouds were rapidly getting closer and Gid was spinning headfirst out of control towards them.

'My wings – I have to learn how to use them quickly, or this could be really messy.' He tried to get his wings to spread out, concentrating as hard as he could; he had to come up with something. 'Please, come on, spread out, do something... spread out... flap, glide, anything!' Gid yelled in desperation. He was now spinning faster and the wind was tearing at his arms and legs, filling his eyes with tears and making it almost impossible to breathe. The clouds were upon him now and he knew that somewhere not too far below him the ground would be racing up to meet him – this was not a reunion he was looking forward to. Anger and frustration at his hopeless situation coursed through Gid's body.

'I won't give up. I must fly somehow. THIS IS NOT FAIR, WHY WON'T YOU WORK? COME ON, WORK!' he yelled, as he passed through the clouds.

His arms were numb, his face was stinging and he was still falling, spinning and flipping over and over. The world was

11

suddenly below his feet and then just as quickly back above his head. He couldn't stop himself; the ground was getting closer and closer, and he could make out the dark shapes of trees and what looked like a big hill surrounded by bushes. Soon he would hit the earth, and at this speed he was sure he would explode on impact like an old tomato being smashed by a speeding car.

'One last chance,' thought Gid. He closed his eyes, pictured his wings spreading out, pretended he was somewhere safe and tried to relax. Suddenly the leathery wings sprang to life and he could feel strange new muscles working in his back as they spread out. He wasn't quite flying but he had slowed down a little. He was now only around 50 metres from the rapidly approaching ground, but he was falling a little more slowly and his head was pointing skywards. Just a few more metres before impact; he was still going too fast.

'Nooo, this is really going to…' SLAM!

'…hurt,' he groaned, as he struggled to his feet and readjusted his leathery wings. The crash had winded him badly, but after initial checks he was relieved to find that nothing was broken, both feet pointed in the correct direction, his neck still worked, both arms were still in place and every finger moved. In fact, there was barely any indication that he had just fallen almost a kilometre from somewhere above the clouds. A year ago, a short tumble from a tree had left Gid in plaster from his thumb to his elbow, and yet now, apart from aching a little, everything was fine.

He sat down to take it all in. He was sat near the summit of a small hill, and below him he could just about make out a few trees and a large cluster of bushes. He had wings, although they weren't as impressive as the pictures he had seen of angels – these were smaller and reminded him of bats' wings. They were brown in colour and slightly torn in places, and from his experience he didn't think they worked very well. He was clothed in thick leathery armour, similar in appearance to a Roman soldier's, apart from the colours – there were no fancy reds and silvers; everything was simply a different shade of brown. He had a bronze breastplate over a brown tunic, and long leather gauntlets with studded knuckles protected his forearms and hands, while a short brown animal-hide skirt covered his thighs.

'This isn't right,' he moaned. 'Wings I can cope with, even this odd armour, but not a skirt – that's just wrong. The gladiator guy from the movies could get away with it. He was solid, and a brutal killer, but my legs are tiny, and I've never even so much as punched someone.'

Long brown boots covered the rest of his legs, and a short sword with an evil-pointed end, again similar to that of a Roman's, hung in a scabbard from a large belt around his waist. Whatever this dream was, it seemed likely that it was going to involve some fighting.

Suddenly, the feeling was back. Something was watching him. It was too dark to see anything clearly but Gid could feel the hairs on the back of his neck rising. He turned around. Determinedly, he placed his hand on the leather-bound hilt of his sword – if something was down there he wasn't about to find out without being ready. He couldn't make out any shapes apart from the bushes, and he could hear nothing apart from his breathing.

Curiosity gripped Gid; he had to know whether there was anything in the shadows. He took a deep breath as a bead of sweat dripped off his forehead and his hand clenched more tightly around his sword as he drew it from the scabbard.

'It's just a dream. I'll be fine,' he whispered to himself, unconvincingly. Gid slowly made his way down the hill. Suddenly, a hot stabbing pain hit the unprotected part of his left leg – then another. His leg went numb and, before he had time to react, the same pain shot through his right leg. He looked down, afraid of what he might see. Just above his knees on both legs, four fluffy-ended darts stuck out, two in each thigh. Both legs were now numb, and by the second he was losing the feeling in his whole body. Any moment now he would black out. As he began to fall over he glimpsed two dark figures moving towards him from the bushes. Gid's last thought was that he had been right – something, or someone, had been watching him.

Chapter 3: Arborinium

'What have you done? You idiot!' the larger winged creature bellowed furiously as the smaller one tried to release himself from the other's iron grip.

'I panicked,' he whimpered. 'We were supposed to watch and wait. Our tribe has done this for generations; I didn't think he would actually show up. He's the stuff of legend, an awesome warrior, a warrior who, I might add, was heading towards us with his sword drawn.'

The larger creature was unimpressed. 'You used your blowpipe and hit him with four sleeping darts – that's enough to sedate a herd of Hogboars. I told you to stay calm. I knew it was a bad idea getting you involved with this.'

'I just...' the smaller creature started.

'I know what you JUST – you JUST panicked. If you weren't my brother I might JUST run you through with my sword right now.'

They had received their orders: sit, wait and watch. That's what they had to do. If he ever appeared, one of them was supposed to run and tell the Elders while the other was to watch him and do whatever was necessary to keep him there until the Elders arrived. They had successfully completed the last part – their hero was going nowhere fast.

'Ok. Here's what we do,' said the bigger one. 'First, you check if he's still alive and remove the darts. You shot him, so you can sort that out, at least. If he is alive and wakes up, he may kill you; that would be one less problem to deal with.'

The smaller creature moved carefully towards the motionless body. 'He's breathing!' he exclaimed with relief, and very carefully removed the darts. The larger creature walked over to them. 'We'd better take him back, and you'd better pray that he keeps breathing.' Then he strapped their unconscious warrior to his back and headed towards home.

Last night's dream had seemed so real! Gid had been sure that he could actually feel the wind on his face as he was falling, and now his legs both felt a little numb, his head was fuzzy and every part of him was aching – even his wings.

'I still have wings!' he thought, shocked. 'What is going on?' Gid slowly opened his eyes, afraid of what he might see. He was in a large, warm bed, covered in furs of some kind, in a small and cosy room. The walls were made from wood – but not planks. It was as if the whole room had been carved out of a huge lump of oak, and it looked to Gid like a small wooden cave. There were two large round windows on the right-hand side of the room, and next to them a small door. The room was about five metres high, and there was a lantern hanging from a domed ceiling high above him. Opposite the windows was another door, and a beam of light from the windows highlighted a painting of mountains above a cool-looking lake. Gid worked out that it must be around midday by the strength of the sun shining through the windows.

'I must still be dreaming.' It seemed the only reasonable explanation, only he felt as if he had just woken up. This really was turning into a very weird dream.

Gid's sword was hanging on a hook on the wall, and below this at the side of the bed was a small table, on which was a wooden beaker full of water. At the side of the bed that was furthest away from the window was a small wooden chest with the clothes that he had been wearing neatly folded on top. A sudden embarrassed fear washed over him.

'Oh please let me be wearing something. I know it's only a dream but I don't want anybody to see me naked!' Gid checked under the sheets and found that he was still wearing his tunic. 'Phew, that would have been a bit embarrassing.'

Wherever he was, it seemed that he was in no immediate danger. He wasn't tied up and they had left his sword with him. 'Well, I'm here, wherever "here" is, and I'm in one piece, at least.' He decided to take a look out of the window to see if he could get any clue as to where he was.

'Whoa!' As he tried to stand, both his legs felt weak. He wobbled and then started to fall. Gid scrambled wildly with his arms, trying to catch hold of the small table in a desperate attempt to stay on his feet. The table gave up the fight to stay upright and flew backwards with Gid, followed by the water-filled wooden beaker. Gid hit the floor with a dull thud and quickly threw his left arm out to catch the beaker, managing to do so without spilling a single drop. 'That was smooth. Man, am I cool?! And people have the cheek to call me clumsy,' he said sarcastically, as he tried to lift himself back onto his jelly legs.

Suddenly the door burst open. The beaker and its contents were once again airborne. This time the water decided to leave its container and head directly for Gid's face.

'He's alive, and um, a bit damp,' shouted a very nervous voice.

'Lucky for you,' replied another.

'Look, I have already apologised, to you, to the Elders – in fact, to everybody who knows the prophecy. What more can I do?' the first voice moaned defensively.

'It shouldn't have happened in the first place. If you weren't such a coward, none of this…' The second voice tried to sound angry but was cut off mid-flow.

'I may be many things but I'm no coward. Take it back.'

'You panicked because he had a sword. What kind of warrior are you?'

'I'm no coward,' replied an angry voice.

'Whatever you say,' the second voice replied flatly.

Gid was now sprawled face first on the edge of the bed, trying to right himself, whilst his legs uselessly struggled to push against the floor. His legs felt very weak but he wasn't sure that he would have stood up even if he were able to, as

17

this was quickly turning into a heated argument. He heard two swords being drawn and decided that enough was enough.

'Excuse me,' he said, in a slightly irritated yet cautious voice. The argument and scuffle between the two figures in his room came to an abrupt stop.

'Look! I'm sure that your argument is very important, but I was wondering if someone could help me up. I'm struggling a little here. And maybe you would be kind enough to explain to me what on earth is going on – where I am and who you are?'

He'd got their attention now, and was feeling a little nervous.

The two characters put their swords away and apologised to each other. 'Forgive us for being so rude,' said the larger of the two to Gid. 'My name is Rahmon.'

'Nice to meet you, Rahmon,' replied Gid, smiling as he hung on to the rapidly slipping bed covers. 'I'm Gideon, but my friends call me Gid.'

Rahmon stood around two metres tall and was all muscle. His hair was long, braided and a dark shade of green, and his eyes were a cold, stony grey. On his back was a large pair of leathery wings similar in appearance to Gid's. He wore a simple dark brown tunic with green trim around the neck. It was tied in the middle by a large black leather belt that held a long heavy sword. In his right hand he held a sharp and deadly looking spear. Rahmon placed the spear against the wooden wall and walked over to Gid.

'Here, take my hand.' Rahmon held out a huge hand and helped Gid back onto the bed. 'This is Tharik, my younger brother, and the reason that you may be feeling a little groggy.'

Tharik was smaller than Rahmon. He was around the same size as Gid and, like his brother, his hair was a dark shade of green, only he had fewer braids. He had the same colour eyes and was wearing a matching tunic. Tharik blushed and twiddled his thumbs behind his back.

'As my brother said, my name is Tharik, and the reason you may feel groggy is because I shot you with enough sedative to knock out a small army. Please forgive me. I didn't mean to – it's just that you were coming towards us with your sword drawn and I panicked. I'm no coward, but you're the warrior from our prophecy, and I was a little nervous.'

None of this was making much sense to Gid. What was this prophecy, and why did they think he was a warrior? Even though he seemed to be wearing the right clothes, he was sure he had never done anything even slightly warrior-like.

The confusion was obviously showing on Gid's face. 'We'll let the Elders know that you're awake, and when your legs feel stronger we'll take you to them. They will explain everything.' Rahmon and Tharik stood in the doorway, staring and smiling at Gid, like children who had just met their favourite superhero.

'My legs feel stronger already, but before we see the Elders there is something I have to do,' announced Gid in an important tone. Rahmon and Tharik looked at each other, then back at Gid, expectantly.

'If we can help, do let us know. We are at your service,' said Tharik.

'Thank you for your offer but I will be ok on my own, I think.' Tharik tried not to look disappointed – he had messed up and wanted to help now in any way he could.

'I need to get dressed,' laughed Gid.

The two brothers left the room. Gid's immediate reaction was to quickly dress and check for any escape route in case he wasn't as safe as he felt. He tried the door by the windows – it opened but there was no balcony outside; only a sheer drop of hundreds of metres.

'Why would anyone put a door there? I could have died!' He was not exactly convinced about the sanity of the people who made his room. 'Well, it doesn't look as if there's any other way out of this, so I may as well follow them.' He gave up any plan of escape, checked the steadiness of his legs, and nervously walked to the other door to join the others.

Once he was out of the room, the two brothers led him along countless corridors, past hundreds of doors, all of which, like the room Gid had been in, seemed to be carved into the wood. They passed many people like Rahmon and Tharik, none of whom seemed to be particularly surprised or bothered by the sight of the newcomer.

'Not the reaction I was expecting,' he whispered to himself. If he was supposed to be some awesome warrior, the people around here didn't seem to know about it, or if they did, they obviously didn't think it was that big a deal. Ahead of them, Gid could make out a huge circular open space. They came to a wooden walkway that followed the wall round this enormous space. The walls were trees – thousands of them all joined together to make what Gid had mistaken for a room. It wasn't a room at all but was more like a clearing in a forest surrounded by giant trees. Gid stood with his mouth open, taking it all in. They were on a walkway around 150 metres up. The corridor they had emerged from had been cut through the trees, and all the rooms, as he had guessed, were indeed carved out of the wood. Below them there were around 20 or 30 other walkways with corridors opening on to them. The floor of this living cave was made up of thousands of roots that looked to Gid like a nest of giant wooden snakes. Above them were at least 100 or so other walkways marking out each floor and leading up to a giant leafy mouth that allowed the sun to pour in. They were in a mountainous hollow tree that was made up of countless intertwined others, and in this giant structure were at least 150 floors.

'This has to be the world's best ever tree den,' laughed Gid excitedly. Rahmon and Tharik looked at Gid and smiled, saying nothing and letting him enjoy the scenery.

'This is Arborinium, the city of trees and home to our people, the Arbitans,' said Rahmon proudly.

'The Elders are up there,' announced Tharik, pointing towards the opening.

Gid was not looking forward to walking up countless stairs to get there, although he hadn't actually noticed any stairway or rope ladder, or, in fact, anything at all that would lead to the other levels. 'This may sound a bit silly, but how do we get up there?'

Tharik looked from Rahmon to Gid with a puzzled look on his face. 'Um, we fly,' answered Rahmon.

As if to demonstrate, a figure flew past their faces heading to the level directly above them. Gid was worried; how could he tell these two who saw him as a mighty warrior that he couldn't even fly?

'Ok, we'd best be going. Just follow us.' Tharik flew off in the direction of the opening, followed by his older brother.

Gid managed to spread his wings, as naturally as if they were his arms, only now he had no idea what to do. He tried to flap the wings but they just moved awkwardly downwards. 'This is not going to get me to the other levels but I guess at least it's a start.'

He had had many dreams where he was flying, only in them he didn't have to think about it. Maybe that was it; he was just trying too hard. Before he had a chance to try again, Rahmon landed next him. 'Is there a problem?' he asked, 'Only the Elders will be waiting.'

Gid's heart sank and his wings folded back into place. There was no way out of it; he had to tell Rahmon that he couldn't fly. 'I'm a bit new to this. You see, I don't have wings when I'm awake,' he said, both cheeks glowing.

'When you're awake? I'm not really sure what you mean. You have wings now and you are awake.' Rahmon was puzzled.

'I mean really awake. In my own world, when I'm not dreaming, I don't have wings and I can't fly.'

Rahmon was starting to think that this mighty warrior was

a little odd. What did he mean by *really* awake? 'Well, everybody has their first flight some time, and to be honest I was wondering what had happened the night you arrived.'

It hadn't actually been the entrance Rahmon was expecting. Seeing Gid plummet from the clouds and slam into the ground didn't seem fitting for a mighty warrior. But it wasn't Rahmon's place to question or doubt; he was merely there to make sure that Gid made it to the Elders. Besides, there was something about this young one, something hidden; he couldn't work out what it was but he sensed a great power in his small frame. Rahmon nudged Gid towards the edge of the ledge like a mother bird encouraging her chick to take its first flight.

'Just believe,' he said encouragingly 'I know it's in you, and I think you know it too.'

Gid stood with his toes over the edge of the walkway, 150 metres above the ground that would stop his fall. He closed his eyes and spread his wings again, leaning forwards until his own weight tipped him over the lip of the walkway. He had 120 metres to learn to fly, 80 metres. Gid tried again to get his wings to flap. Now 60 metres. His right wing flapped on its own, making him spin. With 40 metres to go, his right wing stopped and he plummeted once more. He was now only 20 metres from the floor; he had to do something quickly. He closed his eyes and imagined himself flying towards the upper walkways, gaining speed as he passed each floor. Gid kept his eyes closed, readying himself for impact, but it didn't come. He opened his eyes and found himself hovering about three metres above the ground, being kept there by his rapidly flapping wings. He looked up, focused on the upper levels and flew, each floor passing him in a blur.

'I'm flying,' he yelled. 'I'm really flying!' He was sure he would wake up any second, ruining the best part of his dream.

Rahmon caught up with him, beaming. 'I knew you had it in you,' he said proudly.

They flew to the uppermost walkway where Tharik was waiting. 'What kept you?' he asked. Without waiting for an answer, he headed towards a small, unmarked door. He knocked several times in some kind of secret code. The door opened, seemingly on its own, and a deep voice from inside the room beckoned them to enter.

Chapter 4: The Elders

The room was long and had a low ceiling. Along each wall were paintings of old-looking faces, and every face had a pair of eyes that seemed to follow Gid's every move. The room had no windows but was lit by lanterns that gave off an eerie green glow. Two sturdy-looking guards stood inside the entrance and suspiciously eyeballed Gid as he came in. There was a long wooden table in the centre of the room. A group of people, whom he presumed to be the Elders, sat at the far end on large wooden chairs. One of the group, a lady who looked as old as the city itself, stood up, followed by the others. She was slightly hunched with snow-white hair that reached to the ground, her wings partially wrapped around her as if protecting the brittle frame underneath.

'Welcome,' she said, in a friendly voice. 'My name is Valletia. I am head of the Elders of Arborinium.'

'My name is Gideon, but my friends call me Gid,' he said as confidently as he could. She beckoned Gid towards the group. A knot developed in his stomach and he felt as if he were about to stand in front of a full school assembly and give a speech. He rarely felt nervous, but this frail old lady standing in front of him now seemed to be looking straight into his heart, and he felt a great power emanating from her. Gid could understand why she was the boss – she held an authority greater than any adult he had ever met, and yet there was a tenderness and warmth about her that eased his nerves.

'You want to know why you are here, why you haven't woken up yet and why people think you are a warrior,' Valletia said in a calm, knowing voice.

'Um, yes, I suppose I do,' replied Gid.

'I will do my best to put your mind at rest, but first let me introduce the Elders.'

The lady to the left of Valletia stood up. She looked like a much younger version of the head Elder and shared the same warmth; she had long, fiery red hair that reached to her knees. Her eyes seemed distant and misty, and Gid couldn't quite work out what colour they were – one second they seemed as green as the deepest ocean and the next it was like staring into a storm.

'This young lady is my granddaughter, Romallia. She is an expert in the field of dreams. I'm sure you will have some interesting questions to ask her.'

Romallia bowed and sat down. To Valletia's right stood an old but strong-looking man. His worn figure and scars said enough about him without the need for words: he had obviously been a soldier. He stood, with his back straight, and saluted Gid with his one arm. His head was bald and tattooed with thick black tribal patterns; he was missing one eye and had a long, neat scar across the other. 'I am Artimus, commander of our army and head of security. I am looking forward to meeting you properly, Sir,' he said, followed by another well-practised salute.

'To Artimus' right is Borrea. His job is to ensure that the city is clean and healthy; he has the most taxing and important job of us all. This city is home to more than 3,000 people – 3,000 who would be homeless without him.'

Borrea smiled proudly. He was small and slim with messy black hair, and Gid noticed that he, too, had dirty fingernails and a slightly mucky face. In fact, he had all the trademarks of a good tree climber. 'I'm more of a gardener than anything else; I keep the trees alive and they protect us. If you need to know anything about this city, speak to me – I know this place better than I know my own wings.'

'And last but by no means least is Mallerik. She is in charge of education and is an expert on the ancient scrolls, including the prophecy concerning you.'

Mallerik nodded and smiled, staring at Gid as if studying

an ancient fossil. She had a look of strictness about her. Everything she wore said sensible and neat. Her brown hair was tied back, and perched on the end of her nose was a small round pair of glasses that made her eyes seem huge. 'I have much to ask you and lots to tell you,' she said. 'I hope my sons have been looking after you, and I am very sorry for Tharik's rash actions; he gets that from his father.' At the back of the room Tharik's ears were burning.

Valletia looked at Gid thoughtfully. 'Come with me. I will answer your questions and tell you everything you need to know as best I can.' She turned and walked towards a small door at the back of the room, opened it and walked through.

Gid followed her through the door. It led outside on to an enormous branch as long as a football pitch and as wide as the length of a bus. Even from the outside he couldn't see the whole city; the tangled trees seemed to go on and on either side of him. He could, however, see the ground a very long way down, which made his knees quiver and his head feel dizzy.

'It seems a lot higher from out here,' he said, slightly nervously.

'Yes, I suppose it does. But now you have learnt to fly, if you fall you won't go very far,' replied Valletia politely.

'I only learnt about five minutes ago. How did you know?' he said, puzzled.

'I know a lot about you Gid, and there is just as much that I don't know,' she said. 'Where do I start? Let's sit down; we have a lot to talk about.'

Gid sat down, all ears, waiting to get some answers. He had a feeling that he didn't want to find out a lot of what he was about to hear, but he knew he had to listen. Valletia sat down with her legs dangling over the edge of the enormous branch and gazed at Gid as if trying to read his thoughts. Then she began.

'The prophecy that we have mentioned concerning you was

almost completely destroyed; the little information that we do have is all we managed to save. I will tell you what happened to the rest of it later, but I will start with what we have.' Valletia closed her eyes and breathed in deeply. '"In the year of the ice moon under the cover of darkness he shall arrive. The mighty warrior, who brings balance. The destroyer of falsehood shall descend from the clouds to the hill known as Bidrahar, the tomb of kings. The wrath of the warrior with the innocence of the child shall bring light to this divided land. He will unite all and undo what has been done."' She paused and looked at Gid with sadness in her eyes. 'This is all that has survived of our ancient writings. You are the warrior, Gid; you will bring unity and undo what has been done.'

Gid looked worried. 'It all sounds kind of cool, but honestly, I reckon you might have the wrong kid. I'm not a warrior; in fact, I'm not even a fighter; I'm more like, well, the kind of kid who tries to avoid being stuffed into rubbish bins and getting dead legs. I can take a kicking better than most, so I suppose that's something, at least. Besides, if I really was a warrior, I don't think I would look as stupid in this skirt.'

Valletia gave Gid a warm smile. 'I wish I could tell you more, Gid, but this is all we know. I don't know how you will unite us all or exactly what you will face, but it is your destiny.'

Gid stood up and looked towards the ground so far below, deep in thought. 'What happened to the other prophecies?' he asked as he sat back down.

'Around 3,000 years ago – we don't have an exact date for reasons I am about to explain – but as I was saying, around 3,000 years ago every village, tribe and breed lived in relative peace. Wars had been fought in the land for a long time. Tribes battled for power and land but the battles were short; a balance of power was being established and a sense of order was finally coming to this world.

'At around this time, a child arrived from an unknown

27

world and a rumour started to spread that he was the warrior spoken of in the ancient prophecies. The child called himself Legion and said that he had the power of many men. He did possess an amazing power: he could read a person's innermost secrets and desires. He was welcomed by the Elders of the city of Harrashon, the most powerful city in the land. There he advised the Elders on all matters and was loved by all. For a time everything was peaceful.

'My distant relatives were entrusted with the scrolls and realised that some things didn't add up. For a start, the place, time and year of his arrival were all wrong. There were many prophetic scrolls. One in particular that has been passed to us in stories through generations told of the prince of lies, who held a power that would once again bring war and separation to our world. Word of this reached Legion, who persuaded the Elders of Harrashon that the scroll guardians had lied about the prophecies in order to gain power.

'He turned brother against brother and drove old friends apart with his evil words. Legion's lies spread like a disease through the city. Harrash, the chief Elder, called for all people who believed in their new all-powerful warrior to join him. He declared war on anyone who believed in the old scrolls. Once again, war ravaged the land and lasted for more than 100 years.

'Harrash died in the first year of the wars, and Legion, the powerful child warrior, took his throne. Eventually he became an invincible leader; every tribe that fought against him was defeated. Legion gave the beaten tribes a choice – join him and hand over their land, or die. He took possession of all the ancient writings and scrolls and had them destroyed, along with anything relating to his arrival – all but the one concerning you. From then on the prophecy was kept secret from everybody except a trusted loyal few, and was passed down through the generations. My ancestors fled into the forests of Arbor and hid the last prophecy in a hollow tree that quickly grew into the city of Arborinium.

Legion was unaware that the scroll had survived and saw little threat from his remaining enemies. He left my ancestors alone and called an end to the wars. He lives to this day and sometimes sends raiding parties to remind us of his power. He controls everything outside the great forest. We don't leave and he doesn't enter.

'He is the ageless prince of lies and you are the mighty warrior. Your destinies are linked, though without the scrolls I don't know how; I only have the stories that were passed down to me.' Valletia looked at Gid with purpose in her eyes.

Gid sat and stared into space. This was a lot to take in, and it all sounded like it would make a great movie, but something bothered him more than anything he had just heard. 'I'm not dreaming, am I?' he asked flatly.

It had been in his thoughts from the moment he woke up in a strange bed earlier that morning. Everything seemed so real – conversations, feelings, bruises – and he was sure that his own head couldn't come up with a dream like this.

Valletia took Gid's hand – she knew her answer would hit him hard. He may be a warrior but he was still just a child. 'You are not dreaming.'

'How did I get here, and how do I get home?'

Valletia thought long and hard about her answer. 'I think you should ask my granddaughter; she will be the best one to answer this,' she said as she slowly got to her feet.

'Can I have a moment on my own?' Gid asked. A lot had happened in the last day, and suddenly it was no longer a dream. He was really here.

'Of course,' Valletia replied. 'I will be just inside if you need me.' She went back inside and left him on his own.

Gid spread his wings, crouched low and pushed hard into the air. He flew up fast and headed straight past the top of the city, the wind whipping at his face, but still he flew up, further and further, faster and faster. He could see Arborinium below him, like a huge wooden volcano with hundreds of winged creatures flying in and out like bees around a busy hive. He looked down at the ground and raced face first towards the base of the trees, the speed of his flight turning everything into a blur as he sped down towards the leaf-covered earth. He pulled up centimetres from the floor and flew along, dragging dried leaves in his wake. He turned and headed towards the branch that he had just left, spinning wildly as he ascended, finally coming to rest once more on the giant branch and slumping into a heap.

'I needed that,' he said, with his heart pumping, and a smile slowly crept across his face.

He walked back into the meeting room. Everyone had left apart from Romallia. She was standing by the chairs and seemed to be waiting for him.

'Follow me,' she said as she flew past him out of the door through which he had just come in. He stared momentarily at the door, sighed deeply, and flew back out after her.

Chapter 5: Awake

Romallia flew close to the ground and headed for a huge forest that lay about 500 metres from the city, dodging low branches and tree trunks as she sped along the forest floor. Gid followed closely behind, surprised by how easy flying had already become.

'Keep up,' Romallia teased as she quickly changed her course, heading straight up to the canopy of the densely packed trees.

They burst through the thick leaves and glided just metres above the treetops. 'Nearly there,' she said.

'Nearly where?' asked Gid.

'You will see.' Ahead of them was a clearing. 'Just down here.'

They landed at the edge of a small lake. 'I come here when I need to get away from the city,' Romallia said as she picked up a flat stone and skimmed it over the still silvery surface. 'Seven. I've managed to get them to jump eleven times before, but seven isn't bad.'

Gid picked up a stone, took aim and let rip. It sank without a single bounce. 'I think I've managed two before,' he said sheepishly.

Romallia was strange. She seemed distant, as if she was detached from every problem her world could throw her way. 'I know how you got here,' she said. 'I've seen you before.'

Gid was sure that they had never met, but he desperately wanted to know how he had arrived and how he could get home, so he thought he had better listen. 'Go on,' he said.

Romallia looked up towards the sky, dreamily. 'I had a dream once. I saw you standing with a group of boys, only you didn't have wings. Then a large metal beast on wheels stopped and you all climbed into it, so I followed. I walked up to you and smiled but you couldn't see me. I walked with you into a large building full of children; you were being told about the changing body but you weren't listening. You sat scribbling pictures on a piece of paper – pictures of you but with wings; good pictures. In one picture you were flying towards a city with your sword drawn – the city of Harrashon.'

Gid sat down with his mouth open. He didn't say anything. How could she know what he had been drawing? How was she there? It was impossible.

'I was only with you for a few hours, but when I woke up, more than a year had passed here.'

'I don't understand,' said Gid.

Romallia bent down and picked up a few stones, discarding the ones she didn't want. 'I fell asleep here, and some part of me travelled to your world. I was supposed to see you; I didn't know why at the time. I told my grandmother and she showed me the prophecy.' She stopped speaking and threw another stone across the lake.

'Hmm... nine. That's not bad, is it Gid?'

He was speechless. She had just told him about the morning before he had arrived in this strange place as if it was as normal as asking how his day had been at school. 'That was only yesterday,' he said, confused.

'It may only have been yesterday to you but it was nearly two years ago in this world. As I said, I was only with you for a day and yet my body was asleep here for more than a year. I was 20 when I had the dream and nearly 22 when I woke up. For every day that passes in your world a year will pass here. Right now your body is asleep back in your world. You have been here for one night and half a day, but barely any time will have passed where you come from. While you are here no one will miss you; they will still be sleeping. The way I see it, another year could go by here before it's time for you to wake up back in your world.'

Gid sat quietly, letting it all sink in.

'I think the part of you that is here is what we call your soul.'

Gid nodded. 'We call it a soul as well, if that is the part of me that is here. But how can you know this for certain? I know your body stayed here when you fell asleep, but I couldn't see you, so maybe you weren't totally in my world. Everybody can see me here, so my body might not be back in my world – it might really be here.'

Romallia smiled. 'I just know that it's back in your world. I don't know exactly how; I just know. You weren't supposed to see me in your world, but you are supposed to be here. It makes sense to me,' she said confidently as she bent down to pick up another stone. She was about to throw it when a deep growling sound interrupted her. 'Quick, we need to go.'

There was a sound of breaking branches close by, and a strange mist was slowly flowing across the ground towards them from the dense trees – something big was on its way. As they took to the air, Gid looked back and saw the shadowy shape of a huge animal just inside the line of trees on the other side of the pond. In seconds it was enveloped in the thick, eerie mist.

'What was that?' he asked, his heart pounding in his chest. Whatever it was, it was huge, and it didn't look too friendly.

'That was the Hogboar. Everybody knows of it from childhood stories. It lives in these woods and they say it is an evil creature that kills for fun. We need to get back; our food will be ready soon and I'm starving,' Romallia answered calmly.

Gid stared at her. 'Does nothing bother you? We were seconds from coming face to face with an evil killer beast of some kind and you are thinking about food,' he said in disbelief.

'You were with me. We would have been fine,' she replied.

As they flew back, Gid wondered what people would make

of Romallia back at home. He was known as a dreamer, but she was in a different league. He was sure that if he looked up the word 'vacant' in the dictionary there would be a picture of Romallia next to it staring happily back from the page.

Tharik was waiting for Gid by the door to the Elders' room. 'Romallia, Gid,' he said, and nodded to each of them as they landed on the branch. 'The Elders asked me to wait for you, Gid, and let you know that your food will be brought to your room. They thought you might like some time alone.'

'Thank you, Tharik. You seem to have done a lot of waiting for me. I hope I will be worth it,' he added glumly.

He wasn't sure that he could live up to his warrior reputation, but then again, this morning he thought that getting his wings to work would be impossible, but now he was flying as naturally as if he had learnt to before he could walk.

'I'll see you soon, Gid. If you ever need me, you can usually find me by the lake,' said Romallia as she turned to leave.

'You would go back there even with that monster thumping around? Are you mad?' said Gid in astonishment.

Romallia just smiled, shrugged and flew down towards a lower door.

'She's a bit odd, that one, Gid, but you'll get used to her,' said Tharik. 'Umm, how are your legs doing now?' he asked awkwardly.

'They're fine. A little numb still, but look, don't worry about it. I'm a warrior, remember, and I'm sure I'll be in for worse than that in the future.'

Tharik had waited for a whole year for Gid to arrive, dreaming about meeting this mighty warrior. He had formed pictures in his head of a huge, muscle-bound barbarian with a thick neck, tree-trunk arms and legs, armed to the teeth with weapons and covered in scars from previous battles. Gid may not fit this image, but he had seen him smash into the ground and then stand and walk as if he had simply fallen out of bed.

He had shot him with drugs that would kill any living thing and yet Gid had woken up with nothing more than a headache and slightly numb legs. Innocent-looking or not, Tharik knew that Gid was a warrior, stronger than even he could have imagined. Yes, he looked like a child and seemed a bit unsure of himself, but he knew that this child was like no other in this world.

'I know you don't really believe that you are the warrior we are waiting for, but I know it's you. I believe it and so does my brother; you will soon see. Believe me. If it's not true then how do you explain your arrival? Rahmon told me that you were not convinced that you were awake, but I know you can't believe that any more. If you are here by accident then your arrival is one big coincidence. You are here, you are awake and you are a warrior, trust me.'

Tharik looked at Gid as if staring right into him, smiled, then turned and led the way back to Gid's room.

On the bed lay a plate that looked as if it had been hand-made. On it were some kind of green vegetables, some odd-shaped brown things similar in appearance to potatoes and what appeared to be a kind of red meat.

'Hmm... I'm not too sure about this. The green things can stay on my plate. I hate veg at home and I'm not going to start eating it here.' Gid opened his mouth and bit into the meaty-looking substance. He chewed for about 20 seconds and then swallowed it with a big gulp, holding his nose.

'It tastes like chicken,' he said with relief.

In fact, the meal was pretty similar to a normal Sunday roast except without any gravy or Yorkshire puds. Gid placed the finished plate on the floor and lay back on his bed, letting his stomach feel the benefit of a proper meal. He looked at the ceiling and then closed his eyes. He knew for sure now that this was no dream. His teachers always said he had a wild imagination, but this was too real and too wild. He was here, wherever here was, and he was a warrior. His mum would still be asleep and no one would even know that he was gone. He remembered the American teenager from the news, Brett Johnson, who had fallen asleep and after eight years still hadn't woken up. Gid wondered if that might be happening to him now! Was he in a coma back home? Would he wake up in his teens? He had just become interested in a girl in his class at school and doubted that she would even remember him in eight years. One way or another he would have to get home, hopefully before anyone realised he was gone. He didn't like people to worry about him, and he knew that his mum would panic.

Chapter 6: Mist

It had been a busy day so far – too busy to start missing people – but he still didn't want to be here any longer than was necessary. Gid walked to the window in his room and stared vacantly out, his mind in another place. A thick fog was starting to spread across the ground below; it seemed to be flowing out of the woods and was now reaching the bottom of the city. Every living creature was fleeing from its path, and even the light seemed to be leaving the sky at the eerie mist's arrival. A feeling of security filled Gid and he felt safe and warm in his room, far away from the fog. It reminded him of the time he was camping in his friend's back garden in a storm, knowing that only a few centimetres away was pounding rain that would soak him to the bone. However, in his sleeping bag in the tiny tent, protected by millimetres of thin material, he was quite dry and toasty.

The fog was now so thick that it almost looked as though the city had grown out of clouds. The mist swirled below like a hungry animal searching for its next unsuspecting meal. Tharik had told him that he would be left alone tonight, that the evening was his to do as he pleased and go where he wanted. With every living thing fleeing from this odd mist, curling up in bed seemed like a great idea – after all, he could ask about the fog in the morning! Right now he wanted to forget about everything and pretend that it was as he originally hoped – just a very weird dream.

He stared towards the edge of the great forest, the base of it now completely masked by the thick white blanket of mist, and was just wondering if any creatures were still roaming around in it when his eyes caught a brief movement behind the first row of trees. He stared hard, and to his horror he could see a pair of red eyes staring right back at him. He was in one of thousands of rooms in this tree city and yet these eyes were definitely looking at him. Just above the fog he could make out the top half of a large indistinct shape attached to the crimson eyes.

Gid the 11-year-old child wanted to look away and hide under his blankets, but something inside him kept staring into the gaze – maybe the stare was drawing him in, or maybe the warrior in him was beginning to awaken. One thing was certain: he had to know what this creature was and why, unlike everything else, it was not scared of the fog. He grabbed his sword and decided to take a closer look. Every part of him that was still a kid screamed to stay in his room and hide from those eyes, but he knew that, here at least, he was supposed to be a warrior; he felt an overwhelming urge to explore the fog-covered ground and head into the woods to confront this red-eyed, dark creature.

Gid opened the wooden door that led out of his room. Now he understood why there was no floor or balcony outside! He spread his wings and glided towards the ground. It was still daylight but looked as though it would soon be getting dark.

As he descended, he entered the thick, cold fog and everything disappeared from view; everywhere he looked he could see nothing but white. Once he had heard a climber talking about a white-out fog so thick you could touch it, and he described it as feeling like he was inside a ping-pong ball. Gid now knew exactly what the climber had meant.

The fog lay like a thick blanket, three metres deep, all around the base of the city. Whatever had been glaring at him from just above the fog had to be huge. It must be the creature he had seen with Romallia by the lake. Why had it been staring at him, though? The trees where he had seen the shadowy shape lay only 100 metres or so from the base of Arborinium.

Gid landed softly on the moist ground, drew his sword and headed quietly through the thick white fog towards the forest.

He could see only a few metres around him in all directions and thought of flying up above the fog, but decided that if he could not see anything, then at least nothing could see him either.

'Why am I doing this?' he whispered to himself.

There were no sounds at all apart from his own light footsteps.

Tharik and Rahmon made their way to Gid's room. They had been told to give him time alone but had also been instructed to make sure he didn't leave the city until the Grimbarr mist had cleared. Many people had disappeared in the mist before, never to be seen again. It was common practice in the city to fly back into its protection at the first sign of the eerie fog. It was known to everybody that strange creatures roamed around under the cover of the Grimbarr. Not even the bravest soldiers chanced waiting around outside when the thick white fog rolled in.

Tharik knocked on Gid's door and waited patiently for him to answer, but no answer came. After a few attempts the brothers grew concerned. Rahmon took out a long key, put it into the lock and tried to turn it.

'It won't budge,' he said in frustration.

Tharik pushed the door softly and smiled triumphantly at his brother as it opened. 'It's not locked,' he said smugly.

The brothers immediately saw the open door on the other side of the room. Tharik reached it first. He peered out but could see nothing on the ground below apart from a slight stirring in the mist where something was moving beneath its surface, heading for the forest.

'We'd better tell the Elders! Tharik, see if you can spot him from above, but don't under any circumstances go into the mist or the woods. I'll tell the others. If you see him, shout to him and wait for me – I won't be long.'

The fog was thicker now and Gid had no idea where he was. He thought the forest should be just ahead, but he couldn't see past his nose.

'I'm going to have to take a look from above; this is getting silly – I can't even see my feet,' he muttered quietly to himself.

He spread his wings but the fog seemed to hold him; he felt as if its thickness was weighing him down. He crouched down and tried to push off the ground into the air, but it was no use. The fog had him trapped. He carried on heading in what he thought was the direction of the trees.

Suddenly all the hairs on the back of his neck stood to attention. Although he could only see fog, he somehow knew that he was being watched. Gid tightened his grip on the handle of his sword. The last time he felt like he was being watched he had been right, and it had almost cost him his life. This time he was going to be ready.

He heard something running, close and just ahead. Then it went quiet again, and for what seemed like an eternity he listened but heard nothing more. All of a sudden, something ran behind him, and he glimpsed a brief flash of brown before it disappeared into the thick white soup. To his right he could hear a deep threatening growl, then, as quickly as it started, it stopped again. If something was trying to unnerve him, it was doing a very good job.

'Come on, where are you?' he said quietly, through gritted teeth. 'I know you can see me but where are youoooou–ph.'

Something smashed into Gid's back and sent him sprawling across the floor. He jumped to his feet but before he could ready himself he was hit again, this time in the chest, by what looked like the ugly face of an enormous wild boar. Gid was thrown backwards through the fog and landed on the back of his head. To make things worse, the blow had knocked the sword from his hand and it was now lying somewhere in the thick fog.

For a moment he lay winded on the cold, damp floor, then

he rolled quietly onto his belly, listening hard for any sign of his attacker while searching the ground for his blade, but it was hopeless. He had to get out of this mist if he was to stand a chance of winning this fight. The creature seemed to have no problem finding him, but Gid was now fighting blind and weaponless; the odds seemed to be stacked in favour of his new opponent. Before he could get to his feet, he was trampled by a giant bear-like body, rolled over and left lying face down in mud.

'Show yourself!' he shouted in desperation and defiance.

He slowly stood up, his right arm broken and hanging limply by his side. Another smash in the back sent him hurtling forwards, but this time he managed to land on his feet and quickly turn around, ready for the next blow. Amazingly, the feeling and movement were coming back to his arm. The huge head appeared again, and in a split second Gid stepped to his left and punched the massive jaw with a force that released a deep yelping sound from the half-bear half-boar's throat. The mist swirled in the direction of the stunned beast as it stumbled sideways. Gid ran at a blistering speed with his head down towards the swirling mist and felt his shoulder ram into something soft, and another low yelp escaped from the startled creature as it was knocked into the air. He heard a dull thud and a low groan as the creature hit the floor heavily.

'That's… one… all…,' Gid panted.

He headed slowly towards the sound of the groaning and readied himself for the next attack, but the beast wasn't there – just more fog and a bad smell. Suddenly, a vice-like jaw closed around Gid's waist and he was lifted off his feet and hurled with force through the thick white air. He felt a sudden sharp pain in his back as he smashed into a tree at the edge of the mist-hidden forest. He landed in a crouching position, ready to block the next inevitable charge.

A second later, the beast was in mid-air, leaping towards his head. Gid fired himself upward from the crouch and brought his knee up hard into its throat, sending it spinning into another tree. He leapt after it and smashed his fist into the huge hairy stomach. The wounded creature rolled over and over before once again disappearing into the fog. There was no sound, no movement, no breathing – nothing at all from the direction of his attacker.

Gid caught his breath and walked slowly in the general direction of the wounded creature, the pain in his back from smashing into the tree already easing. He stopped and listened for any clue as to where it was lying. A warm, damp feeling covered the back of his neck. Gid turned slowly and his eyes met the crimson eyes of his opponent. They stood eye to eye, like boxers waiting for the bell, for what seemed a lifetime; the beast's huge upward-pointing fangs were just centimetres from Gid's throat, and Gid's fists were clenched just as close to the beast's. Suddenly, without warning, the creature opened its huge jaws and an enormous slimy tongue shot out and licked Gid's face.

'Uuurgh! Get off!' Gid exclaimed, as he stumbled backwards and fell.

The beast sat in front of him, grunted, then licked him again.

'I said get off! Your breath stinks!' Gid wiped his slime-covered face and gagged. 'That was rank,' he said, and backed off a little.

The fog slowly started to disappear and Gid could finally get a proper look at this stinking, ugly, hog-faced, hairy beast. It sat in front of him like a naughty puppy, its huge face now appearing less fierce. Its body was brown with thick matted hair, and it was about three times the size of a fully grown bear and had yellowy spines down the middle of its back. It had huge paws armed with vicious-looking black claws and it had the face of a hippo-sized hairy wild boar with deadly looking tusks. Gid couldn't help but think that it was now actually looking kind of cute in an ugly sort of way. He let his aching body relax while he got his breath back, and the beast lay down at his side.

'I always wanted a pet,' he said, and laughed, 'even if you do throw me through trees and smell bad.'

He stroked the thick matted fur on the creature's side and smiled. A voice shouted from above. 'Gid, move quickly, it's the Hogboar!' Tharik was above them hovering, putting his blowpipe to his lips.

'No!' shouted Gid! 'It's alright. I think it's my friend.'

The Hogboar looked upwards without moving his head and then looked away, paying Tharik no attention.

'Honestly, it's fine. We had a bit of a scrap but it was just playing. I think it's still a… umm… well, a puppy, I suppose. I don't really know what you call a young Hogboar,' he said and lay back against its huge side.

'A bit of a scrap, you say. Have you seen the state of the place?'

As the mist slowly receded. Gid could now see where the ground had been ripped up and was dotted with small craters. Trees around them were smashed to pieces, with huge splinters sticking out of the once strong trunks. About five metres in front of them was Gid's sword.

'Good job I dropped that, I suppose,' he said, and started to giggle. 'You can stroke it, I think; it's friendly really – I hope,' he said to Tharik.

Tharik landed cautiously and leaned forwards with his hand out. 'I'm not too sure about this. I've heard some stories about this thing, and besides, it smells really bad.'

The Hogboar sat up quickly and licked Tharik's unprepared face. 'Urgh that's rotten,' he groaned, and slumped down next to the slime-covered Gid.

'He likes you,' Gid said, and they both started to laugh.

The Hogboar grunted, slowly raised its huge frame and started to limp towards the trees. The mist was retreating into the forest, and the beast quickly followed. Before it disappeared, the Hogboar paused and turned to its new friends, letting out a deep purr before heading back into the deep, thick and slightly smashed trees.

'We should get back before my perfect brother gives me another earbashing,' said Tharik.

Gid painfully stood up, holding his ribs with one arm and letting the other hang by his side. Every bone in his body ached and seemed to be realigning itself. 'I feel rough,' he whispered weakly to himself.

'You ok, Gid?' asked Tharik, a sudden look of concern showing on his face.

'I'm fine. I think I may have broken a few bones in the fight, but they seem to be mending as we speak. I know now that I'm not completely indestructible, but I seem to mend quickly enough.' Tharik walked over and put his arm under Gid's good arm and led him back towards Arborinium.

Rahmon and a few others were waiting at the base of the great city, and without questioning the two youngsters, they lifted Gid and flew him back to his room.

'Thank you, Tharik,' shouted Rahmon as they flew upwards. 'You did well. You can tell me all about what happened later. I'm sure the Elders will want a full report from you, but first, let's patch up our little warrior.'

Chapter 7: Betrayal

A few days had passed since the fight with the Hogboar. Gid's injuries had healed before he had woken up the next day. The Hogboar and the mist had not been seen since, and the story of the fight had been kept a secret, with only the Elders knowing the details.

Gid had been given some time to familiarise himself with Arborinium and the surrounding areas, with Romallia or Borrea as a guide. Tharik and Rahmon had been sent on separate missions. Tharik had been sent to locate the home of the Hogboar, if indeed it had a home, and to find out whether there was a link between it and the mist, whilst Rahmon was in charge of keeping Gid's arrival secret until the Elders felt the time was right to inform the people.

The only person whom Gid had not formally met was Artimus, the army commander and head of security. Their initial meeting on Gid's arrival had been brief, but he remembered that he seemed to be a scary and very military character. Gid had wanted to talk to him on a number of occasions about the battles he had been in and to see if he could get any tips on how to fight. His battle with the Hogboar had gone reasonably well for a first fight, but knowing how not to get broken and survive a little longer would be pretty handy. He had seen Artimus on a few occasions when he was with Tharik, but Artimus always had some excuse to leave, and if he ever tried to find him he had always mysteriously disappeared, or, at least, no one knew where he was.

'Oh well, I suppose I'll be here for a while. I'm bound to bump into him some time,' he thought as he lay by the pool he and Romallia had visited on his first day. Gid's stone skimming had improved a little over the last few days, with six skims as his current record. He had also found that he could hold his breath under water for a ridiculously long time; he had easily managed around ten minutes on his last attempt, which he now decided to try and better. He checked the surrounding area and stripped down to his small brown cotton tunic. Even though he still had some clothes on, he didn't really like people being there if he was stripping off. 'Ok, one big breath and in I go.'

The pool was teeming with strange blob-like creatures with huge eyes but no visible mouth and which constantly changed from one luminous colour to another. Gid found them fascinating; if he swam close to a group of them, they would compact into a tight ball and mimic his colours. It was almost like staring into a bubbly mirror. Around two minutes had passed and he was in no hurry to resurface.

Tharik appeared momentarily, flying above the tree line over the clearing that had been created by the pool and then vanished again behind the trees, presumably on one of his missions to find the Hogboar. Seconds later, the dark-cloaked, one-armed figure of Artimus appeared from the wood near Gid's clothes. He surveyed the area as if checking that he hadn't been seen and then gazed into the pool, a look of confusion crossing his face as he found himself seeming to be staring at two Gids. He watched for a few more seconds and then ran into the undergrowth, expertly blending in with trees.

'It must have been at least 15 minutes so far. This is awesome; I can't even manage a length of the pool at home.'

It was the first time he had thought of home for a while and he was surprised to realise that at this moment in time he was quite happy to be there at the pool.

'I should be getting back, I suppose, and I should stop talking to myself – people will think I'm losing the plot.' His soggy body climbed out of the pool and started to dress. 'Next time I should bring a towel – or whatever they use as towels... I'm doing it again! Stop talking to yourself, you loony.'

He was supposed to meet the Elders to discuss what he was here to do and how they could help. Gid knew this was a polite way of telling him that they were expecting him to wage war against this Legion guy, or at least look as if he was doing something about it. A strange sinking feeling entered his belly and ended his otherwise pleasant afternoon.

'It's him. He's here. The one they were waiting for,' whispered a nervous, cloaked figure that stood in the shadows before the throne of Legion.

'You are sure it is him? If you are wrong, you and your family will be dead before you have a chance to apologise,' spat a deep, growling voice that had become vicious and sceptical with age and power, its owner hidden by a dark moving shadow that surrounded the huge throne.

'I'm sure. I would not dare to be here now unless I was positive. I told you I would let you know, and now I have fulfilled my promise,' replied a voice that was slowly growing in confidence.

'You have done well, though your part in this deal is not finished yet. Before I grant you power to rule over my armies, you must finish the job. You alone have the trust and clearance of the Arbitans to come and go as you please. I am giving you this chance to gain glory and power. You know what you have to do, so do not mess up; you are well aware of the consequences. Now go, before you are missed.'

At this command the cloaked informant quickly nodded, turned and vanished from the oppressive darkness of the throne room.

'So you have come. The treacherous fools at Arborinium thought they could keep you a secret, but I did not become as powerful as this by letting things get past me. When you die, they will all perish, but for now I will let the Arbitans live in blissful ignorance.'

The shadows surrounding the throne moved rapidly, and Legion, still partially hidden by the semi-darkness, clenched his fists, and an evil smile quickly flashed behind the shadowy veil.

Chapter 8: Traitor

A large fire was burning in a stone fireplace by the far wall at the end of the room. A round hole in the ceiling above the fire let the smoke flow outside to the very top of the tree, making the huge tree-city look even more like a volcano. The Elders' room felt quite cosy considering its size. Gid, sitting in a large padded chair across from Valletia, was feeling slightly more relaxed than he had been earlier at the lake – even the sinking feeling in his belly had gone. The fire was making a low crackling noise and gave off a smell that reminded him of camping.

'I didn't know I was only meeting you. I thought it was going to be a big meeting with all the Elders, and to be honest, I was a little nervous,' Gid said as he sank lower into his chair.

Valletia smiled softly and offered Gid something that looked like a kind of sweet. 'Take one – they taste like bonchas, though I'm not sure you have them in your world.'

Gid placed the red jelly cube in his mouth. 'Mmm… they taste a bit like what we call strawberries and a little bit like caramel,' he replied with a satisfied look on his face.

Valletia left the sweets with Gid and smiled. 'I know you were probably expecting me to ask you to find Legion and destroy him, or something along those lines.'

Gid looked at her completely stunned. 'How on earth does she do that?' he thought, as he placed another sweet in his mouth.

'Well, this meeting is to let you know that this will not be asked of you. You see, the prophecy foretold your arrival, and it also said that you will save us, but we don't know exactly how. It was right about your arrival so I believe the latter part will be right as well. Whatever happens from now on was meant to happen. We ask no more of you than to do as you will. I believe that events will happen as they are meant to.'

'So I'm kind of free to do as I please? That sounds quite easy to me, though so far, doing as I please has been more exhausting than school. Obviously it's been more fun, though.' Gid let out a large yawn accompanied by a full-bodied stretch.

'You look tired, Gid. Our meeting will end now. If you need me for anything, come and find me.'

Gid lay back on the bed in his room and stared at the carved wooden ceiling. '"Whatever is going to happen is meant to happen." Some help that is! I still have the small job of bringing balance, but hey, let's just see what comes up. At least I can get in some practice defending myself against whatever happens in the future – I just need to track down Artimus.' With this final thought, Gid's eyes grew heavy and he gave in to the welcoming pull of deep sleep.

Artimus crouched behind a small tree at the far edge of the forest surrounding Arborinium. The sun was slowly starting to penetrate the thick canopy, signalling the start of a new day. He knew his prey would come by soon – and there was no way it would escape. Years of fighting in the wars had taught him discipline and, most of all, patience. He would sit and wait for as long as he needed to, and if his long hours of following his unwitting prey over the last few days had been worthwhile, his waiting would soon be over. A flapping sound above the trees announced the arrival of what he was waiting for.

Tharik flew down through the trees at the edge of the forest. Before he had even placed a foot on the floor, a hand grabbed his wings and threw him into a large solid oak tree. He lay face down, winded but still conscious. He knew that his only advantage would be to let his attacker think he had been knocked out. His hand that was hidden by his wing slowly reached for the dagger that was attached to his belt.

Something cold and sharp prodded his back. Tharik quickly span around and slashed purposefully with his blade. The blade hit the wooden shaft of a long and deadly looking spear that immediately moved towards his throat. Tharik was now sitting with his back against the large tree, pinned there by the spear, the dagger clenched uselessly in his hand. His eyes slowly moved along the wooden shaft and met the very unfriendly stare of Artimus.

Rahmon flew along the treetops surveying the earth that was visible between the thick leaves. His mission had gone well. A few people had heard strange sounds coming from the fog but had put it down to whatever strange creatures lurked in its midst. Now he was to help his brother find the Hogboar. He had seen Tharik leave and head out over the woods, so he set off after him. He hadn't seen his brother properly since Gid's fight in the fog and was looking forward to working with him again. Sure, Tharik was clumsy and tried too hard at times, but Rahmon had been the same at his age. He would help his brother search for the beast and its home but that was it – this was Tharik's mission and he had no intention of taking over. Suddenly his thoughts were interrupted by the sound of a fight ringing out through the trees below, and he caught a glimpse of two figures.

Talking was getting nowhere and Artimus had heard enough. He raised his spear and thrust it towards Tharik's arm – the one which held the dagger. Tharik let out a scream of pain and dropped the blade, blood running freely down his pierced arm.

'Come with me quietly or die,' growled Artimus.

Tharik reached out, picked up the dropped blade with his other hand and slowly raised himself with his back against the tree. 'I choose to die, old man. I will never go with you. I would be killed anyway. Do it quickly and don't miss. If I don't die now, I swear you will.'

'So be it!'

Artimus had seen Tharik grow into a young warrior and had been close to his family for years, but military service had taught him not to let emotions get in the way. He raised the deadly spear and aimed for Tharik's heart. A sudden swishing sound split the silence, and it was over.

Gid woke up and looked around, no longer hoping that he would be back in his own room at home, and actually quite relieved not to be there. He had no real plans for the day. The meeting with Valletia had taken him by surprise when she said that nothing was really expected of him apart from doing as he pleased. His only real options were to find Artimus, to explore the area some more or to actually do something useful and help Tharik find the Hogboar. He was strangely looking forward to seeing the stinking beast again but hoped it would be a less energetic meeting this time round if they found it.

'Right. The first thing I need is a good breakfast.'

After getting dressed he opened his door, ready for his first mission. So far every meal had been brought to his room and he wasn't really sure where they came from. He opened the door ready to start his hunt for food. The hunt didn't last very long, as a tray of food was once again waiting right outside.

Artimus lay on the ground, motionless, a dart sticking out of his arm.

'Tharik are you ok? What happened?' Rahmon knelt down and felt for a pulse, the horrible realisation of what had happened suddenly hitting home. 'He's dead! The dart was meant for protection in case we found the Hogboar. The sedative was too strong for one of us. I've killed him!' Rahmon placed his head in his hands. 'Tharik, please tell me I have not just killed an innocent man. He was trying to kill you, please say that he was.'

Tharik stared at his brother in bewilderment He had never seen his weak, soft side. Since he was a child, Rahmon had been his father figure, after both their parents died in a fire in the city whilst he was still a baby and the responsibility of looking after him had fallen to his perfect, strong rock of a brother. To see him here, afraid and horrified at what he had done, made Tharik feel uneasy.

'He was going to kill me – you were right to kill him. He is a traitor.'

'What do you mean, a traitor?'

'I was searching for the Hogboar a few days ago and I saw Artimus walking through the woods, acting suspiciously. He kept changing his course as if he was making sure that nobody was following. I managed to fly above the woods and follow without his knowledge. Rahmon, he went straight to Harrashon, to Legion. He must have told him about Gid. I followed him again today, only he knew I was following him. He took me by surprise. I challenged him and tried to find out why he had betrayed us, but he was too strong for me. He wanted me to join him but he was talking to the wrong person. When he realised I wouldn't go with him, he was about to kill me, but you arrived.' Tharik suddenly went very pale and sat down. 'I don't feel too well, brother. I think I may have lost a little blood.' Tharik was sitting in a small puddle of his own blood, and his pierced arm was flopping loosely by his side.

'Let's get you home.' Rahmon collected a variety of leaves from the surrounding vegetation, crushed them until a gummy substance was made and then pressed the mix into his brother's wound. 'Hold this tightly on your arm.'

Tharik obeyed whilst his brother made a dressing from more of the surrounding vegetation.

'Can you still fly?'

'I'm fine. It's just a scratch. I'm just a little dizzy, that's all.'

Rahmon smiled for a moment and then turned his attention to Artimus. He would have to carry his body back on foot.

'Tharik, fly back and give the Elders a full report of exactly what has happened here. I will be back soon.'

Rahmon raised the lifeless body of Artimus onto his broad shoulders and slowly carried him towards Arborinium.

Gid set off, flying high above the trees, the giddy rush of flying stamping a wide grin across his face. A group of children from Arborinium flew below him with wooden swords drawn, and Gid stopped momentarily to watch them play fight before they disappeared through the treetops, their laughs and shouts dying away as they went deeper into the forest. Gid himself was only a few years older than they were, and he longed to once again have homework as his only worry.

He flew fast and low above the treetops, low enough to grab the odd leaf as he sped along. The sun was now high in the sky and blazed down on the enormous canopy. A flock of huge red birds soared into the air and joined Gid before they changed direction and flew silhouetted against the sun as if they were one.

The edge of the great forest was coming into view. Gid spread his wings and brought himself upright, slowing his flight until he was hovering only a metre or so above the canopy. He flew straight up to get a better view of his surroundings. Ahead of him was the forest's end – or beginning, depending which way you were travelling; to his left a rocky outcrop burst through the dense trees, and to his right the hundreds of shades of green treetops spread out as far as the eye could see. At the forest's end, a huge river, or a small channel, separated the green of the trees from the greys and browns of what appeared to be a vast desert skirted by a range of mountains. As he approached the edge, he could make out strange enormous shadows on the desert floor.

'That's odd. There isn't a cloud in the sky and there's nothing around that could cast such large shadows,' he thought.

As he stared at these strange features, they seemed to be

moving closer. The dark shadowy areas were now covering the water's edge on the far side. Then the shadows took to the air and carried on their tree-bound journey. He waited, transfixed as the dark shapes came closer and closer. Then they stopped just at the base of the trees. They were not enormous shadows at all but hundreds of individual yet unrecognisable dark shapes.

The small army of shapes slowly disappeared into the forest, and as they entered, the whole area went silent. Hundreds of strange winged creatures left the shelter of their once safe homes and took to the sky. Gid turned and flew full pelt back towards Arborinium – there was something evil about these ghostly figures and he knew he had to warn the Elders.

Two figures landed on the huge branch outside the Elders' meeting room.

'Gid, what are you doing here?'

'I have to warn the Elders about shadows. I saw them entering the… What happened to you?' Gid stared worriedly at his friend's blood-soaked clothes and bandaged arm.

'It's a long story that ends with me being stabbed and Artimus dying. Look, we both need to see them, so let's go in together. I get nervous in there on my own.'

The two friends took their turns to inform the Elders about everything that had happened so far that day, each report being met with questions and a formal thank you before they were dismissed.

'What do you think they will do?' Gid asked.

'We'll find out soon enough. They don't mess around in that room.'

Sure enough, around 20 minutes later they were asked to re-enter. Valletia rose with a cold look on her face. 'A group has been sent out to help Rahmon. Artimus will be taken out of the forest and buried in the desert land, but not until we have sent out a party to find out what the shadows are and what their purpose is. Gid, you and Rahmon will lead this party. Tharik, you will rest until your arm is better.'

'If it's all the same, I would like to go along,' replied Tharik. 'My arm is ok. I lost a little blood but I was well enough to fly back. I know the forest better than anyone. I've been everywhere looking for the Hogboar and I know I can help.'

'If you feel up to the job I have no objections. You have earned it. You will all leave tomorrow at first light. Today, you will rest.'

Tharik smiled. 'Thank you.'

'You may leave now. Please inform your brother of the outcome of this meeting. I will need to hear his version of events when he gets back.' Valletia turned her attention to Gid.

'You see, Gid, I was right – things are starting to happen. I wouldn't say I expected things to happen quite as they have, but things are happening. I have asked you to be part of the party tomorrow because you know where the shadows entered and also because they must be linked to you being here. If you don't want to be a part of it, that's ok, but I'm sure you'll want to find out what the shadows are as much as I do.'

Once again Valletia was right. Ever since his discovery of these eerie forms he had wanted to go back and find them. The thought of them scared him, but his curiosity was fighting against his fear and winning. 'I would like to go and would have asked to if you hadn't invited me.'

'Thank you, Gid. You can leave now, unless you want to chat about anything.'

'I'm ok at the moment, but thanks anyway. I'm going to go and see Tharik, to see how bad his cut is.'

Valletia smiled. It was easy to forget that Gid was still so young, but every now and again he reminded her what it was like to be at an age where problems seemed to float past unnoticed. 'Goodbye, Gid.'

'Goodbye,' he replied politely, and left the room.

Chapter 9: Shadows

Twenty warriors had been chosen for the mission, some of the fiercest in Arborinium, with muscles piled on top of muscles. They stood in four perfect lines, each five deep. For most of them this would be their first real mission when all their training could finally be put into practice. This was to be a simple scouting trip to observe the shadows, but any kind of action would be better than sitting around or doing more drills.

The warriors were well disciplined, and although the news of Artimus' demise had been a shock, it was dealt with in a cold, professional way by all. None of them had ever suspected their once fierce general of being a traitor, and many still had their doubts, but the past could not be changed and they still had a job to do. No sign of nerves could be detected amongst any of them – they were ready, even though they knew that even the simplest of missions could hold hidden dangers.

Rahmon walked along the rows of warriors, a feeling of pride forming in his chest. These were the best men and women in the army, all chosen because of their discipline and loyalty, and he knew at that moment that the mission would go well – nothing would go wrong.

The first rays of the early morning sun slowly warmed the faces of the small band, and in its orange glow their weapons shone from meticulous polishing and cleaning.

Gid stood with Tharik and watched as Rahmon inspected his troops. Deep down, something told him this was not going to be an easy mission and he had a sickening feeling in his stomach that everything was about to go wrong. Not even the beautiful fresh morning with the sun's warming glow could raise his spirits. He did not want to share this feeling with the others; they all seemed so calm and confident.

The warriors had all been briefed about Gid and, whilst some believed, many had never heard of the prophecy and found it hard to think that a child could be their mighty hero. Many of the group completely ignored him; others shot him untrusting glances. He was not going to show any weakness and feared that his misgivings about the mission would make him seem like a scared child. Maybe it was just nerves – warrior or not, he was still new to his role so nerves were to be expected. Only a few weeks ago he had frozen in front of a school assembly. He had had five lines to say in a very short play about bullying, but not a single word would come from his mouth; he had just stood there and stared blankly whilst his cheeks slowly started to burn. His teacher had finally prompted him after what seemed a lifetime, and he had mumbled his words before leaving the stage as quickly as was physically possible. Now he stood with a whole band of warriors, all of whom had been told that he was probably stronger and better than any one of them. Gid needed a way to take his mind off his fears.

'You look worried, Tharik. Are you ok?' Gid felt that this was a good way of disguising his own concern.

'I'm fine. I have things on my mind but I'll tell you about them later.'

Gid was not really expecting this reply but was relieved that he was not the only one who was not himself today.

After receiving their orders, the troop marched towards the thick trees of the forest and disappeared, expertly blending in with the many greens and browns of the undergrowth. The steady march through the forest was silent; all communication within the group was performed with hand signals and by mimicking animal sounds. After what seemed like hours, Rahmon gave a hand signal that meant all was clear, the sign for the group to rest and eat. Gid sat with Rahmon and Tharik as they discussed the plans for the day.

'If the information you gave us about their last location hasn't changed, then we should be in about the right place to hide and wait for them to come this way. My only concern is that we know absolutely nothing about them or how fast they move, or even how they move. Tharik, Gid, do you have any objections to using this area as a base?'

Tharik looked at Gid and shrugged. 'Seems as good a place as any,' Gid replied, trying to sound like he knew what he was talking about.

In truth, he had no idea where they were or why this area would be any different from the rest of the massive forest that they had passed through. 'The only thing I have noticed,' he added, 'is that it's spookily quiet here. I haven't seen or heard a single creature for ages.'

'I noticed that too, which is why I feel we must be close,' replied Rahmon. 'You said that creatures were leaving the area as these shadows were entering, so it seems only reasonable to assume that they are somewhere in this area. All we can do now is hide ourselves and wait.'

After a short break for food and drink, Rahmon gave the order to hide. Within seconds the warriors vanished.

The day passed slowly but the group's discipline kept them hidden and quiet. Gid was feeling unusually afraid. He may have been surrounded by 20 of the bravest and best warriors from Arborinium, but he felt alone. The light was slowly fading and soon the eerie blue glow of the moon would touch the ground through the gaps in the trees. He was sure that just beyond his vision something was waiting in the trees, something evil and unseen, and though he felt frozen to the spot, he had the strangest urge to go and find out what it was. It was a feeling he had had before, when he was younger – the monster-under-the-bed feeling that makes you draw the covers around your face yet also entices you to take a peek underneath just to see if anything really is there.

Gid was not the only one feeling this; all the warriors were feeling the same senseless fear. Even Jareth, the biggest warrior Gid had ever seen, was scared as he sat hidden in the bushes. His heart was starting to pump loudly in his ears. A bead of sweat formed on his forehead and clung to his clammy brow for a brief moment until it let go and slid snake-like into his eye. A shiver ran down his back and his huge fist trembled.

'This is ridiculous. Why am I so scared? There's nothing there,' he whispered to himself in a broken, jittery voice.

Something moved in the trees. It was only a blur that he caught out of the corner of his left eye, but it definitely moved, and he had to know what it was. His training had taught him to stay with the others, safety in numbers always being the right choice; yet although he felt that he couldn't move and wanted nothing more than to curl up into a ball and move deeper into the cover of the bushes, he simply had to find the source of the movement.

Jareth left his hiding place and headed into the dark shadowy area of trees to his left, a look of pure fear etched on his normally hard-looking face. He walked very slowly with his sword drawn. As he moved forward, he placed each foot delicately down, making sure that not even the slightest sound came from him. Every tiny branch that snapped under his feet sent a cold shiver through his body. Another bead of sweat slowly worked its way down the lines of his face and his heart pounded even louder in his ears. He felt sick and fought hard to hold it back, his hand shaking uncontrollably and his white knuckles showing how tightly he was gripping his sword.

Fear stopped him again, and a feeling of being watched haunted him, but there was nothing there. Still he could not calm himself down, and a morbid curiosity led him deeper into the forest. It was just Jareth and his shadow. But something was wrong. His shadow was not the right shape, and it seemed darker than normal. He stood still and stared, while his shadow seemed to move from the floor and the trees where the slowly dying light had cast it. It was as if it were moving on its own. Very gradually, the shadow stood up in front of him and lifted a shadowy hand towards Jareth's terrified face. He tried to scream but fear would not allow it, and he stood, silent, as the shadow slowly covered his body.

His sword dropped from his hand, his legs went weak and his breathing became frantic. He couldn't take in any air as his mouth was smothered by the thick, shadowy figure. His lungs were burning from a lack of oxygen, everything was going white, and Jareth's once huge, solid frame slumped lifelessly to the floor.

The whole group were leaving their hiding places and heading into the trees on their own, each forgetting all their training, blinded by fear. One by one they were being sucked in by the same curiosity that had cost Jareth his life. A few muffled screams made their way back to a terrified Gid, and then all went silent.

Rahmon sat in the bushes alone, and for the first time in his adult life he was terrified. He could not stop his group from leaving. He wanted to shout orders – he needed them to stay together – but he didn't dare to make a sound. Uselessly, he sat frozen to the spot. He knew that his group would be powerless against this enemy on their own. Like the others, he wanted to leave his position and run, but years of discipline kept him hidden. Two shapes made their way towards his unguarded back, joined seconds later by many more. Before he could react they had surrounded his scared body, lifted it and were carrying it through the forest. Wherever he was being taken, he was to be alive – terrified but alive.

Gid stayed in his place. He was scared too, but fear was no stranger to him – he was still a child. Still afraid of the dark, he knew what it was to fear imagined wardrobe monsters from time to time, and things under the bed. Ghosts still walked through his house at night. Fear had been his companion from the first night his mum had made him sleep with the light off years ago. More recently, fear was only triggered after he had watched a scary film, but it was still a very familiar feeling.

He knew that the wardrobe monsters turned out to be piles of clothes or a badly hung shirt, that the monster under the bed was usually the shape of one of his toys, and that ghosts were only timbers creaking when the temperature dropped at night. What he was feeling now was new, real – there truly was something to be scared of, but it was still just fear. If he had a quilt with him he could hide and make a small hole to breathe through and that would make him feel safer, but for now, the safety of hiding in the bushes would have to do. Gid sat feeling very alone and very scared, and no amount of curiosity would move him.

Gid's back was just visible in the bushes ahead, and the lone figure crept quietly towards it. A hand reached out to touch his shoulder. Gid spun round and pointed his sword at the silent stalker.

'Whoa, Gid! It's me, it's Tharik. The shadows have gone.'

A spark of relief shot across Gid's face. 'I'm so glad you're ok! Tharik, I thought I was the only one left – I could see everyone disappear into the forest, and no one came back.'

Tharik stood and stared blankly into Gid's face. 'They took my brother. They surrounded him – he was still alive and they didn't kill him. Gid, you should have seen his face – he was terrified. I've never seen him scared like that before – he just sat there like stone and let them take him. I followed them from above the trees and I know where they took him. Gid, we have to go and find him, rescue him. We don't have time to go and get help. We need to go now; you can help him, Gid.' Tharik was almost in tears and speaking rapidly.

'Tharik, I agree. We don't have time to get help. I'm supposed to be here to bring balance, to help. I won't lie – I am scared, but I will do my best. I watched everyone before and did nothing. I couldn't move. I won't fail your brother. Come on, you lead the way.'

Chapter 10: Rescue

Gid flew high above the forest canopy, following Tharik at great speed, driven on by anger and fear.

'We should be there soon. I think it would be best if we land and try and sneak in. If they see us up here we'll lose any slight advantage,' said Tharik as he slowly descended and landed on a huge branch of a monstrous tree. Gid followed, seconds later.

'If we keep to the branches up here we should be hidden, and we'll be able to fly out more quickly if we're spotted,' whispered Tharik.

They knew they had a hard task ahead of them and couldn't take any chances. 'Where exactly are we going?' Gid asked.

'Did you see a wall reaching above the treetops as we were flying? It's some kind of circular barrier protecting whatever is on the inside; it seems to be surrounding a city or something. That's where they took my brother. We're not even allowed to fly over it normally. The few who have been seen heading to the walls have never come back, so we're forbidden to go near the place. I know as much as you about what awaits us on the other side.'

In the growing darkness it was becoming impossible to see whether anything at all was moving below them.

'I think we should work our way through the treetops right up to the wall,' suggested Gid. 'Who knows what could be below us?'

'I think you're right. Our silhouettes might be seen against the moonlight from below, but we'll be safer this way. Let's just hope we don't get spotted,' Tharik replied. 'Look – the wall is just ahead. If we get right against it and fly up to the top edge we should be able to see enough of the inside to get a good idea of what to do next.'

Slowly, the pair made their way through the dense branches, unseen. They reached the wall. Huge roots of ancient trees covered its sheer sides, the thick grey veins making the wall look alive, as if each root could reach out and attack. Gid checked their immediate area and flew up to the edge.

'Tharik, there's nothing there. It's just a grassy mound. Are you sure this is where your brother was taken?' Gid asked, slightly puzzled.

'I'm sure,' replied Tharik, as he joined him at the top of the wall. 'Let's fly down and get a better look. This is where we should be,' he added, in a slightly sharp tone.

'What do you mean, "this is where we should be?"' asked Gid.

'I mean, err, well, it just feels like my brother is here somewhere. Look, we're wasting time. Let's just go and have a closer look.'

As the pair descended the other side of the wall, the mound still looked to Gid like a mound and nothing more, but he didn't say anything to his friend, as he seemed convinced that this was the right place. They landed in the thick grass and looked around. There was nothing to see other than the huge dark wall that surrounded them and the mound, but still Tharik was insisting that they were in the right place.

'Tharik, I don't mean to sound rude but there is nothing he…. Whoa!'

As Gid spoke, the ground beneath them opened up and they dropped into darkness. Gid flapped his wings and hovered. Above him, the hole that had suddenly opened was just as suddenly closing again, taking with it the only light. Directly below Gid there was a sudden flash, then another, followed by an orange glow coming from a flaming torch.

'I always carry a torch with me, just in case, especially if we're on a night mission,' said Tharik. 'Rahmon always thought it was a good idea.'

All the emotion had disappeared from his voice. Gid knew that he was worried about his brother. Tharik had not been the same since they left the woods. 'Look, Tharik, your brother will be ok, and we will find him.'

'What, oh yes, yes, Rahmon. I'm sure he'll be fine,' replied Tharik, as if he hadn't really heard Gid's words.

Tharik held the torch out and turned around, letting the light fall on the deep, red, rocky walls. They were in a huge, damp, cold cave that had tunnels leading off in several directions.

'What now? I don't think we can get out again the way we came in. We'll have to find your brother and then an exit, if we're still alive after trying to rescue him. I mean, the shadows are bad enough, but now we're stuck in here with them, wherever exactly they and your brother are,' said Gid in a slightly worried voice.

'My brother is through here, I'm sure of it,' Tharik replied as he pointed to a slimy hole about just over a metre wide heading straight down. Dripping noises echoed from its dark, unwelcoming mouth. It sounded deep. They looked around the cave floor for something to drop into it. Gid found a fist-sized rock, walked to the edge and dropped it. **CLUNK**... **CLUNK**... CLUNK... Clunk... clunk... squelch.

'Well, it's deep, and by the squelchy noise I reckon we may get a bit mucky. It's too narrow to fly down, so I guess we just climb. I don't suppose you fancy going first, do you?' asked Gid.

Tharik raised his eyebrows. 'You're the warrior, buddy. I think you can have the honour. Here, take the torch.'

'Thanks a bunch,' Gid replied, sarcastically, as he carefully lowered himself into the darkness of the hole.

He pressed his feet out in front of him and wedged his back and wings hard against the rock, leaving his hands free to hold the torch and help himself down. The pair slowly worked their way down the dark, slimy throat of the opening. Movement was awkward and they had to make sure that every foot placement was solid. Progress was made harder by the heat and smoke from the torch that stung Gid's eyes and made it hard for Tharik, above him, to breathe, but they needed the light to see where the tunnel ended. Finally, after many awkward minutes, Gid reached the bottom.

'Do you want the good news or the bad news?' Gid asked.

'The good news first and then the bad please,' replied Tharik calmly.

'Well, the good news is we're at the end of the tunnel; the bad news is I still can't see the floor. We seem to be in the roof of another chamber. We're going to have to drop out and hover down, I reckon.'

Gid lowered himself out of the tunnel, opened his wings and slowly hovered downwards, followed closely by Tharik. The thick, muddy brown floor slowly came into view, and in the torchlight Gid could see a football-sized crater that must have been caused by the rock he dropped. 'Well, that explains the squelch; it's a bit on the muddy side down here.'

They had entered a large chamber with just one tunnel that was around knee high leading from it. 'That's the only way we can go, and it's thick with red mud. We're going to have to crawl through on our bellies.' A small smile crept on to Tharik's face.

Gid went first again. He held the torch out in front of him and squelched head first on his belly through the thick red mud. Stalactites hung from the roof of the tunnel, barring the way, and he had to lie on his side to get past them. It was a tight squeeze, and he was beginning to doubt that Rahmon would have been able to be taken this way. Every movement was a struggle – the rock was too slippery to push their feet against and there was nothing to hold on to that they could use to pull themselves through. Their only way to move was by grunting a lot and wriggling like worms, which was hard work.

'I'm almost out, Tharik. I can see another big chamber. There are more tunnels leading out of it, and they seem big enough to walk through. Oh, and there's something else,' gasped Gid, as he worked his way out of the mud-clogged tunnel.

He slowly rose to his feet, removed as much of the thick red mud as he could and headed to the middle of the chamber. In its centre, on a carved stone stand, was a sword handle made of bone, but without a blade. He turned and looked at Tharik. 'We're not here for your brother, are we? We're here for this.'

Tharik pulled himself through the last muddy centimetres and looked at Gid guiltily. 'Look, Gid, please understand. We are here for my brother. I knew this was here, or at least I had heard stories about it. This sword will help us get my brother back. I knew you were more likely to come if you thought Rahmon was down here. The truth is, I was scared. The Elders need this to protect the city. They've sent people before to retrieve it but none have come back. They asked me to find it if anything happened. They believe it has special powers – powers that I'm sure we could use to help my brother.'

Gid looked at Tharik's pleading face and knew that he really believed this sword would help his brother. 'Look, next time just tell me the truth. I will always gladly help. If you'd have told me the real reason for coming down here we would still be here now, covered in mud in a slimy cave. There is one thing though – you do realise that there's no blade to this sword, don't you?'

'It should be in the next chamber. Look, Gid, I am sorry I didn't tell you the truth. And thank you for helping. If I carry the torch and lead the way for the next bit, will you take the handle?'

'No problem. Nothing is going to leap out and grab me when I pick it up, is it?' Gid asked, smiling.

Tharik just shrugged and laughed. Gid reached for the

sword. 'One more thing, Tharik.'

'What?' he replied in a slightly snappy tone.

'How did you know where to find this if no one ever came back?'

'The Elders have a map of the caves.'

'Why did they not just give you a copy? I mean, what if you forgot the route?' Gid asked, thinking that actually having a copy of the map would make more sense. Tharik looked slightly offended.

'It's so that the map won't fall into the wrong hands. Anyway, I got us here, didn't I?'

'I'm sorry. I didn't mean it like that. It was just something that came to me, that's all, but it makes sense now, and you did a brilliant job of finding it. I would have lost us by now,' Gid said, trying to get off the subject.

Gid once again reached his hand towards the blade, still not convinced that the walls wouldn't cave in or that a monster wouldn't jump out at them or a huge boulder wouldn't come thundering towards them the moment he lifted the handle from its stand, the way it happens in the movies. He took hold of the sword handle in his right hand, closed his eyes, held his breath and lifted it from the stand. He stood still for a second, holding his breath, with his eyes closed. Slowly he opened them one at a time and let out a sigh of relief.

'Well nothing has happened yet – the cave is still in one piece and – Ouch! What the?! AAArgh! Tharik, help – the sword, it's digging into my arm! Aargh, get it off me!'

The small bones that made up the handle of the sword were moving like snakes and burrowing into Gid's arm and hand. He pulled at them with his other hand but it was no use. The pain was becoming unbearable, tears filled his eyes and he screamed out in pain. Tharik stood and watched as his friend dropped to the floor and rolled around in agony.

'Tharik, please help me!'

But Tharik did not move. As he looked on calmly, almost

the entire handle entered Gid's arm, the bones now moving below the skin and joining with his own. Finally, it stopped, and Gid lay on the floor paralysed by pain.

Tharik sat on the stand that had held the handle, a knowing and guilty look showing on his face. 'I wish it didn't have to be this way, Gid. I've really grown to like you, but I didn't know what else to do.'

'Tharik, what have you done to me?'

Tears of anger and regret filled Tharik's eyes. 'What have I done? I've betrayed my people,' he sniffed. 'I've watched a great and innocent man die at the hands of my brother. I stood and watched as my brother was defeated and taken prisoner – my own brother – and now I've possibly killed Arborinium's only hope in this war.' Tharik sniffed again and wiped tears from his eyes. 'Why did you have to arrive, Gid? We were fine until you got here. In the eyes of our leaders you were to be this mighty warrior; my brother has waited for years for you. I am nothing, Gid, a nobody; I'm just in the way. Legion offered me power; he recognised the potential in me.'

Tharik clenched his fists angrily and turned his face away from Gid. 'I wish I could say I'm sorry, but it's too late. I've made my decision and I have to stand by it. The price was too high, but I've paid it, and I am Legion's man now.'

With these last words, Tharik left through another tunnel, the light of the torch leaving with him. Gid was in agony, alone and in the dark.

Slowly the pain began to ease and his arm started to feel normal again, although the handle was still inside it. A new feeling was filling him – not of fear or pain, but anger, an anger that he had never felt before. He could feel the blood pulsing through his veins. He clenched his fists and punched out, smashing a rock as his fist blindly hit it. He stood up and started punching out wildly, destroying anything he came into contact with; he couldn't think straight – this new rage seemed to be taking him over.

'Tharik, I forgive you,' he screamed. He dropped to his knees again and pounded the floor, his consciousness slipping away. He lay face down and suddenly felt very alone. Everything flashed white and he finally passed out.

Tharik slumped to his hands and knees outside the cave's entrance, retched and then threw up. He started to sob uncontrollably. Gid's words of forgiveness had echoed through the tunnel and he found himself seized with remorse. 'I am so sorry, Gid,' he said to the air as he wiped his mouth and stood up, his sobbing slowly calming down. 'How can you forgive me? I will never forgive myself for this, but I've done too much to turn back now.'

Steeling himself, Tharik took to the air and headed for the city of Harrashon and to his new master, Legion.

Chapter 11: The prisoner

The shadows flew low above the body of water that separated the great forest from the vast mountainous desert of Sidarahath, the Empire of Ash. They were moving speedily just above the surface, causing the water to form a wake behind them. Rahmon was being dragged along, bound by invisible ropes. His feet splashed in the water, their vibrations rousing monsters from its murky depths. Every time a huge fin or serpent-like body would come too close, a shadow would break away from the main group and fly at their pursuer, causing it to either flee or die – the shadows wanted their captive alive.

Rahmon was helpless. His fear had left but now he felt completely drained and his body ached from head to toe. He started to slip in and out of consciousness, his tired mind unable to stay alert or awake.

The shadows reached land. The harsh, dry heat of the desert had no effect on them, though Rahmon could feel the intense heat as soon as his feet scraped the ground. As they continued their journey with their weary prisoner, they were joined by more shadowy figures that circled above them. Rahmon could make out the blurry shape of huge dragons, though, like his captors, they appeared to be mere shadows of the real beasts. One of them, with a long, thin body shape, a short neck and a massive wing span, dived towards a huge rock. It hit the rock at full speed and emerged on the other side as a huge black formless cloud of thick smoke. Seconds later, the shapeless smoke once again took on the form of the dragon. With his shadowy kidnappers and these huge winged creatures now escorting them, Rahmon quietly said goodbye to any hope of escape.

The shadows crossed the desert plateau, then went over the

mountains and headed into an enormous bone-dry valley. They stopped and finally dropped the exhausted Rahmon on the lifeless ground. Just ahead of them was a huge boulder, about the size of a hot air balloon, that was resting on four smaller boulders. Rahmon watched as the shadows approached the boulder and seemed to bow before it. A thin, wispy voice came from the group of shadows.

'Guardian, we bring you this prisoner. Legion has requested that you hold him here until he needs him or until he dies, whichever is sooner.' Rahmon looked on in horror as a face appeared on the boulder, a face with small, piercing black eyes and a huge toothless mouth. The mouth opened and a deep booming gave the shadows its reply.

'Legion's bidding is my pleasure. Tell your master that his loyal servant thanks him for this opportunity.'

The face then turned to Rahmon, its evil eyes staring through him. The huge rock walked towards Rahmon on its smaller boulder legs with the pace and agility of a mountain lion. Before he could react, the walking rock was standing over him, its huge mouth open. Rahmon tried to move but it was too late – the mouth closed around him, swallowing him whole.

A barred window appeared in the side of the monster and Rahmon's shocked face peered out. He was a prisoner inside this evil living rock. Surely there was no way out and he was, as the shadows said, 'Here until I am needed by Legion or until I die.'

As if reading his mind the booming voice spoke again. 'You will be provided with food and water while Legion wants you alive. If he decides you are no longer needed, I will close up and you will be crushed.'

Further along the valley, on the side of a mountain, two unseen figures had been crouching, hidden by a rock that was silhouetted by the sun, watching the whole incident unfold. 'It isn't our problem,' said one.

72

'You may be correct, but I have a feeling it soon will be,' replied the other.

Seconds later they disappeared over a ridge.

Chapter 12: Destiny

Gid lay on a straw bed in the half-demolished chamber, the light from a freshly lit fire flickering over his face.

'He's awake, or at least, he is making a strange noise,' said an enormous tusked figure as it stood over Gid's body, watching excitedly.

'Give him room, Snorback. You've seen what he did to this cave, and you don't want to be in striking distance if he wakes up in the same mood that he passed out in,' grunted another, larger, tusked figure that was sitting by a newly built fire in the corner of the battered cave.

'I can't wait to meet him properly. Do you think he will be my friend? It's been so long since I had a friend.'

Two more huge hairy tusked creatures walked into the room from a tunnel near the fire.

'Any change?' asked one.

'He made a noise,' replied Snorback, excitedly.

'You shouldn't stand so close. Look what he did to this place,' warned the second huge beast.

'I've already told him that, but even after 2,000 or so years he's still as dim-witted as ever. How are the others?'

'They're still celebrating. It's been a long time. Seems like we have a lot to thank this little winged guy for. I just hope he pulls through.'

As if he could hear these words, Gid slowly opened his eyes and tried to sit up.

'I need water,' he said in a dry-throated voice as he slumped back down on to his back.

'Bring the lad some water – he's coming round,' said one of the group to anyone who might be listening.

Immediately the figure closest to the tunnel entrance disappeared. He came back moments later with a simple stone goblet filled with water and handed it over. Snorback nudged Gid gently – there was no response. He placed an arm under his back, carefully moved him into a sitting position and held the goblet to his lips. Gid opened his mouth and water was poured slowly in. He opened his eyes and took hold of the goblet.

'Thank you. I needed that,' he said after downing the contents. 'Who are you and where am I?'

The tallest and by far most fearsome of the group stepped out of the shadows and looked Gid in the eye. 'My name is Grimbarr. I am from an ancient tribe. Our name and existence has been long forgotten by most. Until today, until you arrived and found the sword, we walked around on all fours and fought daily against the urge to kill and hunt as wild beasts. You have met and fought one of our kind before.'

To the left of the speaker, Snorback shrugged awkwardly and seemed to blush. He suddenly gave Gid a huge, tusky grin.

'You and your kind knew us as the Hogboar.'

Gid sat wide-eyed, unable to speak.

'Our story is long and painful. We were once known as the Cortuskas. A feared warrior race, we were neither allies nor enemies of any tribe. Though we were feared, we were a peaceful people and kept ourselves to ourselves. We have been here longer than any tribe, longer even than stories and prophecies. The tribal wars did not concern us. We were approached on many occasions to join with different tribes, to help them fight, but the fight was never ours to join. One day a child arrived and befriended one of the many kings of one of the many tribes, and as I am sure you will know, he eventually became extremely powerful and he would take his army and destroy any tribe or people who would not join him. The balance of power in this world had always been even. There were wars and conflicts, but although they were many, they were always short-lived. With the arrival of this new power, who called himself Legion, the balance changed – he was the new king of all lands. Our people were left alone; we were still feared even by Legion – or so we thought.

'On one fateful night, in the middle of the hottest month, our part in the history and future of this world changed. Legion sent out his army and attacked a group of our people who were out hunting for food. In battle we can change into huge beasts, fuelled by anger and pure beastly strength. The battle was bloody and lasted for the entire night. For every one of our tribe that fell, Legion lost more than ten of his own soldiers. Our hand in events had been forced. We held a meeting and decided to join the fight to destroy Legion.

'If there was ever a night I could undo, it would be the night we created the sword – the very sword you found. That sword was made out of pure hatred. It is made from the bones of our people who died on that night. Our anger and hatred for Legion made the sword into a powerful weapon, but it was a weapon that would never be used by us. On its completion, my entire tribe was cursed. We changed into the creatures that we become in battle, and our only thought was to kill, fight and eat. We have lived in these caves below our old city ever since – only able to leave or return to them when the tunnels open up to release the thick mists that form deep underground. This fog has a strange effect – it traps and confuses any unfortunate creature that isn't quick enough to leave or who is foolish enough to enter it. We used this mist to catch and kill our food. I am sorry to say that you, too, were supposed to be killed, but even my son could not match your strength. Who would have known that the only being ever to defeat my son would also lift the curse? You saved us, and we are all in your debt. Thank you.'

Grimbarr placed his huge hand on Gid's shoulder. 'I hope I have answered your questions. Do you have anything else that needs answering? If so, I will do my best.'

Gid sat and stared at the figures surrounding him and then

down at his arm. 'I do have one more question. When I picked up the sword handle, it seemed to come alive. The bones pierced my skin and buried their way into my arm. The next thing I felt was anger fiercer than anything I have ever felt before – I thought it was going to rip me apart, but then everything went peaceful, the pain stopped and I suddenly needed to sleep. What happened to the sword?'

'Hmm, I have an idea where the sword might be. Please trust me while I try something.' Grimbarr walked away, bent down and picked up a rock that was about the size of Gid's head. Without any warning, he hurled it at Gid. Gid moved with lightning speed; to him the rock seemed to be moving in slow motion. He swung his fist at it, and as he did so, the bones came from his arm and formed a blade that sliced through the rock like a hot knife through butter, and then retreated once again into his arm.

'What are you doing? I lift the curse from your tribe and you hurl a rock at my head! If that's how you thank people, I would hate to annoy you. You could have killed me!'

Then Gid stared at the two smoothly sliced pieces of rock that had fallen by his feet at the edge of the straw bed. Slowly he took in what had happened. 'The sword came from my arm – it was almost like it was part of me. How did I do that?' He looked hard at his arm, turning it over and then back again. There were no cuts or bruises; in fact, there was no mark at all.

Grimbarr sat down on a boulder that had once been a part of the cave wall. 'Every other of your kind who has found the sword has been ripped apart. We've seen a few try, but the hatred that went into making it was too strong for them. You have something stronger than hatred – you must have a pure spirit, lad. I no longer regret making that sword; it was meant to be. Everything has a purpose. In finding the sword, you have made a strong ally with us, and you have a deadly weapon and new strength that will protect you in battle. When you fought my son, you fought as a mighty warrior; now you will be truly unstoppable.'

'Grimbarr, I am not from this world. It is a long story which I will tell you soon, but for now all you need to know is that there is a prophecy about me. I am supposed to bring a balance to this world. At some point I know I must face Legion; until now I never truly believed that I could do it – I thought that maybe there had been a mistake. Valletia told me that things would just kind of happen and, well, they have: my friend has betrayed me, Arborinium's best warriors have been killed and Rahmon has been taken by the shadows. I have released your tribe from a curse, and the weapon that should have killed me has made me stronger than ever. Grimbarr, I need your help. Arborinium is in danger. They are defenceless – we need to act soon.'

Grimbarr turned to the others in the cave. 'Prepare the tribe. Today we leave this place; we go to Arborinium. Snorback, take as many of the tribe as you need, follow the tunnel to Arborinium and make a new way out. We will wait in the tunnel until nightfall. Legion does not know that we are free from the curse, and this will give us an advantage. Gid, come with me. I need you to tell me everything.'

Gid climbed off his makeshift bed and followed Grimbarr out of the chamber.

Chapter 13: Out of the stone prison

The sun was setting over the desert, casting eerie shadows among the rocks. A large brown lizard with emerald green eyes turned its head towards its two-legged companion. 'Look, all I am saying is that they never tried to find you. Why do you care if this... what did you call him – Rahmy?'

'RAHMON!'

'Ok. Rahmon. What is it to you if he lives or dies? We have a good life here. The shadows leave us alone and there's plenty to eat.'

The wingless two-legged companion glared at the lizard. 'Don't be so unreasonable, Gecks. Rahmon was my best friend. The Arbitans didn't look for me because I was banished. I was a thief, stealing anything that wasn't fastened down. Rahmon tried to talk sense into me but I wouldn't listen. You know the story – I lost three things that I cared for as a result of my stealing. I lost my best friend, my home and the only girl I ever loved. I lost her, she was like...'

'Yes, I know, she was like the air you breathed, the only reason you would wake up in the morning. Oh, and what you wouldn't give to see Romallia again just once, to be able to touch her beautiful hair, blah blah blah...'

'I sometimes wonder why I ever rescued you. It cost me dearly, and what thanks do I get?'

The lizard snorted and looked hurt. 'I don't know how many times I can say thank you for that day,' she said. 'I would be dead if you hadn't rescued me, and yes, you would still have wings – you know I feel bad about the wings – but I have helped you too. You would have died of hunger yourself if you hadn't saved me. I showed you how to find water and food in the desert. I showed you how to find shelter and I taught you to climb. It was fate that brought us together and we have made a good team so far. Gecks and Ash – inseparable friends.'

Ash laughed. 'You're right. I didn't want an argument, and I do appreciate what you have taught me, but I owe it to Rahmon to at least try to save him. I would do the same for you.'

The lizard climbed up onto Ash's shoulder and whispered, 'It's getting dark. If we're going to do this, we will have a better chance under the cover of night.'

Ash smiled. 'Tonight, then. I just hope my plan works.'

As the eerie blue light of the moon shone into the valley, Ash and Gecks strolled casually towards Rahmon's living rock prison. The huge shadow dragons circled high above but paid them no attention. As they drew closer, Gecks stopped.

'I'll climb up to the ridge and keep an eye out,' she said. 'Good luck, Ash. I hope your friend is worth it.'

Ash smiled but gave no reply. Gecks scurried off up the side of the steep valley wall. Ash was now within metres of the huge prison. 'Um... excuse me, Sir,' he said politely. 'You seem to be holding one of my friends captive. I don't suppose you would consider letting him go, would you?'

The rock turned its evil eyes on Ash and charged at him.

'Whoa! No need for that, my friend. It was only a question.'

The rock stopped and glared at Ash. 'You impudent little fool. Who do you think you are talking to? I am no friend of yours! How dare you address me with such disrespectful questioning? Do you not know who I am?'

Ash smiled and put on a deep voice, imitating the rock. 'YOU IMPUDENT FOOL. DO YOU NOT KNOW WHO I AM? You use big words and sentences for a dumb lump of rock, don't you? Oh, and to answer your question – um, no, I don't know who you are. Unless you are my great aunt Veleras. The voice is about right, but I'm sure she was hairier than you, and slightly less attractive.'

The rock charged at Ash, opened its huge mouth and crashed down on top of him, swallowing him whole. 'You will die in here along with your friend. I have never been insulted before, and you will not live to do it again.'

Ash groped around in the dark and found the leg of his friend. 'Rahmon, are you alive?'

Rahmon squinted in the dark. He was unable to see his new prison companion but the voice was familiar. 'Asheroth, is that you? I thought you were dead, my friend.'

'Rahmon, we'll have time to chat soon, but I'm going to break us out of here. I have to do this quickly before the rock realises what I'm doing.'

Ash pulled something from his pocket. Seconds later the small prison was lit up. 'Here – take this.'

Rahmon took a small jar full of glowing insects from Ash. 'I need you to shine the light against the rock – I need to find any small crack. Hold it there – this should be big enough.'

Ash pulled a wedge-shaped piece of metal from his pocket and placed the thin end into the crack. He then pulled out a small rock and struck the wedge hard. The crack grew wider and longer. He hit the wedge again, and this time a loud cracking filled the cell.

'Nooooooo!!' cried a deep voice as the huge rock beast started to crumble. 'It can't be! You cannot beat me. I will crush you!'

But before it could react, the entire living prison cell crumbled into a pile of rubble. Gecks ran down the slope and started digging frantically at the pile of rocks. First she uncovered a wing, and then a hand. The rocks started to move as the two former prisoners worked their way out. Gecks helped them to climb free.

'We have no time to celebrate yet – the valley will soon be flooded with Shadow Forge. We need to climb quickly,' warned the lizard.

Ash sensed the urgency in his friend's voice. 'Rahmon,

quick – we need to climb to higher ground. You cannot fly here. If you do, you'll be killed by the shadow dragons. They only attack things that fly. Follow Gecks – she will know the easiest route out.'

As they climbed the steep valley walls, the ground became swamped with a thick black liquid cloud that seemed to be searching for signs of life.

'We'll be safe here,' said Gecks as they reached a large wide ledge high above the dark, moving ground.

'That was close. A few more seconds and we would have become shadows,' exclaimed Ash, breathing a sigh of relief. Then, turning to Rahmon, he asked, 'So, old friend, what brings you to the mountains? I mean, I know the food is good and the desert is lovely at this time of year, but isn't it a bit far from Arborinium?'

Rahmon smiled. 'Well, you may have lost your wings but you still have your sense of humour. Where are your wings, by the way?' he asked dryly.

'Oh, thanks very much – that was subtly put. It's actually quite a painful subject, isn't it, Gecks?'

Gecks gave Ash an evil stare. 'Don't you dare bring me into this. I will not say sorry again,' she snorted.

'I'm sorry, Gecks, I was only kidding. You know I don't blame you. I'd better explain. After your lot banished me from Arborinium –' Ash paused for dramatic effect and smiled at Rahmon. 'As I was saying, after my harsh banishment, I ended up in the desert on my own. I decided to fly to the mountains to find shelter. I then found out that flying around here was a big mistake – within seconds I was being chased by two of our shadow dragon friends. They act as some kind of guard or trap against any of our kind.

'I landed in a valley in the mountains and found cover in a small cave. I soon learned that the dragons only attack if you fly; they leave alone the animals that walk and crawl through the desert, but if any unfortunate winged creature were to make its way across the water it would be attacked and killed.

'I survived the first night in the cave but I soon needed water. I decided to climb to the highest point in the immediate area. Luckily for me there was a waterfall coming out of the rock about 30 metres up one of the sides of the next valley. As I reached the bottom of the valley, I remember staring up at the cool waters cascading down the rocks in front of me and landing in a deep pool. I have found out since that the water from the pool seeps out into a huge underground cave system, but that's another story. Where was I?'

'Water cascading into a huge pool…,' said Rahmon.

'Ah yes, thank you. I was about to walk over and drink from the pool when I heard a loud rumble, and the stones on the floor around started to shake and jump. I looked down the valley and watched as a huge black wave came thundering in my direction. In front of the wave a lizard was scampering for its life. I had to help it – I couldn't just watch it die – so I flew low along the valley floor towards it. The black torrent was almost on top of the creature when I grabbed it, turned and flew as fast as I could. As I looked up I saw a huge shadow dragon circling over me. We were trapped. The black river would hit us at any moment, but we would be killed by the dragon if we tried to fly out of the way. The pool was only metres ahead. I felt a pain in my back and wings as the river hit us. Fortunately it threw us forward into the pool, and the next thing I remember was lying on a rock at the side of the clear water away from the black river. Gecks was on my chest, unconscious, but breathing.'

Ash stopped briefly and smiled at Gecks.

'The river is called Shadow Forge,' said Gecks. 'It wasn't always here. My family told me that it arrived after the wars. Many people died in battle in these areas. A lot of blood was spilled. The Shadow Forge is the earth's reaction to the pain and death caused by the battles. Anything it touches becomes a shadow, even if it is already dead. The shadow is basically all the bad stuff that is left – anything good dies. Fortunately for us, we landed in the water – it seems to repel and purify the Shadow Forge. When the torrent hit Ash, the water saved us but his wings were gone.'

Ash rubbed his back. 'I was left with burns and no wings, but I found a friend. And also a way to fight against the shadows – the water works on them, too. After a few of them were destroyed by Gecks and me, they left us alone. For a being that is pure evil and creates fear as its weapon, they don't attack if they think you can harm them. You see, they are like any fear or phobia – once you confront it, it's suddenly not that scary any more.

'So what's your story, Rahmon? How did you end up being captured by the shadows and thrown into the bad-tempered rock monster?'

Rahmon told them the whole story, leaving nothing out.

'So you don't know what happened to your brother or the warrior?' Ash asked, sounding very concerned.

'The last I saw, they were still alive. I can only hope that they still are and that they managed to get back and warn the Elders. I, too, need to get back as soon as I can.'

'Well, the way I see it, we have a slight advantage at the moment. Legion thinks you're captured, and now we've met you, you also know how to defeat the shadows. We need to get you back unseen,' said Ash.

'You would help Arborinium even though it disowned you?' exclaimed Rahmon in proud amazement.

'I don't hate them. I learned a great deal through my banishment, and, more importantly, I made a new friend. I was the one who did the stealing. The punishment was a little harsh, but I cannot say that I was innocent. The Elders did what they thought was best: I was made an example of, and I bet the number of thefts dropped after I was exiled,' replied Ash humbly.

Rahmon thought for a moment and then said firmly, 'I will

speak to the Elders. You saved my life and you seem to have learnt your lesson. I never wanted the banishment. I tried to get them to be more lenient but they had made up their minds. I'm sure they will reconsider the punishment. But first, as you say, I need to get back unseen.'

Gecks smiled. 'That's the easy bit. The difficult bit will be getting your people to accept the new wingless wonder here. To get to your city, all we have to do is go through the waterfall. It leads into a huge underground river that goes all the way back to Arborinium and ends in a lake that feeds your trees. We have been through before, exploring the caves and river. Ash even made a small boat from wood that we, um, how should I phrase this... that we "borrowed" from the Great Forest.'

'We should leave now! We have to get back!' urged Rahmon.

'We will go soon, Rahmon, but first we must eat. I'm hungry, and you don't look too well, my old friend,' said Ash, looking concerned.

'You're right, I need to eat. I do feel a little weak,' agreed Rahmon. A grin formed on his face. 'I know a certain girl who will be very happy to see you – as happy as you will be to see her again.'

'I don't know what you mean, what girl? You know me, Rahmon – I live life on the edge – I never get tied down by girls,' said Ash in a manly voice.

'Well, you won't be upset when I tell you that she's married then, will you?' asked Rahmon.

'No, she can't be married. She's mine!' started Ash. 'I love Romallia; she can't have a husband! I am supposed to marry her!' Ash slumped to the floor and sat with his head in his hands.

Rahmon laughed and sat next to him. 'It's a good job she's still single then, really, isn't it? She has waited for you, you know. She always said you'd come back one day.'

'You're not funny, Rahmon. That was cruel,' snapped Ash, his face a bright shade of red. 'So she still has the hots for me, then? Can't really say I blame her. Did you hear that Gecks? She loves me.'

Gecks smiled. 'Yes, yes, Ash, don't we all? What female of any species could ever not love you? You really are irresistible,' she said in a mocking voice.

'Well, that's enough chatter. Let's go and eat. Your place or mine, Gecks?'

Chapter 14: The return

As the blue moon rested high in the cloudless night sky, more than a thousand huge warriors waited patiently at the newly made exit to their caves. Gid stood and looked up, out of the tunnel. He stared at the vivid blue orb that was casting its light over the faces in the tunnel.

'Beautiful, isn't it,' said Snorback.

Gid smiled. 'Yes, beautiful. And life changing,' he said.

'I'm not sure if I would go quite that far. But each to their own and all that.'

'This moon marked my arrival, Snorback. I was to arrive in the year of the blue moon. It was my destiny. My moon at home is a yellowy white, a harmless moon, a moon that means nothing more than sleep. I was just a school kid until this big blue ball changed my future. Since then I have battled you and been attacked by shadows. I have made new friends and lost them, been betrayed and left for dead, and I have freed your people from a curse. I agree, it is beautiful, but for me it is most definitely a life changer. Who knows what that moon will bring my way next?' reflected Gid quietly.

'You're a very bright kid, Gid, but don't worry about that moon. We're here with you now; the moon can only have a good story for you from now on. And I'm sure it will have a happy ending. Besides, I think something far more powerful than the moon is watching over you, my friend,' said Snorback, placing a huge, comforting hand on Gid's shoulder.

'Thank you. I have a feeling you're right. For the first time since my arrival I actually believe I can help this world. Legion's grip on the land will not hold for much longer,' said Gid confidently, as he unknowingly rubbed the hand that now contained his new weapon. 'Snorback, I will go in first and speak to the Elders. If you wait here with the others, I'll let you know when you can enter the city.'

Gid flew silently out of the tunnel and headed along the ground, staying out of the light of the moon. He stopped as he reached the base of the huge city and checked that he had not been seen. Above him, at the ends of some of the highest branches, sat small groups of lookouts, but so far he had gone unnoticed. He had to get in without causing a fuss. The enemy thought that Arborinium was defenceless, and that was the Arbitans' main advantage. Tharik had already betrayed them and Gid didn't know who to trust. If word got out that one of the party had survived and made it back, their advantage would be lost.

He stood with his back to the city and stared upwards. If he could stay close to the shadows that were being cast against the tree trunks, he might be able to make it to his room unseen. Gid flew from shadow to shadow, constantly watching the lookouts. He hovered for a second in a shadow, next to a door about a quarter of the way up. He was centimetres away from the door – too close – and his wing rapped against it. A green glow suddenly came from the small windows.

'I'm coming,' said a voice from inside, and seconds later the door opened, trapping Gid between the door and the wall. He held his breath as the occupant of the room hovered outside trying to see who had rapped on the door.

'Who's there? Come on, show yourself!'

'Is everything alright down there?' yelled one of the lookouts.

'I thought I heard a knock at the door, but I must have been dreaming.'

'Ok. Don't worry about anyone knocking on your door. It won't happen while we're on lookout.'

'Good night,' replied the occupant, and closed the door.

Gid looked up again, sure that he would have been spotted, but the lookout was now deep in conversation with another member of his small group. Gid shook his head in disgust at their carelessness and then placed his hands together as if in prayer. 'Thank you,' he mouthed silently to an unseen listener. 'I'll deal with the lookouts later.'

He flew quickly up to his room, opened the door and slipped inside. Without wasting any time, he headed straight for the Elders' meeting room. He knocked on the door and entered. There was no one inside.

'Of course, it's the middle of the night! Why would they be in here?' exclaimed Gid. 'They'll all be in bed.' But he had no idea where any of the Elders' rooms were. 'I can't just go around and knock on everybody's door,' he thought. 'Who would be awake now? Come on Gid, think…'

He sat with his feet dangling over the walkway. The sun would be rising in a few hours and the Cortuskas army he had brought were waiting for him in the tunnel. He started to panic, like a child lost in a supermarket.

'What do I do?' he asked desperately.

'I don't know, Gid, but if you tell me the problem I might be able to help.'

A dirt–stained hand with mucky fingernails clasped his shoulder. Gid turned his head. The friendly smile on the dirty-faced Borrea greeted him. 'I knew you were still alive, Gid. What happened to the others? Where are the brothers?'

'I'll tell you soon enough. I need to call an emergency meeting before the sun rises. Where did you suddenly appear from?' he asked, slightly puzzled.

'I was up in the leaves counting the bugs. You see, some are active during the day whilst others prefer the night. On nights like tonight I can use the natural light to help me count how many of each species there are in a certain area. If I go up there with a lantern they tend to hide away. If the number of bugs rises or falls too much then the whole balance is disrupted and the city could die.

'There is one bug in particular called a Listinthia Perricala, or fruit wasp. You can fit about ten of them on one fingernail – they are that small. They live and lay their eggs inside a particular fruit called a frune. Without these tiny little wasps we would have no city to live in – the trees would not survive. Tonight is the night that they make their yearly trip to new fruit where they will lay their eggs and then die…

'Anyway, enough about my bugs. I get a little carried away once I start on a subject that I enjoy. If you come with me we can go and wake the rest of the Elders.'

Borrea was fascinating to listen to, and on another night Gid could have talked with him for hours, but tonight there was no time.

Within minutes they had rounded up all the Elders and were heading to the meeting room. Gid told them everything: the devastating defeat at the hands of the shadows, Rahmon's capture, Tharik's betrayal, meeting the Cortuskas and how he had managed to sneak past the lookouts with relative ease. There were many mixed reactions as Gid told them the news: tears, anger and utter shock were mixed with small glimmers of hope. The Elders agreed that the Cortuskas should enter the city immediately. In the morning they would hold a meeting with all the inhabitants of the city to let them know everything, from Gid's arrival to the recent losses.

Gid walked out of the meeting room and on to the huge branch where he had first been told that this was no dream. He walked up to one of the small groups of lookouts.

'Excuse me. I don't want to interrupt your important conversation, but could you please send a message around to each group telling them that they are to see Valletia inside. You are to leave one member from each group to carry on your lookout,' said Gid, sternly.

'You made me jump then, lad. I didn't even see you come outside,' said one of the small group.

'Exactly,' replied Gid, and with that he left the branch and flew to the ground, staying in the shadows.

He reached the tunnel and entered. There was nobody there.

'Hello?' he called quietly.

'Hello, Gid. What kept you?' said the deep growling voice of Snorback from behind him.

He was suddenly surrounded by smiling Cortuskas. 'How did you do that?' he asked in amazement.

'We're masters at hiding, Gid. I showed you that in the fog, remember?' replied Snorback proudly.

'How could I ever forget? I'll never feel safe in fog again!' joked Gid. Then he went on, 'I have spoken to the Elders. We are to enter the city when they signal that the coast is clear.'

'Why does it matter if the coast is clear? We're nowhere near the sea...' asked Snorback, with a puzzled look on his face.

'It's just a saying. It means that we're safe to enter the city without being seen,' Gid laughed. Reaching up, he patted his huge new friend on the shoulder.

'Ahh, now it makes sense. I'll go and tell Dad, I mean General Grimbarr.' He turned to a huge warrior with a missing tusk. 'Go and inform the General that we will be leaving soon.' Snorback had been placed in charge of the troops – a position that he was loving.

A few minutes later the General arrived, dressed in a long red cloak with a black fur trim. It looked slightly odd, as the Cortuskas wore no clothes. Grimbarr must have noticed Gid's interest in the cloak.

'I know. It looks too formal, doesn't it, but it's the only thing I own. I think the red matches my eyes perfectly though, don't you?' he said in what was possibly supposed to be a mock female voice.

'You look lovely, Sir. In fact, the black fur matches your teeth, too,' said Gid cheekily. The Cortuskas who were within earshot were desperately trying not to laugh.

'I like you, lad – you have guts,' laughed Grimbarr. He

patted Gid on the back, knocking him to the floor. 'Sorry, son. I forget my own strength sometimes.'

The Cortuska, watching for the signal at the mouth of the tunnel, climbed down. 'There was a flash from the doors, Sir, like something reflecting the moonlight,' she said as she saluted Grimbarr, Gid and Snorback in turn.

'That's it. That's our signal. Let's go, quickly,' said Gid, as he picked himself up from the floor.

The ground between the tunnel and the city was suddenly filled with a thousand huge shapes as they headed quickly but silently to the city gates.

Chapter 15: A trip down the river

As the moon reached its highest point, beneath the ground the three companions paused halfway across the rocks by the pool as they made their way to the waterfall.

'Mind yourselves on the rocks here – they can be a little slippery for two legs,' said Gecks mockingly.

'Thank you, Gecks, but I think you would have to be really careless to fall in... Don't you think so, Rahmon?' added Ash, as he struggled to hold back the flood of laughter that was ready to burst from him.

'That's it you two, laugh away. I'm sure it must have been hilarious. I could have really hurt myself, you know,' snapped Rahmon as he tried desperately to salvage any pride that he had left. He was sitting on a rock, emptying his water-filled boots back into the pool.

Ash and Gecks could take no more. They both collapsed in laughter and could not stop, no matter how hard they tried.

'Oh shut up. I'm soaking wet and we've only just started the journey. I have nothing dry to wear now!'

This did not help, and the two friends laughed even harder as they tried to apologise.

Eventually, Rahmon began to see the funny side of it too, and joined in. All three of them now sat laughing together, unable to stop.

'Please, no more! It's starting to hurt!' cried Rahmon.

Ash stopped for a second, sighed, then started again. After a few minutes, and many sighs and giggles, they eventually stopped laughing.

'Ok, are we all finished now?' asked Gecks.

Ash and Rahmon were still letting out random bursts of childish giggles, but they were now ready to continue. Rahmon put his soggy boots back on and carefully hopped along the rest of the boulders to the edge of the waterfall.

Behind the waterfall was a steep hidden pathway that led down to a small boat on the bank of the underground river. There would be no need for lanterns, as the whole length of the river and cave was lit up by small, bright green, glowing slug-like creatures that covered the entire ceiling and walls.

'Rahmon, can I borrow your wings while I walk through the waterfall? It's just that I don't want to get wet really, and it isn't as though you need them now, is it?' asked Ash cheekily.

'Just walk behind me and I'll keep you dry. Trust me.'

Ash walked closely behind Rahmon and sheltered underneath his huge wings as the water poured down heavily on them. They made their way carefully down the steep path without incident and slowly pushed the boat into the river. It was slightly unstable, but they climbed aboard and slowly headed down river towards Arborinium.

'The river picks up pace soon as it heads deeper underground. The whole trip will take a couple of hours. There's no need to row – the oars are here for travelling back up river, but to be honest, last time we just dragged it back through the water while we walked along the bank,' explained Ash. 'Gecks, should we let him see the light show?'

Gecks climbed up onto Ash's shoulder. 'Watch this!' she said excitedly, and flicked her tongue out at the glowing slugs.

A sudden burst of light exploded from the point where the lizard's tongue had touched the slug, like ripples on a pond after throwing in a rock. Each ripple was a different vivid colour that carried on as far as the eye could see. It was an amazing sight, and the three lay back in the boat and watched the dazzling, colourful display unfold.

'You could live down here quite easily,' said Rahmon in a relaxed voice.

'We did for a while. There are fish in the river and there's an endless supply of water. There are caves and tunnels leading everywhere down here, and the best part is that the shadows can't come through the waterfall. In fact, I think we're the only three who know about this cave's existence. The only reason we left was to get fresh air again and see the sky. But as a safe haven goes, it can't be beaten,' replied Gecks.

'What happened to your family, Gecks? How come you stay with this one?' inquired Rahmon, pointing at Ash.

'I have no family. When Ash rescued me I felt obliged to help him. I often feel like a nanny, but we look out for each other really.' Gecks fired her tongue at another slug, setting off another ripple of lights.

The rest of the journey passed quickly, with the odd outburst of laughter as one of them pictured Rahmon's face when he fell awkwardly into the pool. Rahmon was beginning to fall asleep when he was roused by Ash.

'We're here!' he said. Rahmon rubbed his eyes and looked around. They had reached a stretch of river that looked like a thick underground jungle.

The massive tree roots of Arborinium came down from the roof of the cave and fed from the river's waters. Ash tied the boat to one of the roots. 'At the top of this root there's a small opening that comes out near the entrance to the city. After you, Rahmon.'

Chapter 16: The Council of War

The Cortuskas sat on the huge roots in a vast room at the bottom of the city. The Arborinium Elders, joined by Snorback and Grimbarr, sat in the middle around a highly polished oval table. Valletia was sitting at the head. She had welcomed the guests and introduced the rest of the Elders.

Both tribes had now been brought up to date with the current situation. Outside the room, two guards kept watch and whispered about the newcomers.

'The building of ladders and hatches for access to the other levels for our new allies the Cortuskas will be done first thing in the morning, This will no doubt cause a stir amongst the people and we will deal with this matter when we have a public meeting. But there are a few points to discuss before then. Firstly, the impending attack on Arborinium – if, or rather when, it will happen. Secondly, security – how can we protect ourselves? Thirdly, Rahmon – we need a plan to find out if he is alive, where he is and if we can rescue him. And, finally, we need to know how to defeat these dangerous shadows.' Valletia was looking tired. The news had quickly taken its toll and Gid could tell that she had not slept much since he had last seen her. She looked tired and kept rubbing her face as she spoke.

'I might be able to help out with the last two points, though I must admit I'm not too happy about being third on the list,' said a familiar voice from the back of the room.

Everybody turned their heads to see the speaker. Valletia stood up with tears in her eyes as Rahmon, Ash and Gecks walked through the crowd.

'Evening Val,' called Ash cheekily. 'Long time no see!' He lowered his voice and spoke to Rahmon. 'Are these people new or have the Arbitans got a lot hairier, uglier and taller since I was banished?'

'Shut up, Ash. Let me do the talking, ok? You'll just get yourself into more trouble,' whispered Rahmon sternly.

'Rahmon, there's Romallia! How do I look?'

Rahmon just shook his head.

Romallia smiled shyly at Ash and then looked away. Valletia stood up, walked over to Rahmon and placed her hands on his shoulders. 'Thank the heavens that you are safe,' she said.

Mallerik ran over, flung her arms around him and burst into tears. 'I'm so happy to see you. I thought you were dead.'

'Where is Tharik? Please say he made it back,' pleaded Rahmon, scanning the room hoping to see his brother.

Mallerik stopped hugging her son and her face became stern. She stared at him, unable to speak.

'What? What is it? Please tell me he's alive. I can't have lost my brother.'

'Your brother is alive, but he is as good as dead. He is a traitor – he set you up, and the shadows were a trap. He left Gid for dead in a cave. He is with Legion.' Mallerik could take no more. She walked back to the table and burst into tears. Romallia slipped over to the table and placed an arm around her.

'Gid, is this true?' Rahmon trusted Gid completely, and his word would be enough.

'He betrayed us all, Rahmon. I'm sorry.' Gid felt awkward. There was nothing he could say to make things different.

Rahmon wiped a tear from his eye. 'Not only have I lost a brother but I have killed an innocent man. Artimus knew that Tharik had turned and he tried to bring him back, but I killed him.' He felt a lump rise in his throat and stared at the floor, momentarily lost. Then, composing himself, he said determinedly, 'I have news about the shadows; I know how to beat them.' Beckoning Ash to come forward, he went on, 'We owe my life and this information to an old friend.'

Ash took a step and gestured politely to the Elders. He suddenly felt a little awkward. 'Hi, um, how are you all?'

Valletia waved him over. 'Come here, Asheroth,' she said in a very official-sounding voice.

Ash bowed his head and walked towards the table, followed by Gecks.

'Is this true? Did you save Rahmon as he says?'

'Well, you know me. I do what I can,' answered Ash, looking at the floor. Rahmon poked his friend in the back. 'I mean, yes, it is true, what he said. With a little help from a friend.'

'We owe you our gratitude and the life of Rahmon,' said Valletia gently. 'I see you have lost your wings.'

'Yes, it's a good story, if you would like to hear it,' piped Ash with some enthusiasm.

Valletia smiled warmly. 'I am sure we'll have plenty of time for your tales over the coming days. Who is your friend?'

'I am Gecks,' said the lizard as she bowed her head.

'Pleased to meet you, Gecks. We owe you a lot. Please treat our city as your home.' Valletia crouched down, leaned closer to Gecks and whispered, 'I'll catch up with you properly later, my old friend. How has he behaved?'

'I think you will find him to be a much humbler person than you remember, though he still has a mouth on him,' said Gecks. She thought for a moment and then continued, 'He is still in love with your granddaughter; he never stops talking about her. And he has become a very good friend. I may have almost died doing it, but you were right to ask me to keep an eye on him.'

Valletia smiled and winked. 'This will be our secret. He must never know.'

'The secret is safe with me!' assured Gecks.

'Romallia, find Gecks somewhere to stay, and take Asheroth back to his old room,' said Valletia, standing up.

'Does this mean I'm forgiven?' asked Ash smiling.

'Of course! Welcome home. Now get some rest – we will need you in the morning.' Just before he left, Valletia leaned forward and whispered into Ash's ear, 'If you ever call me Val again you will be out of here faster than you can say sorry! Oh, and one other thing – look after my granddaughter. She has missed you terribly. Now don't let her down again!'

'Thank you so much,' said Ash bashfully. 'I promise you I am a different person now; I will prove it. Again, thank you.' Ash could not believe his luck.

'Follow me,' said a very pink-faced Romallia from behind them.

Gecks climbed onto Ash's shoulder. 'She's very pretty Ash – too pretty for you!'

'You two were very chatty, what were you discussing?' asked Ash curiously.

'You!' replied Gecks, giving nothing away.

With Gecks on his shoulder, Ash bowed to the Elders and followed Romallia out of the room. 'This is going to be a long climb – my room is near the top,' said Ash to Gecks.

Romallia spoke to two burly guards and then flew up to a higher level. While Ash and Gecks watched her fly away, the two guards gripped Ash under his arms and flew the two friends up after Romallia.

Back in the meeting room, Valletia sat down again at the table while Rahmon took a seat next to Gid. He spent the next few minutes giving a report on his capture and rescue and, most importantly, sharing the valuable information on how to defeat the shadows. In return he was given all the information that had been discussed that evening.

Valletia stood up and spoke. 'Tonight we have won back a small advantage, made new friends, welcomed back old friends and have had Rahmon and Gid returned to us. We will talk more in the morning. We will think better after a good night's sleep. Grimbarr, we have arranged rooms on the ground floor for you and your people. They are normally used for storage and I apologise that they are only basic. Tomorrow we will prepare something more comfortable.'

Grimbarr grinned. 'Lady Valletia, you are very kind. We have lived in a damp cave for longer than I can remember. The rooms will be most welcome. I agree with you about sleep. We can do no more here tonight.'

'If everyone is in agreement, I will call this meeting to a close,' said Valletia.

Gid held up his hand out of habit. 'I have something to add, if that's ok. Valletia, you once said that things would just happen. Well, you were right about that. My being here has definitely put the cat amongst the pigeons.' Gid was met with a number of confused looks. 'Ok, I guess you don't have cats or pigeons here... Forget that bit then, it isn't really important. What I really want to say is this: when I was with the Cortuskas I wanted to get back here and warn you all as soon as I could because I was really scared that something terrible might have happened. I have come to see Arborinium as my home and everyone in this room as my friends. I feel like I have been accepted by all of you and I'm very grateful. I don't really know if I was supposed to take sides, but I have – I am with you until the end. You can count on me! Snorback said that something more than the moon was watching out for me, and I think he's right. My part in all this was written down before I was born; I cannot escape it and I don't want to. I know we can win this and err, well, um, that's all really... I just felt that I should say something. I hope that made some kind of sense.'

Valletia took Gid by the hand. 'This world has been waiting for you for a long time, Gid. You will bring balance. I'm glad you are with us and that our world will be free again. Legion will be beaten.'

The whole table rose to their feet in agreement. Grimbarr picked up a wooden tankard from the table and raised it high. 'To Gid and to the end of Legion!'

The rest of the table stood noisily and joined in the toast. 'To Gid and to the end of Legion!' echoed round the room.

The following morning was an eventful one. Valletia's meeting with the Arbitans had been difficult. Some of the people were outraged that they had been kept in the dark about the prophecies and Gid's arrival, some did not believe the prophecies and thought Gid was a fraud, while others stared at her for the whole meeting with open mouths and unblinking eyes in sheer shock. But the news about Artimus and Tharik stunned them all into silence. Families and friends huddled together as they were told the outcome of the first contact with the shadows. The introduction of their new guests and allies was too much for some, while for others it was exciting to have new faces around.

The inhabitants were instructed to act normally, to continue their daily routines. The farmers were to carry on working in the clearing outside the city and the hunters were to continue bringing food from the woods, only now they would have non-uniformed guards to escort them. No one was to enter or leave the city without permission. A curfew was put in place, and everyone had to be inside the gates before nightfall. The entire city was on full alert – war had once again raised its ugly head.

'Well, that went as well as I could have hoped,' mused Valletia to Rahmon as they flew away from the meeting room.

'Arbitans are tough. We will adapt to the news and these changes soon enough. It looks strange now, though, with ladders everywhere,' replied Rahmon. 'It didn't take the craftsmen long to get things in place for the Cortuskas.'

Gid finished getting ready and rubbed his eyes. Mornings were never a favourite of his. Last night had been pretty sleepless, so this morning was worse than most. He pushed his door open and walked down the corridor towards the clearing. He soon realised that he was no longer just another face. Every Arbitan he walked past greeted him in some way – some gave him flowers, some bowed, some turned their backs, and others approached him to shake his hand or just touch him. One extremely wrinkly old woman with a hairy chin grabbed his face between both hands and kissed his head. He suddenly realised that he was surrounded. Getting anywhere now would be impossible.

'Ouch! Do you mind – that was my bum!' he snapped. He turned round and came face to face with a group of pretty girls who smiled and waved. Gid blushed and quickly turned away.

'Come on, give a hero some room!' resounded a booming voice as Snorback pushed his way through the now dispersing crowd. 'I saw the crowd and thought you might need a bit of a hand!' he chuckled.

'Thank you. I did need it. It wasn't all bad, though. Did you see the girls?' said Gid, puffing his chest out and trying to straighten his hair.

'Not hairy enough for me,' grunted Snorback.

As they walked along the corridor, Gid was aware that they were being watched by thousands of curious eyes. People were pointing, staring and whispering in small groups. Just ahead of them, a group of about ten women and men, young and old, had congregated. They were in deep conversation and hadn't seen the pair approaching.

'If you ask me, I think they should go back to where they came from.'

'They're barbarians, uncivilised.'

'They smell a bit strange – must come from living in caves.'

'You'd think they would have made an effort to smarten up a little!'

'I just don't like the look of them. They don't seem "trustworthy" somehow.'

'I heard someone saying before that they were all

102

murderers and criminals...'

Snorback leaned his head into the crowd. 'We kill off our old people as well, and sometimes we use small furry creatures to wipe our bums. Excuse me please, kind people, I would love to stop and chat but you know what it's like – people to murder, crimes to commit. I do hope you can forgive me.' He smiled politely and walked through the middle of the silent, gobsmacked crowd.

Gid followed him, desperately trying not to laugh. 'Don't worry – he doesn't kill before breakfast,' he added, and waved goodbye.

'I don't know how you didn't punch one of them. You didn't even get angry. They were well out of order!' he said to Snorback once they were out of earshot.

'My dad, um, I mean the General, says that people like that are just ignorant. He says it's best just to be polite and prove them wrong, but I think it's ok to tease them a bit as well. There are lots of them like it in this world, and I expect it isn't much different where you come from.'

Gid nodded. 'We call them racists. There are some in every culture. It looks like there are some in every world, as well.'

'I must admit, though, it is quite nice to know I could rip them all limb from limb in seconds if I ever wanted to,' said Snorback, mimicking the act of strangling someone with his hands.

They continued on to the meeting room, Snorback climbing the endless ladders while Gid flew alongside him. There were four guards outside the door to the room.

'Please state your name and purpose for being here,' announced the largest.

'Gid and Snorback. We are here for the meeting,' said Gid politely.

The guard looked through his list and crossed off their names. 'You may enter, Sirs,' he said, and saluted.

As they entered the room, they were glad to see that they

were not the last to arrive.

'Good morning, Gid, Snorback. Please take a seat. Mallerik and Borrea will be along shortly,' said Valletia warmly.

Gid and Snorback took their places at the table and were joined seconds later by Mallerik, who was carrying a huge pile of books, and Borrea, who was holding a long, dark green vine and a lit candle.

'Let's start with you, Borrea. I know you are eager to share your idea,' said Valletia, once everyone was settled.

'Thank you. I'm sure you are all wondering why I am holding a Climbolus Hydrata?' he said, smiling, and waited for some kind of response. None came. He shrugged and continued. 'Well, this vine grows all through the great forest, and we have lots of it here in the city. It can be used as a water source if you ever get stuck – all you need to do is cut off a chunk about half a metre in length and you can drink from it.

'It also protects itself and the other trees from fire. Watch this.' Borrea placed one end in a beaker of water and then held his candle under the vine. Within seconds, the vine was spraying water out of hundreds of tiny holes. The candle was extinguished and those closest to the vine, including Mallerik, got a bit of a soaking.

'I'm sorry if you got wet, but do you see?' he asked enthusiastically.

There were a few confused faces, but Rahmon was beaming. 'Borrea, you are amazing. You may well have saved our lives. I see what you're thinking but I will let you explain, my friend. It is your idea.'

'Thank you, Rahmon. I would not say "amazing" – I just know plants, that's all. This vine, however – this *is* amazing! If I can tie these vines all through the city and have people standing ready with candles or torches, then we can let the shadows in. I had thought it would be quite impossible to keep them out, and then we would be done for, but if they are all in the city and we start the vines spraying water everywhere, then the shadows and not us will be done for. And not only that, if we have them over the outside of the city too, then if we are attacked with fire, as I am sure we will be, the vine will put the flames out.'

Valletia stood up. 'Borrea, you are a genius. Thank you. Can you get enough vines?'

'They are everywhere. I already sent some of the hunters out to collect as many as possible. I know I should have waited but I thought we could use them for fires even if you didn't like my plan for the shadows.'

'Again, a wise decision. This city would be lost without you.'

Everybody applauded. It seemed that their biggest problem had been the easiest to solve! Gid smiled and nodded at Borrea; he had a lot of respect for the modest gardener, as everyone did.

'Mallerik, would you like to follow?'

'Thank you. I do not have a plan but I do have valuable information. I have been reading through these books about Legion and his battles. It seems that his methods of fighting have changed through the years. When he was young and out to prove himself, he would be very much a part of the battle and would use sheer numbers to defeat his enemies. He became known as a fearsome warrior. As he grew older and his confidence grew, he would take fewer soldiers and still win. Then, as his enemies decreased, he would stay in his kingdom and send out small numbers of troops to attack on his behalf. If they won, the respect and fear for his troops would grow; if they were losing, he would send in another wave to back them up. He would carry on this way until eventually he would be victorious.

'You see, to Legion, war is a game; he could beat almost anyone with sheer numbers in one big battle. But to make it more interesting, he will send in a few soldiers and see if he can win. He likes to judge his enemies' strength. I know he

105

feared you, Gid, which is why he sent in so many shadows. But he felt that even they may not beat you, so he had a back-up plan. Even if all his soldiers could not beat you, he still had something to try – your friend.

'Legion is an expert at judging his enemy, but he thinks we are defenceless. I am sure he will attack soon. It would have come eventually, but in our day and age he needed an excuse – his people would not allow war without reason and he values public opinion. You see, when Gid arrived, we effectively declared war on Legion, and now he has a new game to play. I think we were left alive all these years so that he would still have an enemy to fight; we are a toy to him, and he was just waiting for his moment. He will not use many troops to start with. I believe he will send in the shadows as he sees them as his best weapon, and he will consider that they will be enough. When, or if, they are defeated, he will send in soldiers, and if we beat the soldiers he will send in more. We can last for a while, and we have the upper hand at the moment, but eventually, unless we take Legion himself out of the equation, we will lose.' Mallerik sat down and passed her books around the table.

Rahmon sat at the table, twitching his fingers. He had in front of him a map covering all the areas between Arborinium and Harrashon. On the map he had placed wooden blocks of differing colours representing different troops and their abilities. He had been playing with the blocks for a while, moving them and taking them out, trying different formations.

'She is correct,' he said at last. 'We can last for a while, but the sheer numbers dictate that we will lose in the end. There are, however, a number of things that we have on our side. I believe that with Borrea's plan we can defeat the shadows without too much difficulty. With Grimbarr and the Cortuskas on our side we can deal a huge blow to Legion's armies. They will not be expecting to fight a force as powerful as yours, Grimbarr! They will have made plans to attack a badly

106

defended, unsuspecting city.

'Legion's men will outnumber us by about twenty to one. This sounds bad, but it could actually be used to our advantage. Legion's men will be confident of an easy win, and they have never really been tested, but our soldiers will know that this fight means life or death. We will fight until the last warrior is standing.

'And finally, we have Gid. He is our key to winning the war. Gid, you will have to defeat Legion; no one else in this room can do it. After the first big defeat, Legion will reorganise his army and change his plans, and we will have to counter them – the advantage will move back to him. Gid, you need to defeat him at Harrashon before he can do this. You will need someone who knows the city, who can get you in – somebody with the skill to break in to Legion's palace undetected. You need a thief.' Rahmon looked across the table to Asheroth.

'A reformed thief, actually,' replied Ash. 'Gid, he's right. I've spent a lot of time in Harrashon. I know the city well. I've become a good hunter since my banishment. I used to visit the city to exchange meat and animal hides for clothes and medicines with the local traders. I know my way around and I know the right kind of people. I want to prove to you all once and for all that I have changed. You've been good enough to allow me to return; I would now like to do my bit for Arborinium.' He was determined to help, to somehow repay the Arbitans for his thieving in the past.

Gecks was sat on the back of Ash's chair. She looked at Valletia and said boldly, 'If Ash is going then I am going too.' There was no questioning it. Wherever Ash went, she went.

'I would like to go as well!' said Romallia. 'I don't know why exactly, but I'm sure I am supposed to go with them.'

Valletia looked at her granddaughter seriously. 'Do not let your feelings for Ash influence your decisions!' she said, probing her motives.

Romallia blushed, but replied firmly, 'I would rather not

put myself in danger, but something is telling me that I need to be there.'

Valletia nodded; she seemed satisfied with the response.

Ash stood up and spoke. 'Oh, come on! Have none of you read any books? This is a classic story, if ever there was one. Guy falls in love with girl, guy goes bad, gets banished, loses girl. Guy gets forgiven, finds girl again. Guy and girl volunteer for dangerous mission and either girl gets kidnapped or killed, or guy rescues girl and then gets killed himself. Please, Romallia, I've only just got you back; I don't want to lose you again, and in all honesty I don't want to die either. That would be, well, really, really bad.'

Romallia smiled. 'If that's how you feel then I will stay here while the shadows and Legion's armies attack. I'm sure I could be quite handy with a sword if I have to.'

'You win,' said Ash, and he sat down again, looking a little glum. It seemed that she would be in danger wherever she was.

'I would go with you, Gid,' Snorback offered, 'but the only thing is, I think I may stand out a little, big and hairy as I am. I would love to help you, but my place is here. I love a good fight. And I'm guaranteed a fair old battle if I stay, but I will always be ready to come and help you if it feels right.'

'I am with my son on this one,' growled Grimbarr. 'My people will finally do what we should have done a long time ago: Legion and his army will finally feel the full force of the Cortuskas! We defeated ourselves last time, but it will be different this time and Legion will fall!' He for one would not give in until he had seen Legion's reign come to an end.

Gid stood up and grinned gratefully. 'I honestly believe you could win this war without me! I would not like to face any of you on the battlefield. If my part in this is to remove Legion then that is what I will do, but I have seen something else happen today that I think may have been missing years ago when the wars started. Harrashon itself was the most powerful

108

city in this world even before the wars, or at least that's how I understand it. I think that even without Legion, the king – what was his name, Harrash? – I think he could have beaten all his enemies because all the tribes were fighting for power and not for each other. Nobody joined together to fight against Legion, and the cities just fell one by one because his army was better and bigger. Today the two remaining tribes that were never beaten by Legion have joined with each other to fight against him rather than to fight him alone and lose. I know I must face Legion, but I think a big part of the reason for my being here was to unite his strongest enemies. You have all told me that you believe in me, and now I believe in myself. But more importantly, I believe in you – I know you can win this. Your tribes were strong on their own, but they are unbeatable together.'

Smiles and nods broke out around the table. The boy was right! This was the first time that any tribes had joined together to fight Legion, and if they worked together to come up with a good plan, and if they could believe in themselves as much as Gid did, then half the battle would be won before it even started. This time it could be different; this time it would be different!

Chapter 17: Onwards

The sun was bright in the cloudless blue sky and the air was crisp as Gid stood on the huge branch outside the Elders' meeting room. A cool breeze blew across his face and made his messy hair dance. In a couple of hours he would be setting off for Harrashon and his destiny. Battles would soon be fought once again in this world, but as Gid stared into the endless shades of green of the thick forest city, he felt calm.

'I may never see this view again after today,' he thought to himself. 'But at least I got to see it like this before I left. This is how I will always remember Arborinium.' A small tear formed in his eye and then rolled down his cheek.

He stared up at the perfect sky and sighed. 'I have never done this before and I'm not sure how I'm supposed to do it, but God, if you are out there and you can hear me, I just wanted to ask if you could keep an eye on everyone for me? I don't want to lose anyone from here – it has become a second home to me. If things are going badly can you please give them a helping hand? Oh, and although I'm still not sure about this one, I'm going to ask it anyway. Will you go easy on Tharik? I know what he did was really bad – he betrayed us all – but I don't really care about that any more. You see, he is as much to thank as I am for the advantage we have at the moment. We wouldn't have met the Cortuskas, Rahmon wouldn't have found Ash and we wouldn't know how to beat the shadows, and also Legion would know exactly what he was up against – he thinks Arborinium is as good as his – and it's all because of Tharik! But more than that, he was my friend and I forgive him. Am I supposed to have my eyes closed and hands together when I say this stuff? If I am I'd like to say sorry for that as well. Oh, and before I forget, can you look after me and keep me safe too? I don't mind admitting that I'm a bit scared. Well, I think that's all for now. Thank you... oh, and Amen.'

A weight that Gid didn't realise he had been carrying suddenly lifted.

'That was beautiful, Gid. I'm looking forward to getting to know you better on our journey.'

Gid turned to look for the owner of the voice. 'Who said that?'

'I'm sorry, Gid. I didn't mean to startle you,' answered a cluster of leaves just above his head. The leaves moved as Gecks appeared from their midst. 'I was out here watching the sunrise – it was beautiful. I think I must have fallen asleep because the next thing I knew you were standing below me talking to something or someone up there,' she said, pointing her nose towards the sky. 'I've seen many people do that before. Who exactly were you talking to?'

Gid smiled and shrugged. 'I don't know, really. We call him God. People often talk to God when they need something or when they're in trouble.'

'We have a similar story here,' replied Gecks, 'only the place is not called "heaven"; they just call it paradise. Do you believe it, Gid?'

Gid was thoughtful. 'I've never really thought about it much. I suppose that everything that's happened to me recently has just got me thinking. And besides, it can't hurt, can it? If God is real, then I've just asked for some help – and, who knows, we might get it. If God isn't real, then I've just been speaking to the sky. To be honest, I was feeling a bit nervous about facing Legion and I needed to speak to someone, and it kind of helped. I don't feel that bad any more, just kind of peaceful. It's probably because it's such a nice day, but then again, it might be more than that.'

'That's a good way of looking at it. I'm nervous too; it will be a tough task to even get to Harrashon. I'm all for any extra help. I might just ask this God myself; like you say, it can't hurt, can it? Deep down I have a good feeling about it all, you know. Legion has had his time and it's definitely now time for a change.'

The pair stared out over the forest and watched as a flock of yellow birds flew wildly around chasing insects through the air.

Rahmon, Valletia and Grimbarr had spent most of the night going over plans. Everything seemed simple when they read what they had written down, but putting it into practice would not be so easy.

Today, anybody who could not fight would be moved into caves below the city. The shadows would not be able to enter the caves from the desert end – the waterfall would destroy them, and Borrea had vines running all along the entrance from the city end and had lit a fire below them that was sheltered by huge leaves. The heat from the fire caused a constant downpour of water from the vines, making a watery barrier that would block off the shadows' only other entrance. The people would have plenty of food and water with them, and the city's builders had been busy making shelters and beds.

Anyone who was fit enough was given weapons, mainly consisting of a sword, a small wooden shield and a crossbow. Every citizen of Arborinium was trained in combat from the age of 16 until their eighteenth birthday when they had the option to become a warrior or to find a trade. Those who chose a trade would now be fighting alongside the warriors and the Cortuskas. The loss of their best warriors was a blow, but there would still be an army of around 2,000 Arbitans and 1,000 Cortuskas, all willing to fight to the bitter end.

'All we can do now is wait. We have plans and we have an army. We can continue training until the last minute. In the end there will be a victor. It will be hard but I think we can do it,' said Rahmon, as he stretched back and yawned.

Valletia looked at Grimbarr, huge and extremely fierce looking. If his looks were any reflection on his skills, and the skills of his people as warriors, then they would have more than just a whisker of hope of winning.

'You have my word that every last one of the Cortuskas will be with you all the way. We are generally a peaceful and friendly people, but in battle we are deadly,' he said in his deep, gruff voice. 'I feel that our plans are good – they should work. You seem to have a knowledge and a skill for seeing every outcome of the battle and adapting your plans to suit. I am glad and proud that I will be fighting with the Arbitans.'

The door to the meeting room opened and the grubby-fingered Borrea entered. 'It is done. The vines are in place and lanterns are in each room ready to be lit.'

Valletia smiled. 'Excellent, Borrea. How are the shelters coming along in the caves?'

'I have around 200 workers down there. They should take no longer than one more hour.'

'I am always amazed. You are a credit to the Arbitans, and you will be rewarded greatly when the battle is over. Thank you, Borrea, and please sit down. We have some plans written and I would like you to read them and see if you can think of anything to add or anything that you would change,' said Valletia, passing the papers to Borrea.

'I will read them, but I am not a military man. I'm sure that what you have here will be just fine,' he replied modestly.

Gid and Gecks had left the branch and were now with Ash and Romallia. They were to meet with the Elders and the Cortuskas by the ground-floor entrance and set out from there. They were to travel on foot for two days until they reached the river. From there they would travel down river, posing as fishermen heading to Harrashon to trade goods.

The river was not the most direct or fastest route to the city, but they would be less likely to run into Legion's warriors this way. It was more important for Gid to get to the city in one piece and undetected than it was to get there quickly.

They were all very quiet as they made their way towards the giant roots on the ground floor. All the Elders were standing in a long line leading to the huge doors, waiting for them. Next to the doors were two large cloth bags with rope shoulder straps, and laid beside these were fishing rods and a map.

Valletia walked over to them. She had a tear in her eye and was fighting to control her emotions. 'We have put together a few items that you may need for your journey. It should take you about four or five days to get there,' she said, her voice trembling a little. 'Ash knows the way so there should be no problems. This isn't to say that it will be an easy journey – there are many dangers in the forest and on the river, so stay alert. We have no plans for you, Gid; finding and defeating Legion is very much in your hands, though I'm sure your companions will help in any way they can. All that is left now is for us to say goodbye and good luck.' She hugged them one by one, saying a final goodbye to each.

They passed along the line of Elders and Cortuskas, every one of them wishing them good luck and shaking their hands.

'As I said before, my friend, I would love to come but I will be best here helping in the fight,' Snorback said before grabbing Gid and giving him a huge, rib-crushing hug. 'Thank you again for freeing us. I hope we will see each other again soon. I like you, Gid, and I don't often find a friend who can beat me in a fight.'

'I'll see you soon, my friend,' choked Gid. He could say no more – the moment and occasion were too much and he was trying desperately to hold back tears.

'Gid, if you find my brother, will you give him a good hiding for me – and then bring him back! Tell him it's not too late; he needs to face up to what he has done, but we want him back,' said Rahmon. Then he leant closer and, trying to raise

Gid's spirits a little, whispered, 'And keep an eye on Ash; he has a tendency to find trouble even in the friendliest of places!'

The last goodbyes were said. Gid and Ash picked up the bags, rods and map, and the huge doors were opened. Gecks climbed on to Romallia's shoulder, they all turned to say farewell to their friends and then headed into the forest towards the river.

Chapter 18: Solving a problem

Bright shafts of sunlight shone through small gaps in the otherwise dark throne room. One dust-filled beam lit up the aged and evil smile of Legion, his other features masked by the darkness of the room. He was talking to a tall, skinny, grey man with long, thin, grey wings, leathery skin and arms long enough to allow his thin, claw-tipped fingers to touch the floor. It was Ergerin, the feared leader of Legion's armies.

'If everything Tharik has reported is true, the city is almost defenceless,' said Legion in a sly voice. 'We will need to teach them a lesson. I have enjoyed having an enemy – it keeps me young – but I will enjoy destroying them. I think we should toy with them a little, send in the shadows and maybe some soldiers. It will be very pleasing to see the mighty Arbitans crumble, even more so when I destroy them with as little force as possible. I am, however, a cautious leader, which is why I am still in power. I think I will also send soldiers to cover all routes in and out of Arborinium; I will not underestimate my enemy. And besides, this may be the last battle for many years, so we may as well enjoy it. Ergerin, see that my orders are carried out.' Legion passed the leathery grey creature a scroll containing the plans for the destruction of Arborinium.

'Your will is mine, my lord,' said Ergerin in a deep, rumbling tone that did not match his skinny frame. 'I will ensure that the soldiers are informed. When you give the order, they will be ready. I will not fail you. Arborinium will fall.'

Legion placed a bony hand on the creature's shoulder. 'You may go. Send Tharik in when you leave. I need to talk to him.'

'Yes, my lord,' he answered coldly. Ergerin hated Tharik. He was in charge of the armies, not some bratty traitor from Arborinium. As far as Ergerin was concerned, Tharik was scum for betraying his brother, even if he was an enemy.

Ergerin left the room and passed on the message to Tharik without even looking at him. Tharik was nervous. He had completed his tasks easily but now he was having doubts about his ability to lead an army. He walked to the huge wooden door that led into Legion's throne room. He rested his head on the door and rubbed his face nervously. 'Come on, get a grip. The hard part is over; now it's time to reap what I've sown.' He gathered his confidence together and pushed the door open.

He could see Legion at the far end of the room with his face half lit up by the sunbeam. 'Ah, Tharik, how are you? Come here. I need to talk to you.' Legion beckoned him over.

'Yes, my lord,' said Tharik, moving forward in trepidation. The last few days had been hard on him – although he craved authority it was to come to him in ways that would haunt him forever. Gid had become a good friend, and he loved his brother, but greed and a lust for power had taken over, and now he was beginning to wonder if he had made the right decision. The throne room was always eerie and dark, and Legion's presence seemed to make it oppressively dark. There was an authority about him that had come through his deeds as well as his reputation: he was merciless and cared only about himself. Tharik envied the way he showed no sign of emotion – right now he would give anything to be free of the guilt he was feeling.

'You look nervous, Tharik,' said his new master, as if reading his thoughts. 'I gave you a hard task – in fact, an almost impossible task – to bring me Arborinium. I must say, you have surpassed every expectation I had. Arborinium is ready to fall. Its generals are dead and captured, and the one spoken about in the prophecies is no longer with us. I am very impressed. This does, however, cause me a problem.' He stared at Tharik in silence, as if waiting for his reaction.

'What do you mean "problem", my lord? There can be no

problems now – I made sure of that.' The hairs were standing up on Tharik's neck and a sickening feeling was working its way through his body.

'You, Tharik – you yourself are the problem. You have been excellent, but you betrayed your city, your friend and your own brother just for power. My problem is this: they trusted and loved you, and you betrayed them. You will never be satisfied – you are too ambitious. I cannot spend my days watching you, checking that you are still with me. If you can betray your own flesh and blood then you can also betray me. I cannot trust you.'

A look of horror spread across Tharik's face, his throat went dry and words failed him. He had nothing to say in his defence.

'What do I do with you? I will not make you a general. You will be given no power or authority from me. I cannot send you back – you know too much. However, I do not want to dispose of you, as you are still valuable to me. What do I do? There is one solution. Guards!'

Legion waved his bony hand and four enormous guards came from the shadows and grabbed a shocked and frightened Tharik by the arms. 'You will pay for this! I betrayed friends and family for you. Believe me, I will not rest until you die. If I get the slightest opportunity, I will kill you.' Tears welled up in his eyes – a mixture of anger, shame and humiliation coursing through his veins.

'I had better make sure you don't get the opportunity then, hadn't I?' mocked Legion. 'Goodbye, Tharik. I hope my prison is to your liking. Take him away. Make sure he is well looked after and keep him in good health. I have something very special lined up for our little power-hungry friend.'

The guards dragged Tharik out of the room as Legion looked on and smiled maliciously.

Chapter 19: Lizards

The forest was extremely dark but thick shafts of light were finding their way in through the dense vegetation, lighting up the ground and tree trunks in patches. The four new companions had to cut through thick vines and bushes that cut and scratched their skin as they slowly made their way towards the river.

'I still don't understand why I couldn't have just flown to Harrashon. This is hopeless – it will take us years to get to the river – that is, if you haven't already got us lost,' moaned Gid as another spiky branch whipped his cheek.

'Look, Valletia asked me and Gecks to go with you, and in case you've forgotten, we don't have wings, and no amount of flapping our limbs is going to help. Besides, if you were to be seen, then any advantage we have would be gone. We've been over all this already.' Ash was also wishing for wings, but he was tired and fed up of Gid's moaning. 'You whinge a lot for a hero, don't you?'

Gid went to argue back, but then he realised that Ash was right – he had done a lot of complaining over the last few hours. 'I'm sorry. I just want to get to Harrashon and fight Legion, and I need to get it over and done with. The longer I have to wait, the more nervous I get.'

Romallia and Gecks followed a few steps behind, letting the guys be manly and hack at the trees while they went over the plans for the journey. A few moments later they reached a steep grassy slope that led down towards a small black stream.

Ash smiled proudly and puffed out his chest. 'See, I told you we weren't lost. This will take us to the river. I think it's time for a well-deserved rest and some food. What do you say, Gid?'

'Sounds good to me; I'm starving!'

Gecks climbed a nearby tree and surveyed the surrounding area. 'We shouldn't stay for long; this region is home to a distant relative of mine – the Salamodo Lizard. They grow to over a metre high and three metres long. They live and hunt in packs of about 50, eating anything they can find.'

'If we stick together, Gid and I could fly you to safety,' said Romallia. 'Can they climb trees, Gecks?'

'Luckily for us, no. But they will stick close by and keep tracking us until they get bored or we fall down!'

Gid flew up to a high branch that gave him a clear view. He could see clearly enough in all directions to notice any sudden movements. 'If I wait up here I can be a lookout, and if there's any sign of movement I'll let you know.'

Romallia looked at the others. 'Why don't we just join him in the tree? If these Salamodos can't climb, we'll be safer up there. It also looks far more fun up in the branches than being stuck down here on the ground. Ash, you can climb up there, can't you?'

'I was born in a tree, Romallia. Of course I can climb!'

A short time later they were sat high in the branches, the sun shining down through the leaves and warming their tired bodies. With food in their bellies and the sun on their faces, the group soon fell asleep. The sun changed position as midday turned into afternoon and the temperature dropped slightly. Gecks was the first to stir and set about waking the others. 'Come on guys, we need to get a move on. I don't want to be stuck around here when it gets dark – it just doesn't feel safe.'

'I know what you mean, Gecks,' said Gid. 'It feels like we're being watched, but I can't see anything out there.'

Ash leaned over with a serious look on his face and stretched out his arm. 'What's that?' he said quietly.

Everyone looked to where he was pointing.

'What?' asked Gecks

'There's nothing there,' added Gid.

Romallia stared dreamily at the spot, imagining what Ash

might be seeing.

Ash leaned in closer to Gid and whispered, 'Just there, by the stream.'

Gid searched the area with his eyes but saw nothing.

Suddenly, Ash grabbed Gid by the arm and shouted. 'Rraaagh!'

Gid's heart jumped, and the blade in his arm flew out like lightning, slicing the branch they were all sitting on. All four of them came crashing down in a heap on the floor.

'Is everyone ok?' asked Gecks.

'Gid, what in the name of Arborinium just happened?' asked Ash, rubbing his back.

'You made me jump, you muppet! It's my sword – it comes out of my arm when I need it. You're lucky I only sliced the branch off.'

A muffled voice came from just below them. 'Um, excuse me guys, but if you don't mind finishing off this conversation in a minute, I would be very grateful. It's just that you're both sitting on me.' Romallia struggled to push them off.

After a few minutes of rubbing bruises and readying themselves, the small party set off once more down the stream. But now they were not alone – a group of around 60 huge black lizards were following them silently, creeping through the thick bushes.

'I don't want to alarm anyone but, well, how do I put this without causing panic?' ventured Ash. 'I just looked behind us and, well, I think we're being followed by a large group of carnivorous lizards.' He was grinning, but his shaky voice showed that he was not joking.

Gid spoke in a low voice. 'Gecks, climb on to my back quickly and hang on. Ash, give me your hand. Romallia, take his other hand. After three we need to fly up through the trees but stay just above the canopy. If we see anyone or anything else then we'll have to head back into the trees – we mustn't be seen. Ok, ready? One, two, three!'

As Romallia and Gid carried their passengers up off the floor, they were leapt at from all directions by the Salamodos. Most of them collided in mid-air, but one managed to grab Gid by the leg. It held on for only a second, though, before Gid's blade sliced down through its head, the lizard falling to the ground with a loud thud. The body was immediately pounced on and devoured by its brothers and sisters.

The pack of killer lizards finished eating and sniffed the air. Quickly they picked up the scent and headed through the undergrowth, following their prey that was now out of sight above them.

'We can't stay up here for too long – we could be spotted and we might lose the stream,' said Gid as he looked around, checking the area. 'Besides, I think someone here ate all the pies!' he added and smiled at Ash.

'I have no idea what a pie is but I think you're trying to say I'm out of shape or a bit on the heavy side! I'll have you know that I'm actually very fit for my age,' replied Ash defensively.

'Gid is right – I need to stop soon. You may be fit for your age but you're not a little kid any more,' added Romallia.

Gecks said nothing. She hated flying and was gripping tightly to Gid's back.

'I don't think it's my weight; I think it might just be you two. You can't cope with carrying me – maybe you're just not as strong as you thought.'

Gid grinned and turned to Romallia. 'You know, I think he may be right – I'm just too weak. How about you? I reckon we just drop him before we all fall from the sky.'

'Sounds fair to me, Ok, after three. One, two...'

Ash knew he had lost this one. 'Very funny. Ok, I'm sorry. Yes, it's me, it's all me; I'm just too heavy. Happy? Now please don't drop me!'

As he spoke they flew over a small clearing. The stream was still below them and, more importantly, there was no sign of the Salamodos. They glided down and landed in a large tree with thick bushy branches.

'We'll be safe up here. I don't think that we should venture to the ground just yet. The Salamodos are amazing hunters and it won't be too long before they sniff us out,' said Gecks as she climbed down from Gid's back, happy to be out of the sky.

'Everybody be very quiet. We are definitely not out of the woods yet,' whispered Gid.

'You are quick, you know, Gid. I mean, what gave the idea that we are not "out of the woods"? Was it the trees, by any chance? I know I'm being picky here, but technically this is a forest,' replied Ash sarcastically.

'It's just a phrase, Ash. It means we're not out of danger yet. Ok? Do you understand now, or do I have to talk to you like a baby? Look, Ash – big soldiers are walking down the forest path with nasty-looking swords!'

Ash suddenly went very quiet. Romallia had already hidden herself in the dense leaves of the tree and Gid was slowly moving deeper into the branches with Ash close behind. Gecks slipped through the branches, watching the large troop of Legion's soldiers. She was in no danger of being spotted as her skin blended in perfectly with her surroundings; even if she was spotted, she was a lizard, and in these parts lizards were not uncommon. She listened as the soldiers stopped and started to set up camp. She reported back to the group what she had heard.

'The soldiers are a back-up plan. All the information the Arbitans have is correct. Legion intends to send in the shadows first, followed by a small group of soldiers. This group are a back-up in case anything goes wrong. I couldn't quite make out everything they were talking about but I think there are more groups like this. We need to warn the Arbitans and if possible stop this group before they have a chance to help the shadows.'

They all sat quietly, thinking about what should be done. 'We need a plan. We must be able to stop the soldiers. Gid, surely they would be no match for you – I mean, you fought Snorback and won – these are nothing in comparison.' Ash was sure this would be the best plan of action.

'But if Gid is spotted, and if any one of them gets away, then our mission has failed. We cannot risk it. Still, there must be a way.' Romallia sat with her hands clamped behind her head, thinking hard.

Gid stared blankly ahead at nothing in particular. 'I have an idea,' he said calmly. 'It could be a bit risky but it might just work.'

Chapter 20: Water

From the outside, Arborinium seemed no different than on any other day: people were still heading in and out of the woods or tending their vegetables and livestock. Inside, it was a different story: it was like a ghost town – no living soul could be seen, but hundreds were there, preparing for the oncoming battle. Some were sitting quietly going over their particular roles; some were nervously waiting, unable to think about or do anything other than worry, while others sat calmly, singing quietly to themselves. But all were well hidden away.

The sun had almost set; all that was left of the day was a small orange glow along the treetops trying to hold off the blue night. The Arbitans working outside slowly gathered up their day's produce and tools and made their way cautiously back into the relative safety of the city. One or two looked round anxiously among the once safe trees surrounding them, but nothing moved or leapt out from their dark depths.

'We need to wait until they are all inside the city walls. If they are all in one place it will be harder for them to escape; if any do get out, we'll be waiting for them on the outside,' said a huge, scarred warrior dressed in a black hooded cloak with enormous wings protruding from the back. He was holding a well-polished cutlass in his right hand and a small whistle in his left. From his hiding place high up in the branches of one of the trees he had watched for hours without moving, waiting for the right moment to give the signal.

'This isn't right,' grumbled a vicious-looking female warrior, also in a black hooded cloak. 'Why are we the ones who have to mop up? We are warriors; we should be in there destroying the Arbitans, not these shadows. They weren't good enough or quick enough to avoid the Shadow Forge when they were alive, so why should they get all the fun now that they are dead – or whatever they are! They're second rate, if you ask me – just scum that couldn't make the grade when they had the chance.'

Seconds later, the dark shadow of a hand crossed her face, and the life drained instantly from her. She slumped forwards and almost plummeted from the tree, but was held up in mid-air, her wings gripped by the same hand that had killed her.

'If anyone else has a problem with us or is not convinced of our powers, speak up now,' hissed the bone-chilling, sinister, wind-like voice of the shadow. It looked around at the other warriors hiding in the trees. 'No one else wants to speak, do they? She dared to call us second rate.' The shadow glided gently to the ground and hid the lifeless body in the undergrowth.

The lookout stared ahead at the city and watched the last figure enter, unfazed by what had just happened. He lifted his whistle to his lips and blew. An eerie sound, like the wind howling through an open window, echoed through the forest. He stopped blowing his whistle and watched as the shadows on the ground grew slightly and moved towards the huge doors at the base of Arborinium, then slipped up to the doors and then disappeared through them. The lookout turned to the other warriors. 'They're in. Get ready for the screams, and watch out for anyone who tries to escape. This should be over soon!'

Inside the city, the shadows moved along the huge roots at its base, ready to kill any living soul that they came across. 'Something is wrong; we just saw the workers enter. Where are they?' hissed one of the shadows.

'Split up and search the whole city. They must be here somewhere. Follow any sound. I can smell fear in the air – they are here,' shrieked another with shrill authority, suggesting it was in charge.

The shadows floated through the city, spreading out in all directions, searching every corridor and room. Everywhere the smell of fear was strong in the air, but still there was no sign of the Arbitans.

The leader floated over the roots at the base of the city, sniffing the air, when something caught its attention. A very faint sound was coming from below the roots.

'Shadows!' it bellowed with its tempest-like voice. 'They are below the city!'

Another shadow from a level higher up screamed, 'The smell of fear is thick up here. It seems like the whole city is afraid. They must be all around us.'

All the shadows agreed – the Arbitans seemed to be everywhere, but they were not showing themselves.

'There is definitely something below the city – I can hear them. Shadows, come to me now. We move below,' hissed the leader.

'NOW!' yelled a voice from somewhere above.

The shadows stopped and stared up towards the source of the voice. Rahmon was standing on the highest level of the city, staring down at the invaders.

A tiny drop of water fell past his face. The shadows' piercing eyes stared at this single droplet as it fell towards them. Suddenly they realised what was about to happen. The air was now full of thousands of water droplets falling speedily on them. It was as if the whole city was inside a huge rain cloud as the water cascaded towards the floor. Fear crossed the misty face of the leader as it realised that it was doomed. 'Nooo, this cannot be happening!' it yelled. Screams bellowed out from the evil army as the water seemed to burn right through them. Within seconds they were all destroyed, the only sign of them being the mist that filled the air, like steam coming from hot ground after a rain shower.

Rahmon smiled The first part of the plan had been flawless; the shadows were vanquished in a matter of minutes and the Arbitans had not suffered any casualties. He banged his fist hard on a vine above his head, and it echoed through the city to give the signal to stop the water and prepare for the next battle. When the drops stopped falling, he headed back into his hiding place.

'Did you hear those screams? You can say what you like about the shadows, but I'm glad they're on our side. The Arbitans didn't really have a chance,' said the deep voice of a skinny, hooded warrior with long bony arms and dark eyes.

'I suppose we should go in and mop up – if there is actually anyone left to mop up, that is,' added another, snickering.

The lookout had not let his eyes drift from the city; he was expecting to see at least one or two Arbitans escape from it. 'Something is wrong…' he mused, placing a hand to his face and stroking the ends of a well-groomed moustache.

'What's up with you, Krast?' asked the warrior with the dark eyes. 'You only play with your facial hair when you think something bad is going to happen. But then, you always think something bad is going to happen,' he added mockingly.

'Something isn't right. Whenever the shadows are involved, a few things normally happen. Their enemies – usually adults – come out of hiding because of sick curiosity and then get picked off one by one; sometimes they can't move because they're frozen with fear. This usually happens to the bravest and strongest who have fought the feeling of curiosity. Or they flee in terror, which is the usual reaction from the young. Arborinium is full of children – we've seen them playing in this forest and flying in and out of the city. Why did none of them leave? It doesn't seem right,' answered Krast. But he knew the other warriors well and realised that their pride and the lust for any kind of a fight would outweigh his misgivings and caution. It was useless trying to convince them, even though he had been right in the past. And this time he was more sure than usual that it would be bad.

'You worry too much. You love the fight as much as the rest of us, and you're better than any others in this army. Things always work out – this will be no different. Maybe nobody survived long enough to escape. There were a lot of shadows this time – almost all of them. If they've got themselves into trouble, which I highly doubt, then we can be the heroes for a change. Now be a good man and get ready to give the signal, before our warriors turn on us out of boredom,' laughed the commander of the small but brutal army of warriors. He smiled and patted his second-in-command firmly on the back.

Krast sighed. 'As you command, Sir. I just hope you're right.' Krast did not sound at all convinced.

Chapter 21: The plan

'How many more days' marching until we get to Arborinium?' asked an important-looking soldier dressed in shiny silver armour with a long purple cape covering his shoulders. 'The troops are getting weary, Sir, and morale is low.'

'Soldiers are soldiers; they will cope,' replied a wise-looking general, his dark eyes staring into the distance. 'There will be plenty of time to relax soon – the Arbitans are our last real enemy. When they are defeated, who will we fight? Will this world even need an army?'

'All is quiet, Sir. The soldiers can bed down for the night. Lookouts are in place and relief guards have been ordered to take over at four-hourly intervals,' panted a brutally battle-scarred soldier. He looked as if his entire body might fall to pieces at the slightest touch.

'Good. You may give the order to sleep,' replied the first soldier in the purple cape.

Moments later, a high-pitched screech pierced the soldiers' camp, informing them that their time to rest had come.

'Finally! I thought this hour would never arrive,' sighed a short but muscular soldier as he warmed his hands by an open fire.

'That's all you think about, Qwod – sleep, sleep, sleep,' replied another voice from somewhere in the shadows.

'That's not true; I also think about food quite a lot. But sleep is my favourite.'

'I would say women are the only things I think about – well, women and killing people in battle.'

The figure behind the voice from the shadows emerged into the light of the fire, collected his sword from where it was resting on a log and slowly walked back into the darkness. Within minutes, all the fires had been extinguished and every soldier, apart from those on watch duty, had disappeared into their temporary shelters.

The night was silent and a warm breeze blew over the camp. One of the guards was leaning lazily on a long, deadly looking spear, desperately trying to keep herself awake. About 20 metres away from her, another guard had dozed off, only to be woken seconds later by the sound of his own loud snoring. It had been a long march to this point, and every soldier in the camp was feeling its effects. The camp was now rumbling with the sounds of deep snores from tired soldiers, sounds that should be enough to scare off any enemies in the area.

In the moonlight, the guard with the vicious spear caught sight of something moving towards the camp from the thick forest. 'Come and take a look at this,' she beckoned to her colleague who had just woken himself up again. 'It looks like we're about to be attacked by a little lizard.'

'Where? I can't see anything – it's too dark,' replied the guard who had just made his way over to take a look.

'It's just there, running towards us; I can't believe you can't see it. Look down the length of my finger – surely you can see it now!'

The guard squinted as he stared down the length of his companion's finger, and his expression suddenly changed as his eyes finally focused on the lizard, who was indeed heading at a great speed for their encampment.

'I reckon we should wake everyone! One little lizard like that could rip this place apart. Quick – sound the alarm,' he joked.

'I think you're right. I mean, look at it – it looks pretty ferocious to me.'

'I'll make a bet with you. We have one arrow each. If you kill it with your only arrow, I'll do your next guard duty; if I kill it, you'll do mine.'

'It's a deal. We both have to loose our arrows at the same time, though. It won't be an easy shot – it's moving pretty quickly and the light isn't great. Are you sure you're up to this?'

'It will be easy for me, bad light or not, but you may struggle, being a lady and all,' he teased, trying to get his challenger wound up before the vital shot. But she just smiled.

'The pressure is all on you then. I mean, you wouldn't want to be beaten by a lady, now, would you?' she replied.

'Ok, you win on the wind-ups, but let's see who is the better shot!'

The guards loaded their bows and took aim. 'Ok, on the count of three. One… two…'

The countdown stopped. Gecks was in both their sights and at a distance where they could both hit her easily, but behind her the whole ground seemed to be moving rapidly towards both the lizard and their encampment.

'What in the name of Harrash is that?'

'I'm not sure, but it's heading this way. I think we really should sound the alarm now!'

The little lizard ran straight past the guards and into the camp, dodging tents and the smouldering fires.

The huge, dark, fast-moving shape was now in clear view of the guards, though now they could see that it wasn't one shape but lots of large, individual bodies moving in a tightly packed group. Dozens of giant lizards were thundering down on the encampment and would be on them in seconds.

'I don't have my whistle. Quick sound the alarm now!' screamed the female guard at her colleague who was standing like a statue, staring at the oncoming attackers.

For a moment the guard just stared blankly.

'What are you doing? Use your whistle quick before it's too late,' she yelled urgently.

The guard suddenly snapped out of it. He reached for his whistle and placed it to his lips, but in his panic it slipped from his hand and fell to the floor. He reached down and tried to find it, but the darkness was not helping. He scrambled about with his hands, frantically trying to locate it. Suddenly, without any warning, he slumped over and lay in a heap on the dusty ground.

'What the...? Get up, quick!' The female guard bent down to see what had just happened to her friend and saw the feathers of a dart sticking out of his neck.

'It's an ambush,' she said quietly to herself.

The other guards around the encampment were now staring in her direction with looks of horror across their faces. She turned to see what they were glaring at and realised that her time was up. A huge lizard, dribbling saliva from its razor-sharp teeth, was right behind her. In a flash she shot her loaded arrow straight into its gaping mouth, and it collapsed, writhing in agony on the floor. But seconds later more came in its place. She let out a short scream as the lizards pounced on her and her dead friend. Before the other guards had time to react, the whole encampment was engulfed in a swarm of ravenous killer lizards who took no time at all to find their prey in their flimsy tents. Screams filled the air as the lizards devoured anything that moved. A few of the soldiers tried to take flight and escape the lethal slavering jaws, but they were all too slow.

Gid sat and watched as Legion's soldiers were rapidly destroyed. His face showed the horror that he was feeling as he sat and witnessed the ugly end to the short but devastating struggle between the ferocious lizards and the stunned and unprepared soldiers. Moments earlier, his expression had been one of elation as he witnessed the plan working almost perfectly. From the second that the dart hit the guard's neck, everything had gone far better than he could have hoped. Gecks had made it through the guards just before they were taken out, and the soldiers were losing, badly.

The horror he was feeling was now not the shock of what he had seen, but of disgrace as he realised what the plan had led to. This was no way for any soldier to die. Legion's troops hadn't had a chance to defend themselves or escape. Not long before, he had watched them as they sat and shared drinks with each other, even coming close enough to hear one group of warriors chatting about their lives and what it would be like to be back at home with their families. Most of them had not seen home for a long while, and now they never would.

Gid covered his face with his hands and rubbed his eyes. 'What have I done?' he groaned, fighting to control his feelings.

'You have given Arborinium a better chance of surviving,' assured a friendly voice from the bushes behind him.

'Gecks, you made it. That at least is good news!' But his relief suddenly changed to uneasy disquiet. 'Gecks, what side am I on? Am I a good guy or a bad guy? The soldiers who died were just ordinary people and our plan has wiped them out. I'm confused. I thought good guys were supposed to be "good". Nothing that just happened was even slightly heroic.'

'Gid, listen to me. You must understand that if they had lived and attacked Arborinium they would not have hesitated to destroy every single one of the Arbitans. War does seem to blur the lines between good and evil. They would have done their job for Legion, given the chance. They themselves may not have been, as you say, "bad", but they were soldiers trained to kill, and I can guarantee that they would have done their job without stopping to think about what their enemy was like. You have done what you needed to do; your plan did its job, just as they were waiting to do theirs.' Gecks could tell that the events had hit Gid hard.

'I'm just a kid, Gecks. I'm not supposed to be responsible for killing soldiers. I should be playing with my friends. When they die in a play-battle, they get up again at the end and go home for dinner. Why do people have to die? I won't let it be like that again. I will defend us if I have to, but I'll give the enemy a chance next time. I may be a warrior here, but I am no killer. I will fight for you, but next time Legion's men will be given a chance to fight too.'

'He would not do the same for you,' mused the lizard.

Gid looked her in the eye. 'Thank you, Gecks.'

She looked puzzled. 'Thank you for what exactly?'

'For showing me why he is the bad guy and I am the good guy. I will fight fair and he won't; it's not much, but it does show me that I am different to him.' The little comfort this had given him was enough to bring a small but slightly sad smile back to his face.

'Gid, you are clever beyond your years. I only hope that after all this you can return to living your life the way it should be lived at your age.'

'I am living a real-life adventure, with me as the hero. I always dreamed about this, but it's funny how my dreams were never quite as serious. I half-wish that it was still just a dream, but it's not, is it... This is very real, and people will get hurt, for real.' He sighed and absent-mindedly rubbed his eyes.

'We should go soon, Gid. We still have a long way to travel and we should make the best of the darkness while we still can. We'll reach the river in a few hours, where we will meet up with a trading boat that will be following the inland rivers and canals, doing business with some of the open-lands nomadic tribes. But the boat will only wait for us until first light tomorrow.'

'I thought our trip was a big secret. How did Valletia let the traders know, and how do we know they can be trusted?' Gid was suddenly unsure about how secret their journey actually was.

'The traders meet up with the Arbitans regularly. Tomorrow is one of the dates that they normally meet. As to the question of trust – well, that remains to be seen. We obviously don't have anything to trade, but I'm hoping that they will let us tag along with them; that way we won't be so easy to spot. The traders are no fools, mind. If we lie to them, we'll be on our own, so it's more a question of how much truth we tell them.

'Information can be traded as much as materials, and we'll be giving them a good bargaining tool in the form of you if they run into Legion's men; they may trade information about you as well as weapons, so the less they know the less they will have to trade. Oh, and they're notorious for being extremely good thieves!'

'Let me get this right – we don't actually have anything to barter with the traders apart from information that could put us in danger, especially if we run into Legion's men? And what's more, the traders are also quite likely to try and rob us blind? And we don't even know if they will let us tag along anyway!' Gid looked dubiously at Gecks.

'Yes, that's about right.' Gecks beamed back with a sharp-toothed, lizardy grin.

'Great,' Gid replied sarcastically. 'I can't wait to meet up with them now, it should be fun…'

'Don't worry, Gid. I'm not about to let them know anything, apart from the fact that Legion has attacked again. Our story is simple: we have been sent out as spies. Spies obtain information, information that we may wish to trade with them at a later date.'

Gid frowned. 'I'm not sure I quite understand what you're telling me.'

'If the traders think we could give them information in the future, we become valuable to them, and hopefully this will make them less eager to pass on information about us. What could we give them if we were captured by Legion?'

The intense frown on Gid's face showed that he was still far from convinced. 'I'm sure I'm missing something, but I'll have to trust you on this one,' he replied with resignation.

Gid made his way back through the bushes while Gecks sat casually on his shoulder. It was time to find the other two and let them know that rest would have to wait a little while longer. Although Gid was apprehensive about the rendezvous with the traders, he was looking forward to meeting a group that were on neither side in this war. If they knew what had just happened with the lizards and the soldiers, would they tell him he had done the right thing or would they hate him? Gid knew he wouldn't be able to ask them, as it would be giving away too much information and drawing too much attention to their party, but he was curious nevertheless. But all these thoughts would have to wait; he and the others had a way to go before they met the traders, and his head and body were starting to feel the effects of the last few days.

Chapter 22: The cell

'Wake up sleepy!' yelled a skinny, yellow-eyed jailer dressed in a dirty brown tunic, as he threw a bucket of cold water through rusting steel bars over his new guest. 'I hope the room was to your liking. I know it's not what you might call spacious, but we use only the best quality stone to make these beds, you know.' He sniggered at his joke and grinned with rotten, yellow teeth, satisfied that the prisoner was both awake and angry. He was going to enjoy this.

'If you ever do that again, I will kill you!' seethed a cold, wet and now furious Tharik.

'I must be a very lucky man,' he sneered. 'That must be at least the fifteenth time I've heard that threat. Most of the threats came from warriors, not snivelling little boys, though. So please forgive me if I don't break down crying with fear.' The guard turned from Tharik's tiny prison cell and looked towards two highly polished metal doors behind him. 'Can you hear that?'

Tharik listened hard. At first, all he could hear was a dripping noise coming from somewhere behind the jailer, but then he heard footsteps. They were slowly getting louder. 'I can hear footsteps, but what's so strange about that? I have heard them before, you know,' he said, trying to sound unconcerned.

'That, you little worm, is the sound of the end of your life as you have known it until this day. You know, I actually feel sorry for you... you may be a traitor to your own people and a puny little wimp, but what is waiting for you – well, I wouldn't wish it upon anybody.' His eyes showed that what he said was true.

'I'm not as weak as you think; I can take whatever Legion can throw at me,' asserted Tharik defiantly.

The guard grinned evilly, the hint of compassion now gone. 'Then you will be the only person who ever has. All the others died horribly; the experiments just never worked.'

'What do you mean, "experiments"?' Tharik suddenly looked very worried, his brave disguise falling away.

'I've said too much already, but you'll find out soon enough. Sounds like your escorts have arrived.'

The metal doors swung back to reveal two tall soldiers wearing long, dark, hooded cloaks. The jailer opened Tharik's cell. 'Time to go!'

Tharik stared at the jailer and then at the two hooded guards. If he could surprise them, he would be able to get through the open doors and then, hopefully, find a way out. It was now or never.

Tharik pounced like a lion at the jailer, who stumbled backwards and fell, smashing his head on the unforgiving stone floor. This time the threat had turned out to be true: the jailer would never get up again. 'Fifteen must have been your unlucky number,' snarled Tharik. 'I told you I'm not as weak as you thought.' People always underestimated him and he thought that was why he always succeeded.

Before the guards had time to react, he was leaping straight at them.

Tharik felt a sudden pain in the side of his head and a flash of white light crossed his eyes. He fell limply to the floor, his vision failing and the room turning black. He had been hit. It was all so quick; he should have been on his way out of the doors, but instead he was losing consciousness on the cold stone floor. He could hear the dripping sound from earlier, growing fainter, and then there was nothing – only a silent darkness.

'Why do they always do that?' asked one of the guards, rubbing his knuckles.

'I don't know. Maybe they know deep down how much you like to knock people out. That's the only reasonable explanation,' replied the other.

'Quite nice of them really, I suppose. I would hate it if they came quietly – it would take all the fun out of it,' said the first. Then he pointed to the lifeless body of the jailer. 'What do we do about him?'

'Tell the cleaners, I suppose. It was about time he was replaced; he was beginning to smell.'

Tharik's limp body was picked up off the stone floor and thrown over the shoulder of one of the guards. Then they turned towards the metal doors and departed, closing them on the lifeless jailer, laid outside his once beloved cells.

Chapter 23: Impasse

Krast waited for the first signs of movement to come from the city. The shadows were taking a lot longer than he had expected. 'They should be out by now; something has happened. Get the soldiers ready – we're going in!'

'Ok, you bunch of sissies, you heard the man. The shadows have not come out – so we go in. We'll do this the right way. On Krast's signal we take the city from the top. When we're sure we can move on, we search the city level by level. Legion wants no prisoners – this is extermination.'

Krast glared at the commanding officer. 'That was not an order! Legion said nothing about not taking any prisoners. What do you think you are doing?'

The commander turned to Krast with a look of distaste on his face. 'Getting a little soft, are you? Next you'll be asking me to send the troops in with gifts. If the shadows have been defeated, do you really think these people will go easy on us? My orders stay: we go in, they die, and we come out.'

'You cannot do this. We are soldiers, not murderers.' Krast was furious.

'The order stands. If you don't like it you can die with the Arbitans.'

The commander raised his hand high and then pointed towards the awaiting city. Krast raised his whistle and blew; a high-pitched shriek resounded across the night sky.

The trees around the city slowly seemed to come alive as groups of soldiers left their hiding places and flew up into the air in front of the growing moon. Their plan was to fly in through the opening at the top of the city and, once inside, break off into smaller groups to search out their enemy. If the shadows had been successful there would be no battle for them to join, but something told the soldiers that this was not going to be the case. It was with some trepidation that they entered the city. If the invulnerable shadows had been defeated, how were they going to win?

Groups of soldiers landed on every level and quickly split up, checking every corridor and room with the speed and efficiency of a well-disciplined army. In no time they had checked every floor except the ground.

'What's going on here?' asked the soldiers. 'There doesn't seem to be anybody in the city.' The only living things were the thick vines that covered the walls and ceilings.

'We still have one level to check – we may get to fight yet!' boomed the commander.

'I would advise your men to be cautious, Sir,' urged Krast. 'Something is not right. Look around.'

'I am looking around and all I can see is a lack of what should be here – warriors and civilians!'

'Exactly. There's no sign of life, but I feel that we're being watched. And another thing, Sir – look at all these stepladders leading to and from all the levels in this city. The Arbitans can fly – why would they need steps? Please, tell your men to be careful!' Krast was almost pleading with the commander now.

'You may be right; something is not right. But these warriors are well trained – this is their job and they will carry on searching until we find someone to fight, or until we find out what has happened. That includes you, Krast. Do not try my patience any more.'

Together, all the warriors moved towards the lowest level. They glided down and landed on the roots at the base of the city where there were two sets of doors – one set leading to the outside and another set leading to somewhere further in and unknown.

Two warriors walked hesitatingly towards the large wooden doors. Each placed a hand on a handle and slowly started to open them. All eyes were on the doors. But some eyes should have been watching the other levels. The vines covering the walls and ceilings were unwinding, revealing feet and then legs and hands, hands that were holding weapons. Torsos and heads finally appeared as the Arbitan warriors, who had been cleverly concealed by another of Borrea's strange but useful plants, disclosed themselves. This was all happening so slowly and quietly that it was completely unnoticed by the warriors below.

Their eyes were still fixed on the doors where a small gap had appeared between them, just big enough to see through. As the two warriors pulled harder on the handles, the gap widened, and now something was becoming clearly visible. Something was standing on the other side of the high doors – something huge and hairy.

Instantly, the doors burst open from the other side, and the two warriors holding its handles were smashed back into the walls and crushed. Sharp splinters from the doors exploded across the warriors, who clutched at their weapons as hundreds of Cortuskas came charging through. The closest soldiers were thrown aside and trampled like ants.

The first to fall at the hand of Snorback was the commander. His bravado and ferocity soon changed to cowardice when he was faced with a beast as fierce looking as a Cortuska. He feebly held his sword out in front of him in trembling hands. Snorback flicked the sword out of his quivering grasp and leaned forward, growling in the commander's face. The commander reacted in the only way he could – he fell backwards and scrabbled about desperately trying to find his weapon. Snorback turned to face a small group of soldiers who had been frozen to the spot with fear as the rest of the Cortuskas destroyed their comrades. The commander found his sword, and knowing that the ideal opportunity to attack would be whilst his enemy's back was turned, he lunged for Snorback. Without even turning his head towards the commander, Snorback threw his opened palm backwards, slapping the commander off his feet, into the air and across the root-covered floor before his sword had a chance to strike its blow.

The commander lay in a crumpled heap several metres away from the mighty Cortuskan warrior. On seeing this, the discipline of the soldiers was quickly broken. They tried to retreat, but were trapped. Some managed to open the huge doors to the outside world, the warriors spilling out over one another in crazed attempts to flee. The Cortuskas took on the form of wild beasts; they were an awesome sight, and on the ground they had no equal. Many more warriors would soon fall to the Cortuskas' brutal strength.

Some of the warriors who remained inside managed to free themselves from the barrage and take to the air. They now noticed the Arbitans waiting above them. They drew their swords and prepared to fight as the Arbitans swarmed down on them. The air was filled with flashing sparks and the sound of metal crashing on metal as the soldiers flew in spirals, fighting desperately against each other. Wings fell, followed by tumbling warriors, and shouts of anger and pain filled the now frantic air, joined by muffled screams and wild grunts from below.

Rahmon locked swords with one warrior, and then kicked him hard in the stomach. The warrior fell backwards and managed to regain control, but it was too late – he was pierced by the huge blade wielded by Rahmon, and his lifeless body fell to the ground far below, to be trampled by the huge beasts. Rahmon was felling warrior after warrior, flying frantically in all directions, picking them off one by one. His blade met yet another. This time, however, it was he who was sent flying backwards. A sword wielded by one of Legion's warriors came flying towards his chest. He batted it away with his blade and returned the effort with a well-aimed strike of his own, but this blow, too, was blocked by his challenger, sending blue sparks flying through the thick air. The two warriors were now locked in a fierce battle, and Rahmon crumpled over as he felt a foot hit his chest, and a second kick to his head sent him flying towards one of the lower levels. He hit the floor feet first and sprang up to meet his opponent who had pursued him. Rahmon punched the attacker under his chin, sending him spinning backwards, head over heels. This fight was not going to be easy. But then he had never battled anyone like Krast before.

Krast had never been in a fight like this one either; everything he tried was countered by his opponent. His lungs were burning and his arms were feeling heavy. He needed to buy himself some more time. Quickly he flew towards the opening at the top of the city, taking out two Arbitans on his way. He looked down and saw that his worthy opponent was hot on his tail. They flew out of the city and looped, swirled and darted in all directions, constantly trading fierce blow for fierce blow, each throwing everything he had into the fight. Every move they knew was blocked, and every block they managed was followed by another. Their breathing was heavy, their arms ached and their long hair was soaked with sweat; the air they breathed was not enough to fill their starving lungs, and a faint taste of blood settled in their throats. Still they battled on, neither giving any ground, neither able to carry on much longer.

'Who are you?' panted Krast, as he blocked a lunge aimed at his thigh.

'My name is Rahmon. I am the commander of this army. And you?' growled Rahmon through gritted teeth as their blades clashed again.

'I am Krast, a respected warrior. You must be loved by your people,' he said, gasping for breath as he aimed a slice at Rahmon's arm that was just batted away.

'I am! I will fight to the death for these people – you and your kind will not win today; evil will lose.'

Krast managed a smile as he continued to exchange blows with Rahmon. 'It may shock you to know that at home we are

145

not classed as evil. At home I am as much a hero as you are here.' He ducked to avoid a blow aimed at his head, and continued, 'I have a family that loves me as much as you are loved by your people. The only difference is who we fight for. Legion is my boss, I live in his kingdom and I fight out of duty for my family. You fight for Arborinium, probably for similar reasons.'

Rahmon was stunned. He had never thought of it like this before, and he could no more fight to kill this worthy warrior than he could attack one of his own friends. Rahmon drew back.

'We appear to be two of a kind – equally matched, equally loved and equally respected... What do you suggest we do now?'

'I saw my commander fall to the beasts below earlier, which makes me their new leader. I will call off my men if you do the same.' Krast looked at Rahmon intently. Rahmon nodded and said he would tell the Arbitans to stop.

Krast continued. 'However, this will mean that Legion will realise the threat you pose – it will not be the end of the fighting. He will send us back, and in bigger numbers, until you are all defeated.'

'No doubt,' agreed Rahmon, 'But there need be no more bloodshed today.'

The enemies lowered their swords and shook hands before each called off his warriors.

'What will you do? Do you think Legion will allow you back if you have not won this battle?'

'If this battle was mine to lead from the beginning, then no! But I was only the second-in-command. Still, I will need to get my family out of the city as soon as I can. It is easy to lose favour with my leader.' Krast knew that Legion would be furious, and he would probably bear the brunt of the anger. That he could cope with, but he could not put his family in danger. 'I hope to meet you again; maybe we can continue this fight after we have rested!'

Rahmon smiled. 'You can count on it. Maybe one of us is a match for the other, or perhaps we are just equals. I suppose there is only one way to find out…'

When the fighting was called to cease, the amazed warriors obeyed their leaders but were baffled as to why. This had never happened before. Battles always lasted until one side lost. Truces were never made on the battlefield, or at least there never had been before – not until this day.

Chapter 24: The experiment

The room was slowly coming into focus. Lights and sounds were the first things that Tharik could recognise, immediately followed by the feeling of being trapped. As his eyes tried to focus, he could make out bright lights, a table holding sharp instruments, straps holding his arms and legs to a chair and a woman, dressed in a long white gown and holding a long and painful-looking syringe. A hand came to rest on his right shoulder from behind him.

'Tharik, good to see you are back with us. I thought for a while that the sedatives had been too strong. It would be no fun at all if you had died. Maybe next time you will struggle less.'

Tharik could not see the source of the voice, but he knew straight away that it belonged to Legion. His head felt heavy and his eyes were struggling to stay open. 'What are you going to do to me?' he stammered, though he didn't really care what the answer was. He simply wanted to fall asleep again.

'You are about to become part of a very important experiment. Many have died so far in the trials, but I am hoping that we have it right this time.'

A knock at the door interrupted the conversation. One of the guards that Tharik remembered from the prison cells entered the room. 'Forgive the interruption, Sir, but Krast is back and the news does not seem to be good.' The guard bowed and held the door open for Legion.

'I am sorry, Tharik, but I will not be able to hold your hand through this next stage. It seems I have more urgent matters to attend to. You will be in good hands with Vastria. She is an excellent surgeon, though so far she has not made the best scientist – she isn't mad enough, you see. I think that is why the previous experiments all went so painfully wrong.

Hopefully this time there will be less of a mess.' A cruel smile crept across Legion's face as he remembered what had happened before. 'Well, good luck,' he continued. 'Maybe I will see you soon. If not whole, then at least I will get to say goodbye to bits of you.' Legion laughed cruelly, obviously amused by his own sick sense of humour, and moved towards the door.

Tharik watched the cloaked back of Legion leave the room. His drowsy head had not allowed him to appreciate the biting humour in the remarks; instead, a sick and shivery feeling was resting in every part of his body. There would be no more brave ripostes from his young lips. Tharik the warrior was hiding somewhere deep inside Tharik the boy's body. A tear formed in his eye and a lump filled his tightening throat.

Vastria walked over to Tharik's chair and started to tap the veins in his strapped down forearms whilst she delicately held the syringe in her teeth. 'That is a very good vein,' she said, as she removed the syringe from her mouth. 'I will tell you a little of what is about to happen. In this syringe is Shadow Forge. We have been injecting it into different warriors in the hope of creating something new – preferably a new, stronger soldier. As Legion stated, the tests have not been that successful so far. For some reason, the Shadow Forge has made most of our subjects explode. I say "most" because the last test was very promising: a young warrior with a name that escapes me at the moment. Let's just call her number 34. Number 34 reacted very well at first – she managed to turn completely to shadow and escape the bonds holding her to the chair, and she then reformed completely... or almost completely. It is hard to describe, but if you can picture a portrait that has not yet dried being smudged with a cloth... I can tell by your expression that you know what I mean.' Vastria slowly squeezed the syringe, letting a tiny drop of Shadow Forge drip from the end. 'Well, that is how I would describe her; she became a "smudged" version of her former self, and then – you have guessed it – she exploded. But that was before, and I am sure I have adjusted for everything correctly this time – though I must admit I say that every time...'

'Please don't do this!' pleaded Tharik. 'Oh Rahmon, please forgive me,' he murmured to himself.

Vastria merely placed a finger on his lips. 'Hush now,' she said, and plunged the syringe into his arm. A strange tingling sensation spread slowly through his body. It was not an unpleasant feeling – in fact, he felt strong, stronger than ever.

He stared down at his arms, and with a thought he effortlessly turned them into shadow. He slipped his now phantom-like limbs out of the straps before again turning them back into solid skin and bone. A woman in the room was holding a syringe, saying something to him and smiling; at first he smiled back, but then he remembered the injection, his fear and her cruelty. He grabbed her by the wings, tearing them off and throwing her across the room.

His main thought was to find his master, Legion, and do his bidding. A smaller thought was telling him to find someone called Rahmon, though he didn't know why.

Legion sat on his throne in the dark room. Two large guards stood on either side of Krast, who like them was on one knee with his head bowed before their leader.

'Speak,' hissed Legion.

Krast rose to his feet. 'We lost, Sir,' he said, and paused, waiting for a reaction from Legion. There was none, so he went on. 'The shadows vanished, and I can only assume that they were destroyed. We searched the city but no one was to be found. We were ordered to search the last room. As we opened it we were attacked by huge brutal beasts that walked on two legs at first, but then changed their form to attack on all fours. We stood no chance on the ground, and as we took to the air we were assaulted from above by the Arbitans who must have been hiding.'

Legion placed a closed hand to his mouth, in deep thought. 'But you escaped?'

Krast felt uncomfortable, 'In a way, Sir, yes.'

'What do you mean, soldier?'

Krast was starting to regret his decision to call the men off. 'We were about to lose, Sir. We had lost our commander. I took charge and called the men off. I decided that it would be more beneficial to get this information back to you, and spare the rest of the men. The Arbitans knew we were coming, Sir. They were ready for us. We did not stand a chance.'

'Are you a wise man or a weak man, I wonder?' Legion replied through gritted teeth.

'I beg your pardon, Sir?'

'Guards, bring in this man's family. I gave one simple order. Defeat the Arbitans, and yet they live. Not only that, but so do a large number of the soldiers I sent. Tell me, Krast, how long was it before you decided to flee? Did you really judge the situation well or did you flee in panic?'

'It was a lack of judgement from the commander that led us into trouble in the first place. I always weigh up a situation, Sir, then I work out what would be the best course of action. I try to think of every possible outcome and then choose the best option. I think I did what was best, Sir. I am no coward; I have always fought well for you.' Krast knew that he was treading dangerously. Legion did not like to lose, and someone was going to be blamed, and as he was the last person in charge he had a feeling he knew who that person would be.

'Krast, I know that you are a very skilled warrior, but you came back with many warriors who could easily have fought on. My army does not lose a battle while there are still men alive to fight. I am grateful for the information that you have brought back to me. However, I feel that as a leader you showed weakness – you did not want to lose the men, and in a battle, compassion is weakness. For this reason, I am going to use you as an example.'

Krast's heart was trying desperately to burst through his chest, and every nerve was dancing in his body, but he did not let it show. He stood with his arms behind his back, resolutely keeping his eyes on Legion.

'Where is this man's family? I asked for them to be brought in. They can die with you. I owe you that at least,' hissed Legion.

Krast still stood staring at Legion; not even these hate-filled words made him flinch.

A large guard walked into the room, showing obvious signs of fear. 'I... I am sorry, Sir, but his family was not there; they appear to have left the city,' he said as he unconsciously rubbed his forehead.

Without any warning, Krast revealed two blades that he had concealed in the sleeves of his tunic and threw them out sideways – each found its mark in the necks of the guards who stood at his sides. He leapt towards the guard who was standing by the door, grabbed his sword, embedded it in its owner's thigh and flew as fast as he could out of the doors, the building and then the city.

Legion had not had a chance to react. Krast was good, and he had been ready for this outcome; he was always ready.

'I feel that maybe he was wise rather than weak, after all, wouldn't you say?' said Legion sardonically to the injured guard who was staring at the sword sticking out of his leg. 'Oh, and you are free to go and bleed somewhere else.' He waved a thin grey hand at the guard who was still slumped by the door.

A shadowy figure came and stood at Legion's side and placed a solid hand on his shoulder. 'What has happened here, my lord?' it asked. As it turned its head, it changed from skin to shadow and then back to skin once more. Its black eyes stared at Legion.

'Well, this is good news, very good news on an otherwise stressful day. So, you are still with us then, Tharik.'

'I am not Tharik; that name came with weakness. Now I am something new. There is no light in me any more, no feeling, no weakness – Shadow Forge runs through my veins and it is my strength. I am now Darkness.'

Legion smiled; this was better than he could have hoped. 'Welcome, Darkness!'

'I have one question: who is Rahmon? I cannot get this name out of my head.'

'Rahmon was Tharik's brother and he is your enemy, an enemy you will meet soon enough.' Legion clenched his fists as he began planning out the next battle with the Arbitans.

Chapter 25: Pirates

The first beams of the morning sun were creeping slowly through the dense trees. The once quiet forest was alive with the songs of thousands of insects, and from time to time the loud booming howls from strange furless monkeys echoed through the treetops. The night-time prowlers were now asleep, and it seemed as if every living thing was celebrating the relative safety of the light of day.

'Gid, can you see the boat just ahead?' asked Gecks.

Gid looked through the trees and followed the path of the river to where Gecks was staring. 'I see it. There seem to be a lot of people around it. I wasn't expecting that many traders.'

Ash crouched next to Gid. 'They are not traders, my friend. They are soldiers. It looks like our free ride has just been taken.'

Romallia stood still; her eyes were misty and her skin clammy. She took in a deep breath, shook her head and looked at the others. 'We are in danger,' she warned.

'Are you ok? You were somewhere else for a moment there,' asked a concerned Ash.

'The Arbitans have won their first battle and now Legion is furious. He has sent his soldiers out across the land trying to obtain information. He knows about the Cortuskas; he also knows about you, Gid. I do not know his plans; I only know that we are not safe here. The traders are to be taken as prisoners, as a punishment for dealing with the Arbitans. Their goods are to be taken to the city.'

Ash looked puzzled. 'How do you know all this, Romallia?'

'I saw it and heard it as I looked at the soldiers. It just kind of entered my head.'

'What should we do, Gid?' prompted Gecks.

'Romallia, do they know that we are supposed to be

meeting the traders? Do they know we are here?' Gid needed to know what kind of danger they were in.

Romallia went blank again for a few seconds. 'The traders did not know that Arbitans were definitely meeting them and the soldiers know nothing.'

The group watched as the traders were bound together by their hands and feet and led away from the boat into the open land in the direction of Harrashon. Two soldiers stayed with the boat, preparing to take it by river towards the city. There were a great deal of valuable items on board that they would divide between them when they got it all home.

Gid smiled. 'I think our journey may have just got a little easier. Can any of you steer a boat?'

They watched the main group of soldiers fly off into the distance, taking their prisoners with them. As soon as they were out of view, Gid would hijack the boat from the remaining, nonchalant two.

He flew to the boat, unseen, and said in the gruffest voice he could manage, 'Untie the ropes from the mooring. We should take this boat back as soon as we can. There's some good stuff aboard and I'm not in the mood for sharing.'

Without thinking, the two soldiers obeyed, and the boat slowly began to make its way down river; there was no need for sails as they drifted along at a steady pace towards Harrashon. The morning sun was warm, and the weary soldiers were looking forward to an easy trip back home.

'It's a beautiful day,' said Gid chirpily, as he sat next to the now lounging soldiers.

'Yes, it is. The sun is just the right temp... Hang on, who are you? We took the crew captive!' The soldiers leapt to their feet, hands ready on their swords.

'My name is Gid and I am stealing your stolen boat.'

The soldiers looked at each other and laughed. 'Do you believe the cheek of this? It seems this little boy wants our boat! Ok son, feel free. Take it from us.'

The soldiers drew their swords. One of them was still laughing so hard that he wiped a tear from his eye. Gid moved so quickly that all the soldiers saw was a blur before their heads were smacked together.

'What just happened?' asked the soldier who minutes before had been wiping laughter tears away from his eyes. As he came to, he realised that he was sat inside the boat in his underwear with his hands tied around a post behind his back. The other guard was in the same situation but had not yet woken up. 'Oh, we are going to be in so much trouble when Krast hears about this...'

Back outside, Romallia and Ash were dressed in the soldiers' uniforms and keeping a look out for any more of Legion's troops.

'I've just stolen a boat! I guess that makes me a real-life pirate,' giggled Gid excitedly.

'A what?' asked Romallia.

'You know – a pirate, "Yaargh, shiver me timbers, avast ye mangy dogs!" No, umm, you must know, a pirate. Hooks for hands, eye patches, wooden legs, big moustaches, beards and stuff?'

Romallia, Gecks and Ash just stared at him; he had obviously gone completely mad!

'You guys are no fun; I might just make you walk the plank, you sort of "sky and land lubbers". From now on you will call me "Captain Gid, the scourge of the..." um, "the big long river"!' Still they stared at him blankly. 'Ok, just plain old "Captain Gid" will do. Please.'

'Ok, Captain Gid, what duties would you have us do?' asked Romallia.

'Um, I don't know. How about swabbing the poop deck?'

'What exactly does that mean, Captain?' asked a rather bemused Ash.

'I don't know, just find some deck that is a bit poopy and swab it. Does that make things a bit clearer for you, you "lily-

156

livered son of a scurvy rat"?' Gid was not entirely sure he had all this pirate stuff quite right, but it sounded piratical, and that was good enough for him.

'Extremely clearer, Captain,' laughed Ash, revealing a big toothy grin. 'I think he's gone crazy, but I like him like this,' he thought.

The boat continued its lazy trip down river, passing a bland, brown, flat landscape showing no signs of life. Romallia, Ash and Gecks relaxed on deck whilst Gid hobbled around on one leg with a wooden pole under one arm, a home-made patch over one eye, shouting 'Yaaargh' a lot and keeping his other eye peeled for the scurvy enemy.

Suddenly he stopped and stared into the sky. Two figures were approaching from the direction of Harrashon. 'Guys, we have company. Ash, go below deck and watch the prisoners. Romallia, stay in view – your uniform should fool them for long enough.' Once again Gid's childhood was put on hold whilst he prepared for battle.

The fierce-looking figures were now in clear sight; they were unmistakably female warriors from Legion's army. They circled the boat but would not land. They could tell that something was amiss.

'You there, on the boat!' shouted one coldly.

Romallia pointed a finger to her chest and gave them a shocked look.

'Yes, you. Where are our comrades?'

Gid was hiding behind a large pile of boxes and material getting ready for the attack, but was suddenly halted by their next statement. 'Look, I don't know who you are, but we need to get word to our friends. We are not here to fight; we are loyal to Krast.'

Gid had not yet heard of Krast, but he felt instinctively that these two were not the enemy. He came out of his hiding place. 'You can land safely, but one false move and your friends are fish food!'

The warriors looked at each other, slightly confused. 'I am not familiar with this "fish food". I don't quite understand, but I can assure you that we mean no harm.'

Gid had been saving that threat for a good while now for just this kind of occasion. He was less than impressed with its effect. 'Look, just come aboard. You can trust me.'

'We have no time for friendly introductions; we need to speak to our friends.'

They went below with Gid and Romallia and found their tied-up, half-naked and well-guarded comrades.

'Bit warm were you, boys?' asked one of the female warriors with a glint in her eye.

'You know how it gets out on the river – just felt like cooling off a little. Oh, by the way, there were at least 30 of these guys when we were captured.' The bulky warrior was trying to come out of this slightly embarrassing situation with at least a little dignity left intact.

The female warrior turned to his captors. 'When you hear our message I can assure you that you will believe we are not a threat.' Then she relayed their story of the battle at Arborinium and the following consequences that involved Krast.

The prisoners were untied and their clothes given back. The largest of the prisoners seemed to have forgotten his brief spell as a captive already. He stepped forward and spoke. 'Krast is my commander, and I am loyal only to him. What is the plan?'

The messengers looked at Gid as if wondering whether or not to disclose any more information in front of the strangers. As if reading their minds, Gid spoke first and told them that they, too, were against Legion and fighting for Arborinium.

Bit by bit, as the two parties began to trust each other, their stories were shared: Harrashon was divided between those warriors who were loyal to Legion and those who were loyal to Krast. The soldiers loyal to Legion knew nothing about this division. Soon there would be two battles – one fought at Arborinium and one in Harrashon. Around a third of the soldiers Legion had sent to Arborinium were loyal to Krast, and the Arbitan city now had a more or less even chance of survival, surprise being the enemy's only real advantage.

After discussing strategies with the warriors, it was decided that Krast's men should take the boat into the city so as not to raise suspicions.

'How did you know that we were not soldiers from your army?' asked Romallia.

'A number of things gave it away. Firstly, you were not flying a flag to say that this was a captured vessel. Secondly, you are a woman, and we knew that this boat was taken by our friends. And finally, you were standing up, waiting for us as we approached – these two normally lounge or sleep – you were not lazy enough! Anyway, what was your plan? Were you just going to follow the river right into the city?'

Gid blushed and nodded.

'If we could tell that you aren't soldiers from high in the sky, you can imagine how easily you would have been caught when you got up close to the city. Lucky we found you, really. When this boat gets into the city we will have to sign it over. It will stay in the harbour under guard until tomorrow. In the morning all the contents will be checked and inventories will be made, and then it will be moved into the city stores where we can claim it. We can get you into the city and the harbour, but once you're there you'll be on your own.'

'How do we know we can trust you?' asked Romallia.

The warriors conferred with each other and then spoke. 'We have information that could help you. In the morning, Legion is sending his war machines to Arborinium. He has many huge devices – some for storming walls, some that spew flames and some that fling boulders into the enemy. I have never seen a city withstand an onslaught from these machines. In the end, time is always on the side of the attackers when they are used, and eventually they break through.'

Gid looked worried. 'I have had to defend a city many

times against machines like these...'

Everyone looked at him with interest and surprise. He was referring to his computer game back at home.

Ash was waiting for the advice. 'Well, come on, Gid. How did you win, how did you stop them?'

He blushed a little, 'Um, I never did. I always lost.'

'Great, thanks for that. I feel much better now!' Ash shook his head in disbelief.

'There is a way to defeat them,' said one of the female warriors who until now had been silent.

All eyes were on her. 'I helped build them. When they are being moved, it takes a lot of warriors, and they are only constructed properly as we get closer. It means their weight is distributed more equally and they are easier to move. If anyone were to attack in the open before they arrive at a city, the army could be defeated and the machines destroyed. The only advantage they have is the sheer numbers and strength of the soldiers who move them. It would take a pretty fierce group to beat them, but it could be done.'

Romallia grinned. 'We happen to know quite a large group of very fierce warriors,' she said triumphantly. 'The Cortuskas! They won't be able to fight the soldiers in the air when the battle starts at Arborinium, but I don't think anything could beat them on the ground.'

The warrior who knew these machines inside out volunteered to fly to Arborinium and inform them of their oncoming threat. 'I only hope they trust me; I am still an enemy in their eyes.'

Romallia assured her that she would be safe. She was to speak to Valletia or Rahmon and no one else. They would know exactly what to do.

Throughout this encounter, Gecks had been out of view and stayed silent. She had been watching and listening out for any sign of danger or deceit. Satisfied that all was well, she climbed onto Ash's shoulder.

'Cute pet!' commented the bulky warrior. 'Does it have a name?'

'Yes, his name is Ash. I found him in the mountains,' shot back a grinning Gecks.

'I'm sorry. I didn't realise lizards could talk. I meant no offence!'

Ash laughed. Gecks smiled at the warrior. 'None taken. I am a one-off; there would be no way of knowing I could talk. I just wanted to be sure that we were amongst friends before I did speak.'

The newly formed party headed on towards Harrashon with their flag flying high.

Chapter 26: Friend or foe

Arborinium was a short distance away, through the forest, and Krast was keeping his eyes peeled for any lookouts. So far he had seen no signs of life, but Rahmon had already proved to be a formidable adversary. The fact that he could neither see nor hear any Arbitans meant very little. Krast knew that he had probably been spotted a long time ago and that it was only a matter of time until he was captured – the waiting was the worst part. As if reading his mind, a dart flew out of a bush and hit him in the neck; within seconds his head was feeling heavy and his eyesight blurred. He tried to call out and let his assailant know that he was a friend, but no words would escape his lips.

Moments later – or so it seemed – his eyesight returned, though his head and body still felt groggy. He realised that he was lying on a bed in what seemed, by the number of lights and odd-looking instruments on long wooden tables, to be a medical room. Either that or he was about to be tortured.

'Why are you here?' asked a familiar voice. Krast gently turned his head and found Rahmon sitting next to him.

'I am no enemy, Rahmon. I need somewhere safe for myself and my family. You must have realised what I was heading back to when I returned to Legion, defeated and with soldiers still unharmed and willing to fight. I could think of no other place to go to.'

Rahmon placed his hand on Krast's shoulder. 'Your family is safe and you are amongst friends. The soldiers escorting your family arrived a while before you and told us of the situation in Harrashon. Please forgive my lookout for your present condition; he was only doing his job, and he did it well.'

Krast smiled. 'I understand completely. What was I hit

with? I kind of like it!'

'It's a form of tranquilliser; it knocks you out but also leaves you with a very peaceful, happy feeling when you wake. It makes prisoners more cooperative when they come around. I'm happy to have you here, Krast. You are a welcome newcomer to this city, though you are obviously going to be under close watch. Any sign of a plan or betrayal and you will be back in here, feeling a lot worse.'

Krast was now smiling even more broadly. 'Once again, I understand. Oh dear, I can't stop smiling.' With that he burst into a fit of uncontrollable giggles.

'Unfortunately this will wear off in about an hour, leaving you with a slight headache. I'll be back to check on you soon, my friend. You have some anxious visitors waiting outside; I'll show them in if you feel up to it?'

Krast managed to stop giggling. 'I feel great,' he said, and then the giggling started again.

Rahmon showed a beautiful purple-haired lady and two young purple-haired boys into the room. 'I will leave you now. If you need anything at all, we will endeavour to help – this city is as much yours now as the Arbitans'.' Rahmon bowed and left the room, and as he walked away he could hear Krast's giggles, now joined by the heart-warming laughter of the rest of his family.

Rahmon was only a few feet from Krast's room when he was stopped by one of his warriors. 'We have another visitor, Sir; she is out cold in the next medical room. She came in the same way as the last one. She is alone, and before she passed out she asked for you or Valletia – and she mentioned Gid.' The warrior bowed and left. Rahmon rubbed his face and left his palms resting over his eyes as he slowly massaged his scalp. 'Well, I guess it can only be a good thing. I just hope Legion doesn't have anything to do with this,' he whispered quietly to himself. The new arrival would be coming round soon, and once again he would be waiting at the side of the bed to be ready as soon as she woke up.

He walked slowly to the room and stepped inside, waiting at the doorway as if held there by some invisible force. The woman lying in the bed was beautiful. She had long, bright red dreadlocks and pale skin; her eyes were closed and peaceful looking.

Rahmon had never felt anything like this before. Through all the years of looking after himself and his brother, and now the responsibility of being in command of the army, he had never had time to think about females, but something deep inside him now stirred as he saw this warrior lying in the bed.

The doctor in the room saw him standing in the doorway. 'Everything ok, Sir?' she asked.

'Pardon? Um, I mean, yes, yes, I'm fine, just a little tired. Is she ok? You are keeping a close eye on her, aren't you?'

The doctor gave him a knowing smile. 'You seem concerned, Sir; you're not usually in the habit of doubting my work.'

'I don't doubt your work. It was just a question. I'm sorry if you thought I was being rude.'

'Pretty, isn't she?' The doctor was beaming.

'Huh? Um, I suppose. I don't know really... I, um, leave me alone please…' Rahmon was blushing.

'I'm sorry, Sir. I just think it's sweet.'

'Well, you can leave now. I'll wait here until she comes round.' Rahmon was smiling.

'Good luck, Sir.' The doctor winked at him and left the room.

Rahmon sat down by her side. He could not stop the feeling that was working its way through his body and coming to rest in his chest. He had no idea what he would say when she came to, which seemed to be taking far too long.

After what seemed like hours, the warrior finally opened her eyes. Rahmon would normally wait for the person to come round properly before making his presence known, but he could not wait. 'Hello there. Um, how are you feeling?'

The warrior turned to look at the voice. Rahmon saw her eyes and wanted to gaze into them; they were beautiful. His mind was telling him that they were just eyes, but his heart was having none of it. Yet for some strange reason he could not look at them; he was nervous, and it seemed that her eyes were looking right into him.

The warrior looked back at him, trying to look him in the eye. 'You're a handsome one, aren't you? What's your name?' The grin on her face was growing.

'My name is Rahmon. I think you are feeling the effects of the dart – it will take a while to wear off. What is your name and why are you here?' He was desperately trying to remain professional but was failing miserably.

'I am just fine, thank you. In fact, I feel great! You didn't ask me that, though, did you? I may be a little bit giddy from the dart, but I think you told me that. Why won't you look into my eyes? Are you shy? I think you like me, don't you? I can't stop myself from grinning! This feels odd but I like it. What was your name again?'

Rahmon was feeling helpless. He did not know where to look. Part of him wanted to run away, but another part never wanted to leave this girl again.

'I was asking you what you were doing here,' he said, focusing on her chin.

'I am lying in a bed feeling rather happy. What are you doing here, and why are you looking at my chin? I have two eyes, you know! You're shy, aren't you? I won't bite, you know, unless you want me to. You asked me why I'm here, didn't you, and what my name is?'

Rahmon was glowing red; no amount of training as a warrior had prepared him for this. 'I did, yes. Are you going to tell me?'

'Tell you what?'

He was rubbing his face again. 'What is your name and

165

why are you here?'

'Ooh, you are a grumpy one, my little grumpalump! Ok, handsome, here's the low-down on the down-low. I was about to tell you something, wasn't I? Hmm… Think, girl, think. Ah yes, I remember. Are you ready for this? Oh, my mouth feels rather strange…'

She opened her mouth wide and mouthed the word 'strange' in slow motion, smiled and then burst into uncontrollable giggles. After a few desperate attempts, she finally regained control. 'My name is Rowley, and I am here to give you an important message about war machines.'

'Rowley…' Rahmon repeated. 'War machines? What of them?'

'I am feeling a little too light-headed to explain right now, but there are some on their way here. I cannot stop smiling. You are lovely, you know. I like your eyes.'

Rahmon was beaten. He knew she was still feeling the effects of the darts, but he would hold on to her words anyway. She liked him, and that alone was making him smile. 'I will let you rest a while; when you feel better you can tell me what you need to.'

'I told you – I feel sort of great! My message is this: I hope it makes sense; I am feeling a little woozy, you know. Legion is sending his war machines to destroy this city, and I know how you can defeat them, and you have friends who can help.' At these words she started to laugh uncontrollably. 'I'm sorry; it's not funny but I can't stop myself!' Tears of laughter were streaming down her cheeks and a huge grin stretched from cheek to cheek.

Without thinking, Rahmon spoke: 'You are beautiful!' He was shocked at his own words, and he felt as if his face was on fire. He only hoped that she had not heard him.

'Thank you very much. So are you,' she replied, and once again started to giggle, then she yawned and slowly drifted off to sleep once more.

Rahmon decided to let her rest before he asked any more questions. He would wait by her side for the sole purpose of keeping an eye on her. It had nothing to do with his new-found feelings, he told himself – he was just being 'professional'.

Chapter 27: Harrashon

Gid sat hiding with the others under a pile of fabric in the cargo hold of the boat. From above they could hear the sound of large gates opening and the mumble of voices. They were entering the city. The hatch to the cargo hold opened and a voice spoke. 'We'll be in the harbour soon. You're in luck – the guard at the city gates was one of us, and the first guard who will quickly check the boat when it enters the harbour is also loyal to Krast. We'll let him know that you are down there. However, we do not yet know who will be watching the harbour tonight. You'll have to find a way out of the boat and the harbour on your own. Tomorrow is market day so you should be able to blend in easily with the crowds it attracts. The market will still be happening even on the eve of battle; Legion is confident that the Arbitans will fall quickly and does not see the need to place the city on any alert. Life will go on here as normal – or so he thinks. I wish you all the best of luck and hope we meet again.' With these words the hatch closed again and the friends were left hiding until nightfall.

At first, the waiting was exciting for Gid. What if they were seen, what if they had been led into a trap, what if someone decided to check the boat early? However, as the minutes and then hours ticked by, his anticipation gradually changed into boredom, and then sleep.

'Gid, wake up. Gid!' Romallia whispered as she tried to shake him into life. 'Ash and Gecks are on deck. The sun is setting behind the city. It looks amazing. Don't worry – they're both well hidden.' She left Gid and headed outside.

'I think I may have had a little doze,' Gid said to himself, stretching, yawning and rubbing his eyes with his left hand. He had a long crease down his right cheek, and his right arm was numb from where he had been lying on it. He slowly came round, then ventured carefully out onto the deck and hid with the others behind a pile of boxes.

As the sun set, it cast a warm glow over the silhouetted city. The tops of some of the larger buildings in the city could be seen climbing high into the orange sky. There were huge, imposing towers, probably around 20 of them, made from dark, solid stone. Each had a flat roof that was occupied by warriors. It was obvious that the ruler of the city had no intention of ever being caught by surprise. These towers acted as lookout stations; you would have to be invisible to approach the city undetected. Towards the centre of the city, a statue stood on an enormous plinth, rising higher than the lookout towers. The evening light was shining on it, casting shadows across the low clouds. The statue depicted a wounded warrior lying at the feet of a tall, faceless, winged figure. The figure's right hand held a roll of bandages, and the left hand held a shield high above its head as if protecting the two characters.

'I don't understand the statue, Ash,' said Gid. 'Why is the tall figure protecting the wounded warrior? I mean, it's all very nice, but I thought Legion was a bit, well, nasty. There's nothing to show that he is nasty in the statue. That is – if it is supposed to be Legion.'

Ash smiled. 'You're right in thinking that the character is Legion. The wounded warrior is supposed to be this world, and Legion is trying to make the people believe that he is the protector of our world and that he will heal its wounds. It makes it easier to live in the city; people quickly forget the evil things he has done. It's easier to pretend that everything is ok, that he is some kind of hero, than to face the truth.'

'He's a very clever leader, isn't he?' Gid said in a pensive, concerned voice.

Ash smiled ruefully. 'Clever, deceitful and evil,' he said

'How are we going to get out of the harbour? There are guards everywhere.' Romallia's practical question reminded

169

the boys of their current situation.

It was true – there were guards everywhere. At first glance the city seemed to be under constant surveillance. Getting out of the harbour was not going to be easy.

The group watched the guards until it became dark and noticed a few things that might help when they came to leave the harbour. The guards on the towers were not watching the city itself – their attention was concentrated outside the city walls. The guard patrolling the harbour was wandering from boat to boat, briefly checking the deck and then disappearing inside for a few minutes, presumably checking the contents and seeing what he could steal. There were around 50 boats in the harbour, and around 20 between them and the guard. Getting out of the harbour was no longer looking like a problem.

'We can easily travel along the jetties and hide on the boats before the guard surfaces. If we move as soon as he enters a boat, we should easily make it from the harbour without being seen.' Ash was apprehensive. 'It just seems a little too easy.' They had made it this far with no major difficulty, but nothing ever ran this smoothly, so he was expecting trouble.

'Ash, you're right – it does seem a bit too easy,' Romallia said sympathetically. 'But I know why. I still don't understand how I do this, but I can sense what people are feeling. I keep getting little snippets of their thoughts. For example, the guard on the closest tower is thinking about food; the guard nearest him is thinking only about keeping watch; the next one is – well, I'm not going to repeat her thoughts; the guard in the harbour just wants to scavenge and then go home. No one is thinking about us; they have no idea we're here, never mind what we're here for.' She was proving to be invaluable.

The guard in the harbour was making his way into another boat, and as his head disappeared from view, Gid and the others made a dash for a large stack of fishing baskets near the harbour entrance. They made it behind them just in time, as the guard surfaced once more with a small bag tied to his back that had not been there before. Ash peeped around the baskets to watch him and accidentally knocked one of the baskets off the pile. It crashed down on to the wooden decking and then rolled into the water with a soft splash. The guard turned suspiciously and started walking quickly towards them. The group huddled together. Romallia shot a cold glance in Ash's direction; he shrugged, pulled a sorry face and said, 'Oops.'

'Leave this to me,' whispered Gecks.

As the guard approached, Gecks ran out from the baskets and through his legs. He jumped and then started to laugh. 'Stupid lizard. I thought someone was trying to sneak in and steal from the boats – or worse, trying to steal from me! I'm getting too old for this.' The guard turned and walked back to the boats.

'That was a bit close…' Ash had a sheepish grin on his face.

The next time the guard entered a boat, they ran quietly out of the harbour.

A long, dark road lined with buildings led from the harbour to a huge open square in the centre of the city. Most of the buildings were single storeys, made from white stone with small, square, open windows. There were a number of inns and bars around the square, with warm glows coming from inside. The night was getting cooler and the streets of the city were quiet; a few small groups of people were sitting under lanterns on stone benches in the square playing board games and chatting quietly.

'It seems alright here, doesn't it – almost kind of peaceful – I mean, for an evil city, of course.' Gid smiled and looked at his friends.

They all looked back at him with blank faces.

'I'm not saying I suddenly like Legion or anything; it just feels like I'm on holiday, you know?'

He was met with the same blank expressions.

'Ok, ok, I know I'm not on holiday; I just like the place. And

171

don't worry, I'm not thinking of moving here or anything – I'm still going to fight Legion. I just reckon we should try to enjoy the city while we can.'

'Gid is right; the city itself is a great place. I know some good places to go at night. I'll take you to a tavern I always used to visit. On second thoughts, maybe that's not such a great idea... I still owe some money to some not-so-nice people there. Hmm, perhaps we could go to...' Ash led the group across the square and down several small alleyways. Harrashon was a maze of dark alleys, perfect for someone to lie in wait for people who had strayed from the main streets. Ash warned them all to be on guard as they wandered through the many identical alleyways.

After several minutes, they arrived at a small, white building, not unlike all the others they had passed. Ash knocked on a small, green, wooden door. He knocked several times in some kind of secret code. A wooden hatch slid open, two dark eyes peered out and looked at the group, and then the hatch closed again. The door opened and the group stepped into a large but cosy, dimly lit room with a bar at one end. Small groups of people sat around on brightly coloured cushions, talking, smoking from long pipes coming from tall bubbling bottles, and playing the same board game that the people in the square were playing.

'You guys sit there and I'll get us some drinks.'

Romallia sat down, and Gid sat opposite her with Gecks on his shoulder. A few moments later, Ash returned with a tray of glasses containing green liquid. 'Here – drink and enjoy! I've sorted us some rooms for the night. This is one of the few places where I'm owed a favour and not the other way around.'

'What is this stuff? It tastes lovely.' Gid licked his lips.

'It's juice made from a fruit that only grows in one area just outside the city. I thought you might like it; it's a favourite of mine. It has a lovely warming effect and makes it easier to forget your problems.'

'I hope it works. I've been thinking about what we're supposed to do here and I can't let myself believe that it will all go as smoothly as it has so far. And I'm not really sure that Legion doesn't know we're here. I'm thinking it will be a good idea to go with Valletia's advice to me, just to let things happen. I know I have to get into the palace to find and hopefully defeat Legion. I was trying to think of ways to get in, and unless you have any really good ideas I think I've decided on a way. It's not really the most imaginative but it's the best I could think of. I was going to just walk up and knock and ask to see Legion.' Gid had his serious face on again, but now there was less worry in his eyes.

The group stared at him as though he had gone crazy.

Ash thought for a moment. 'It's one way, I suppose, and you would most definitely grab his attention, but before you go with that I reckon I might be able to help. I've thought of some ways too, and I think I could climb into one of the towers and find a door somewhere and let you in. If you flew up, you'd be spotted, but if I climb I might be a little more discreet. The only problem is that I have no idea what to do if and when I get in. The only other way I can think of is through the water pipes below the city; I've heard that there's a pool inside that's fed by the river. But again, I don't think that's a great plan as I have no idea how long the pipes are, and we'd probably drown trying to go through them.'

'Ah, now that's not a bad idea. I don't mean the drowning part. You guys couldn't swim in there, but I could. And to be honest, I don't want you guys coming in; I need to do this on my own, and I don't want you to put yourselves in any more danger.'

Romallia gave Gid an angry glare and then relaxed again. 'Gid, we are with you all the way, and if we can help we will; everything we know is in danger, and we will do what we can.'

Gecks nodded and smiled her lizardy grin. A speaking lizard would have drawn unnecessary attention from the other customers.

A warm feeling slowly spread through their bodies as the drinks started to take effect, and the conversation soon changed from what was going to happen to how far they had come already, and then to idle chatter. It was clear that whatever was soon to happen would, in one way or another, involve them all, that they were in it together and would finish it together. They all knew that tomorrow was on its way. The inevitability of it was bringing them closer, but for the next few hours they could pretend that they were just a few good friends enjoying an evening.

They relaxed and talked for many hours in the comfort of the tavern until their eyes grew heavy.

'I don't know about you guys, but I'm off to bed,' yawned Gid.

Ash opened his drowsy eyes and nodded in agreement. Romallia and Gecks had already drifted into sleep.

The following morning was a complete contrast to the serenity of the previous night. The sun was blazing down, and the once empty and peaceful square was now full of market stalls. There were so many smells in the air – sweet fruity smells, strong eye-watering spicy smells, the smell of cooked meats and the calming scent of incense mixed in with the smells of hot people and strong perfumes. There was a lot of shouting from the owners of the stalls, as they each tried to attract custom. There were so many different looking people with different skin colours and fashions. Gid could tell that most of this world's inhabitants had ended up living in Harrashon, probably because at one time or another their own cities and tribes had been defeated by Legion.

As they slowly made their way through the bustling market, they noticed the constant presence of soldiers. They seemed to be watching the crowds intently, though the people did not seem to notice them. Years of living under the watchful eyes of the army had made the inhabitants of the city indifferent to their presence. Ash, however, had noticed something slightly different about the soldiers. A number of them were not watching the market and the people quite as intently as the others. Some of the soldiers were watching each other; they would nod discreetly, or smile, as if they were sharing a secret.

'If you watch carefully, you can tell which of the soldiers are with Krast,' Ash explained. 'Legion's soldiers haven't noticed anything yet. Krast's men need to be careful though; if I spotted them, it won't be too long before one of Legion's guys does too.'

As if hearing Ash's comments, the soldiers loyal to Krast suddenly acted. They took bright green strips of fabric, which had been hidden in their belts, and tied them to their upper right arms. They would now be easily identifiable to each other in what was about to happen.

From somewhere in the distance a voice shouted, 'For Krast!' This cry was quickly taken up by all who were loyal to him around the city. Legion's troops, who had been completely unaware that anything was going on, suddenly found themselves being attacked by soldiers who, only seconds earlier, had been their allies. It took only seconds for the bustling market to turn into a scene of chaos. Stalls were overturned, vendors vainly struggled to pack up their goods, and many people stole what they could from the stalls. Most people were fleeing the scene, running and flying in all directions.

Legion's soldiers could not defend themselves properly. The attack had taken them completely by surprise, and the crowds around them were preventing them from being able to use their long swords. Krast's men had come armed with extra weapons, including short daggers and clubs. Legion's men were losing quickly, but soon, once the crowds had thinned and the battle took to the air, the advantage of numbers would switch back to Legion. Krast's soldiers would have to make the most of the fight while they were winning.

Soldiers were fighting all over the city, in buildings, streets and in the many alleyways. These vital seconds before the fight went skywards could mean the difference between victory and defeat for those loyal to Krast. The streets were filling with injured soldiers from both sides, and those who were struck in the fighting in the air above the city were now falling into the rapidly dispersing crowds below.

'Gid, now is your chance. We need to get you to the pool's supply tunnel while the soldiers are occupied. No one will see you. Romallia, Gecks and I will have to find another way in, though this may be easier while the attention is on the streets.' Ash knew that this was a perfect opportunity; the entrances to any areas leading to the palace were normally well guarded, but with the current fighting, they would have a chance.

Chapter 28: Ambush

A confident and battle-hardened commander stood by the last obstacle that remained between his men and the Arbitans. He had served for many years and was confident that they had the upper hand; he surveyed his men proudly and smiled.

'Not far now; the forest of Arborinium lies just over the waters. Make no mistakes – when these boats land we need to get the war machine parts off sharpish. Once we're close enough to the target we'll assemble them and let loose the might of these beasts. There has not been an army that has not crumbled once we attack. The shadows may not have beaten these warriors, but we'll deliver a devastating blow.'

All that lay between the warriors and the boats was the expanse of desert, an expanse that appeared to be clear of any enemies. The skies around them were still patrolled by the eerie shadow dragons, preventing any of the soldiers from taking to the air.

There were around 5,000 wingless soldiers, from tribes defeated long ago by Legion, boarding ten of the largest boats. Four thousand winged warriors were in charge of the many war machines. The rest – around 10,000 or more – would fly ahead and ensure that the forest was clear. The advance group would fly over the water and then the trees and find places to land and scout the area.

The machines and their soldiers would be transported by the remaining 40 boats, and then the parts would be carried towards the city before being assembled. The plan was simple: power, speed and numbers would win.

At the water's edge, the advance group took to the air, now safe from the reach of the dragons. The skies darkened as the vast number of winged warriors momentarily blocked out the light of the sun.

The boats carrying the ground soldiers were now loaded and ready to cross the water. Twenty boats lay anchored, waiting for the machines to be loaded. They had arrived less than an hour earlier; everything relied on timing, and the crew on the boats were lowering the gang planks and getting ready to help the soldiers carry the heavy machines on board. The soldiers were now only 500 metres from the boats.

This time Legion wanted it to be over quickly; the Arbitans would have no chance to organise their defences.

As the warriors in the sky started to disappear from view, the boats carrying the soldiers set off at speed, with the wind behind them. Back on land, the commander and the remaining soldiers made sure that the rest were well on their way and started to organise the loading of the machines. 'Everyone in their positions. This is to be done as quickly as possible. All machine parts are to be loaded and unloaded at the same time. We will form one long line all the way – one line of attack. There will be no stragglers and no one racing ahead; we will work as one and destroy the enemy as one – nothing will stand in our... way.'

The ground beneath their feet started to vibrate; small stones were dancing on the dusty ground. One of the soldiers placed her ear to the ground. 'It sounds like something is moving below us!'

For a moment, everything went silent. The listener lifted her ear from the ground and held up her hands, shrugging. 'It was probably a small earthquake, but whatever it was it has stopped.'

A loud, earth-rumbling, crashing sound burst from behind them. 'What the...?'

The ground ripped apart, rocks and dust flew into the air, and the rumbling grew deafeningly loud. There were more explosions of rock a short distance away from the line of stunned soldiers.

'What is it? What's going on?' Unease was quickly starting

to spread through the soldiers, an unease that would soon turn to panic – and then dread.

The first of the huge Cortuskas burst from the ground. Grimbarr had lost his friendly appearance and replaced it with the ferocity of a warrior. All eyes were on him, his huge figure gripping the attention of every soldier. Many more Cortuskas were now pouring from the holes, forming one long line of fierce, monstrous warriors.

The machine parts were dropped to the floor and trembling hands quickly drew swords. One small group took to the air, panic replacing sense and discipline. The forgotten threat in the sky soon showed its ugly face as the shadow dragons tore through the terrified soldiers.

'Hold your line!' yelled the commander of Legion's troops who was responsible for the war machines.

The remaining soldiers were now pinned between two fierce enemies above and on the ground. The line of Cortuskas now stood facing Legion's troops; they were only 100 metres apart.

Grimbarr tilted his head skywards and roared. A thousand Cortuskas joined him in the shout and then charged at the enemy.

'Get ready, lads,' shouted a worried commander, 'They are never as fierce as they look – and besides, we have the numbers.'

The Cortuskas leaped into the air, and as one they changed into the beasts known as Hogboars. Sheer dread flowed through the waiting soldiers like a wave of terror emanating from the beasts crashing upon them.

The Cortuskas smashed into their enemies, sending them flying backwards. Each Cortuska was outnumbered by four to one, but it meant nothing.

Grimbarr smashed the line first. He smashed his tusks into one terrified soldier, then turned on another who still had his hand on an undrawn sword. The next soldier, braver than the others, ran at Grimbarr, sword held high. Before the sword could be brought down, Grimbarr rose up on two feet and smashed his huge head into the soldier's chest. The sheer might of the Cortuskas was too much for Legion's men.

The line was broken. The battle was fierce and it was happening too quickly for any of the soldiers to be able to regroup.

Everywhere in the battle, Legion's men were falling; they had no way to beat these beasts. Bodies were sent flying and were trampled as soon as they landed on the hard ground. No amount of discipline or training could help them now.

A small group had managed to bring one of the Cortuskas down. 'Quick, jump on it now – it's our only chance!' They pounced and stabbed until there was no more movement. Snorback ran wildly at them, smashing one of the soldiers full in the back. He changed into his two-legged form again and pounded every soldier in sight. His right fist smashed through the chest of one soldier as his left hand grabbed another by the throat and he used the body to strike another across the head.

Some of the Cortuskas had turned their rage towards the boats and smashed them to splinters in seconds; masts were left hanging and many were crumpled on their sides in the surf. The ground troops who had set sail earlier were still close enough to make out what was happening to their comrades and boats, but there was nothing they could do to help.

A few of the remaining soldiers had managed to form a small group, trying to find some kind of safety in numbers. They managed to bring down three more Cortuskas, but were soon fighting off more. One by one, the small groups were smashed. There were suddenly no more soldiers to fight. Most lay motionless, and the others were too injured to continue.

The short but fierce battle was over. The machines were trampled during the fight and Legion's soldiers had been defeated, but it had come at a cost. Four Cortuskas were dead, and though this was a small price compared to the defeated soldiers, each of the Cortuskas felt the loss of their comrades. The time to grieve was not yet upon them, however, as they still had to help their new allies in the fight for Arborinium.

Snorback walked slowly towards his father, 'Um, I am not coming to Arborinium; I need to help Gid.'

Grimbarr smiled. 'You feel it too? I reckon a little help may just tip things our way. The air feels restless; I hear its whisper. Everything is in the balance; Gid will need some help. If you have to go, I will not stop you.'

Snorback gripped his father's shoulder. 'I really hope this is not goodbye. I just know that I will be needed.'

'I am a very proud father today. Go and do what you must do. Take 400 comrades of your choosing, and good luck, my son.'

With his warriors chosen, Snorback turned once again into his beast form and ran with his 400 select companions as fast as he could towards Harrashon.

Chapter 29: Making an entrance

A large and rusted metal grate covered the entrance to a dark tunnel. In the dim light, the water looked cold and dark as it disappeared from view.

'This is going to be horrid, isn't it? How long do you reckon the tunnel is?'

Ash tried to look confident, but then his expression changed to one of complete honesty. 'I really don't know; I wish I could say, but I really don't know. It's about half a mile from here to the palace, but the tunnel may not follow a straight line. Look, are you sure you want to do this? We'll all understand if you don't.'

'Of course I don't *want* to do it; I'm not mad. But the thing is, I think I have to do it. Anyhow, it's you guys who need to be careful – this is the easy way in!'

Romallia smiled. 'Well, Gid, we may not find a way in, but if we can find the slightest chance, we'll take it. We have the eyes of Gecks and my new-found talent for knowing what the enemy is feeling, not to mention a top-class guide and warrior in the form of Ash. We'll be ok.'

Seeing that Gid still looked a little concerned, Gecks piped up, 'I'll keep an eye on these guys, Gid, don't you worry. I've managed to keep Ash alive so far, after all, and that in itself is a miracle. I won't let anything happen to them.' She blinked and smiled. 'See you on the inside, my friend.'

Romallia leaned forward and kissed Gid on the cheek. 'Good luck!'

Gid blushed and turned his head, only to see Ash puckering his lips. 'Don't you dare!' he laughed, backing away.

Ash chuckled and patted him on the back. 'Good luck, Gid, and see you soon.'

Gid slipped down into the neck-deep water of the river and

shivered. He gripped the grate and pulled it away from the tunnel mouth with ease. 'Here goes nothing!' he said as he turned and waved to his friends and then let the water carry him into the darkness. His head was still above water, but about 20 feet in front of him the roof disappeared into the river. 'This is it, then,' he said to himself, took a deep breath and put his head under.

There was no light and virtually no sound. The water was cold but not uncomfortable. He soon realised that any idea he had about swimming was out of the question; the current was too fast and he had to keep his arms out in front of him to stop himself smashing against the walls. The tunnel was getting tighter and Gid moved his legs directly out behind him and his arms as far out in front of him as possible, moving faster and faster. From time to time his wings caught on the ceiling and he tried to draw them more tightly to his body.

Around five minutes passed, which to Gid felt like a lifetime, but at least his breath was holding. Suddenly his hands hit something in front of him and he came to a stop. The river water was still pushing hard against him but something was blocking his way.

He felt in the dark with his hands, moving his fingers along the blockage, trying to find a way to free it. Then he realised what it was, and snatched his hand away and nearly screamed – the blockage was a body, or at least it was once; now it was just bare bones and rags. He started to panic. The way ahead was blocked and the tunnel was too narrow to turn in, and even if he could turn, the current was too strong to swim against.

Panic soon turned into a strange calmness, even though the air in his lungs was now trying to find a way out. It is one thing to hold your breath in a safe place, but being stuck in a tunnel with no immediate way out had had the effect of making his breath want to escape.

The knowledge that this really could be it was helping him

keep a level head. He grabbed at the bones and ripped them out of his way. After the first few were freed, the rest suddenly took off with the river and he was moving once again. He could hear a rumbling sound, and it felt as though he were speeding up. The water around him started to roar, and then he was airborne. Bright light hit his eyes and fresh air slapped his face as he felt himself falling through space, gasping for breath. He breathed in deeply just before he hit water again.

Something slammed against his back. He looked around and saw movement below him. Light was shining through the water above him and he headed for this. As he surfaced, he could see that the river was cascading into this underground reservoir from a tunnel about ten metres above him. 'That explains the falling!' he thought. The light came from a strange jelly-like substance that coated the inside of the roof and walls.

The water stirred and a dark shape moved towards him. Afraid, Gid instinctively swam at the creature and punched it; he felt his hand hit flesh, and the surface of the water erupted.

A hairless, scaly, green face was staring at him, rubbing its jaw. 'What is your problem?' it shouted. 'First of all you land on me. Then when I come to see if you are ok, you punch me in the jaw!'

'Um, sorry. I thought...'

'You thought? What you thought was, "Oh, there's something in the water; that must mean it wants to eat me. Everything in the water eats people so I'll just punch it in the mouth!" Well, Mr Fisty, let me tell you something – this pool here is my home. I live a nice quiet life down here. I used to get a few of your kind in here but they were never the breathing kind. I reckon someone must have blocked off the entrance. You came falling in here, still breathing, and I thought to myself, well, that's not something you see every day now, is it? Let's see if this chap needs a hand, and then you cracked me one. Thanks a bunch.'

'I really am sorry. I, um, well, I'm sorry. I... are you ok?'

'I am not as cheery as I was when I woke up, but I'm alive. Why are you down here?'

'I need to get into the pool at the palace.'

'Why would you want to do that? Are you sneaking in like some kind of assassin?'

Gid smiled weakly and then paused before he spoke; if he let the truth slip out to a stranger, he may be putting himself – and, more importantly, his friends – in danger.

'Do you get a lot of assassins falling into your pool?' he asked, trying to deflect the question.

'No, but I reckon I must get some of their victims. It's a shame, though; I wish someone would have the guts or strength to rid this world of that man, if he can be called that.'

'What man would that be?'

'The man who wiped out my kind. I am the last one. Legion killed everyone – well, his soldiers did. Legion saw us as some kind of threat, so he poisoned our waters. I was looking for an area for my new family to live and found this pool, but when I got back I found everyone dead – my wife, my children, my entire race. I would try to kill Legion myself, only I can't breathe for long enough on dry land. So I live my miserable life in this pool, so close to Legion but powerless to do anything. I'm waiting and hoping to have my revenge through another, but no one is powerful enough to kill him.'

'I am,' said Gid, with grave determination.

'What?'

A serious look had set onto Gid's young face. 'I said *I am*. You've been waiting for your revenge, and, well, here I am. The Arbitans have waited a lifetime for me to arrive and now I have. I'm on my way to kill Legion right now.'

Gid was stunned by his own words. He really was on his way to kill Legion! The words ran over and over in his mind. Until this moment he was on his way to 'stop' Legion; now he knew that stopping meant killing.

'You? But you're only a child. Though you did make it here

185

alive without the help of gills to breathe under water, and from your punch I know that you're strong, and quick – but still only a child! Look, I don't dare to dream of what your reasons are – the desire for revenge can be a powerful weapon – but don't let it get you killed.'

'Legion has done nothing to me, my family or my people. I am not even from this world. I am here to get rid of Legion and for nothing else. It's one of those "destiny has brought me here" kind of things.'

'I honestly never thought that the first time I met a hero he would punch me in the mouth...' mused the creature.

Gid put his hand to his head. 'Look, I have said I'm sorry. To be honest, I held back. I could have killed you. My arm does this cool thing where it turns into a bony sword – look.' The sword erupted from Gid's arm and the white bone blade sparkled in the light.

'I'll sleep better now knowing that I was so close to dying – I suppose I should thank you for not cutting off my head!'

'You don't have to thank me.'

'Really? I was being sarcastic... Anyway, if you need to get into the pool I can take you; it's not far from here. And if any of Legion's men happen to be nearby, please throw them in. The thirst for revenge is almost gone from me, but it seems a shame not to satisfy what I have left!'

Gid suddenly looked puzzled. 'Why have you never gone into the pool and just waited until they entered it, if you can get in there?'

'It isn't used any more. I had the idea myself of lying in wait, but the pool is pretty much an ornament now – just a big water feature, but I do wait in the hope that one day I'll hear a splash coming from that direction.'

'If I see anyone I'll throw them in as fish food, I promise.'

'Fish food? Do I look like a fish to you?'

There was a brief silence while Gid decided how to respond. 'A little bit. Well, you do have scaly skin and gills...'

186

'That's rich coming from "bat-man"!'

'Holy scaly skin fishman, let's get to the Batmobile,' sniggered Gid.

'What?'

'Never mind. Let's just get going. And just so you know, where I am from, that would have been funny.'

'I bet your world is a real scream.'

'Are you being sarcastic again?'

'Yes, very – it's a talent I have. Follow me!'

The creature took a handful of the glowing green jelly-like substance from the cave wall that was lighting up the reservoir and handed it to Gid.

'It gets a little dark down there,' it said.

The scaly figure ducked its head under the water and swam quickly towards the cave wall at the far side of the pool. Gid followed as best he could, but although he was a good swimmer, this creature was designed for water, and even using his wings to push himself, he could not match its speed – and there was no competition in gracefulness.

They ducked their heads under and swam down deep and then along the very bottom of the pool. It was dark, but the glowing jelly was giving just enough light for Gid to be able to follow. They swam towards and then through a huge horizontal crack in the cave wall. It felt to Gid as though he had just been swallowed and was now swimming down the rock's throat to its belly. The pressure of the water was starting to affect him; his ears were ringing and he had a cold pain behind his eyes. He knew his breath would hold but was not convinced that his head would.

He needed to rest, he thought, as his vision began to blur and fatigue crept over him. Small lights seemed to be flashing in front of him and he was in danger of fainting. He stopped in the water. He was disorientated and his head hurt, but at the same time he felt strangely at ease.

A scaly hand grabbed at him from out of the gloomy water

and pulled him forwards.

Moments later he was being dragged upwards, the pain in his head started to disappear and his eyesight returned to normal. The strange green swimmer signalled for Gid to stay where he was and then continued to swim up until he was just a small speck above his head. It returned a few moments later and beckoned for him to follow. Gid rushed up towards the surface and took a deep breath as he finally broke through. 'What just happened to me?'

'The water was very deep and I think the pressure got to you. To be honest, I've never known one of your kind to survive at that depth,' his new companion replied.

'Thanks for the warning!'

'You're still alive, aren't you? What's your problem?'

Gid ignored this and asked, 'Where are we?'

They had surfaced in a large, shell-shaped pool and were still in a cave, but the walls had been carved into 20 huge, dark pillars leading up to a ceiling, painted to look like a bright blue, cloudy sky. Chains hung down from large metal hooks on each of the pillars, and attached to the chains were glass balls big enough to stand in. The balls contained a jelly-like substance similar to the green goo in Gid's hand, only it glowed deep red, giving the cavernous room a warm, almost welcoming, feel.

At one end of the room, a flight of stairs large enough to fit 20 people across standing shoulder to shoulder, led off, up and out of view.

'Well, this is as far as I can take you. It's a shame we're alone in here – I was really up for a fight!'

'You may be in luck,' Gid said quietly. 'Listen...'

They lay in the pool, quietly listening. The sound of hard-soled boots on rock echoed through the room and they could hear a hushed voice complaining to another muffled voice somewhere in the distance.

'I know someone has to keep an eye on the pool; I just wish

t wasn't me. The others are fighting outside and I'm going to be stuck down here guarding water,' it moaned.

The muffled sound replied to the grumbling.

'I'm not moaning; I just want to be involved. Besides, nothing has come through that tunnel in years – nothing ever does, and yet we still have to guard it. Well, see you in a few hours; it's your turn next.'

The echoing steps were growing louder, and then in the distance, at the top of the stairs, a large winged soldier armed with a spear came into view, making his way down.

'I have an idea; swim out of view and trust me,' Gid whispered excitedly.

The soldier walked slowly towards the pool, his eyes adjusting to the red light. 'Eye eye, what's this?'

Gid was floating face down in the pool. The guard walked cautiously towards the water's edge and scanned the depths. He prodded Gid's body with the sharp end of his spear; there was no movement. He tried again, just to be sure.

Gid spun around and pulled both the spear and the guard into the water, then climbed out onto the side.

The guard splashed to the surface with his fists. 'You'll pay for that, whoever you are!'

Gid smiled. 'I wouldn't worry about me if I were you. Turn around.'

The guard kept his eyes on Gid; he wasn't stupid enough to fall for that. Scaly green hands reached slowly out of the pool, grabbed his wings and pulled him under.

Gid turned his back on the now eerily silent pool and headed for the stairs.

Chapter 30: Battles

The fighting in Harrashon had taken to the air, and the brief advantage that Krast's men had had in the streets was rapidly disappearing. Slowly but surely, the fight against the huge numbers of Legion's loyal warriors was taking its toll.

'Everyone to me!' shouted the voice of one of Krast's leading warriors.

The rapidly decreasing group flew to the call and gathered around their temporary leader. 'There are less than 1,000 of us left. Our enemies outnumber us five to one; you all know what we must do – we all fly up and we do it together. Is everybody clear?

As one, the group of warriors fled in a spiral towards a thick cluster of clouds, with Legion's army following close behind.

The small group sliced quickly through the clouds and stopped 30 metres above them. Directly below them, as if standing on the clouds, hovered another army with swords ready. The leaders of both parties smiled at each other.

Legion's warriors were quickly pursuing their prey and they were almost at the clouds; it would all be over soon. Krast's men had put on a brave display but it would all end in vain.

As the warriors burst through the dense cloud cover, they spotted their targets waiting above them and readied themselves for the final clash of steel. They were so intent on destroying their enemy that they did not notice the rest of the soldiers waiting, now behind them, until it was too late. Legion's warriors were sandwiched between a now larger force than their own. The battle was not going to be quick and easy, but they would make sure that it was at least bloody.

The sky was full of more than 10,000 battling warriors.

Sparks from clashing swords lit the clouds like small lightning bolts. There seemed to be no order to the battle – every soldier was fighting for his or her own life. Groups of warriors were winding between each other with swords flashing out, striking and blocking at frightening speeds. Two warriors were so intent on winning their fight that they did not notice the ground racing towards them until their bodies crumpled into it. Limp, dismembered corpses were falling from the clouds, which now seemed to be raining blood.

From below, it was impossible to tell who was winning. The silhouettes of battling warriors looked like large flocks of birds flying in unison, searching for somewhere to roost. Loyalties were now pitting friend against friend, brother against sister, and neither side was ready to back down.

A group of around 100 winged warriors were fighting inside a large, dark grey, angry cloud. It seemed as if nature itself was being angered by the fighting. The sky around them was glowing yellow, and their hair was starting to stand on end as the electricity built. Then came a bright white flash followed by a deafening crack of thunder. Many were hit directly by the lightning, their fight now ended, but still the rest slashed and sliced, parried and blocked.

Some warriors who had fallen injured from the sky were now fighting on the ground, many with missing or crumpled wings, intent on destroying their enemies.

Another flash filled the sky and was followed by more falling bodies and heavy rain.

Two skilled swordsmen were exchanging blow after blow, flying quickly and skilfully through the air, no weakness showing in either's technique, each matching the other perfectly. They flew into a thick part of the cloud, and white vapour poured between them. As one of the swordsmen raised his weapon, there was a loud, bone-crunching bang followed by a scream as he smashed into another warrior hurtling towards them.

On the ground below the fighting, Romallia, Ash and Gecks were making their way up the stone steps that led to the huge, wide open palace doors.

'So we are going with Gid's other plan, then – to just walk in through the front door,' said Gecks.

'It seems that way,' replied Romallia, grinning. 'I know I thought it was a stupid idea, but trust me – I have a good feeling about this.'

Ash did not look convinced.

They boldly walked through the doors into a huge, unnaturally dark hall. The doors slammed behind them.

'Very original!' shouted Ash, trying to hide his fear.

The darkness inside seemed to be moving, and it was now too murky for them to see each other. Gecks climbed onto Ash's shoulder, and Romallia grabbed his hand tightly.

'It's the shadows, but try not to worry. They use fear as a weapon, so if we stay calm we stand a chance,' said Ash, a little calmer now that he knew what they were up against. 'How do you feel, Gecks?'

'Scared,' said the honest lizard as she shivered on his shoulder.

'Romallia?'

'Terrified. And you?'

'I can safely say that without water I am more than very worried,' he said.

Romallia gripped his hand tighter. 'What do we do now?'

'I really don't know.'

Romallia suddenly let go of his hand. 'Romallia, are you ok?' gasped Ash.

'Ash, you know that I can sometimes sense how people are feeling? Well, I'm feeling something new; I still feel scared but somehow it's making me feel stronger – the shadows are scared too! They haven't attacked us yet because, well, because they think that I can kill them.'

The power of fear that the shadows possessed was being

absorbed by Romallia. Ash and Gecks suddenly felt a lot better as, with amazement, they saw the movements in the darkness cease: the shadows themselves were frozen to the spot with fear.

'Ash, something is happening to me. I feel so angry, so strong, but I can't hold it in. My hands are shaking.'

There was a sudden, silent explosion of blinding light and wind. Ash and Gecks were knocked off their feet and temporarily blinded. Romallia dropped to her knees, exhausted.

After a few moments, Ash was slowly starting to see again. The unnatural darkness of the room had gone, and light was now shining in through a large round window above the doors. All over the walls there were scorch marks, like the shadows of warriors burned into the stone.

'Romallia, are you ok?' Ash crawled on his hands and knees towards her. Gecks was climbing the walls and looking more closely at the scorch marks.

'I'm fine; I feel great – like every horrible feeling I have ever had has left me.'

Ash looked around the room again and grinned. 'Remind me never to make you angry in the future – and please warn me if you're ever in a bad mood. Come on, we should probably get a move on, if that's ok with you?'

'I think Legion must know that Gid is here; this was a trap. He must have thought this would be how he would have entered,' said Gecks as she crawled back down the wall.

'Great, so this trap was set for a legendary warrior and we walked right into it. I have a feeling we're likely to walk into more!' Ash was not feeling too happy. 'But hey, there's only one Gid and there are three of us, right?' he added sarcastically. With the front doors still slammed shut behind them, the only way out of the hall was at the far end between two large stone pillars, an open door leading into a torch-lit stone corridor.

At first glance, there seemed to be no danger, so they walked cautiously through the entrance. The door did not slam and there were no shadows; in fact, apart from being very long, there seemed to be nothing out of the ordinary at all about the corridor. They walked its length, and at the far end they found another open door leading into an enormous circular stone hall. The ceiling was around 60 metres above them and, apart from the shape and size of the room, there seemed to be nothing special about it either.

As the three companions stepped in, however, this door did bang shut behind them. 'Not again,' groaned Ash. 'Well, let's find out what trap we've sprung this time.' He had his hand ready on his sword.

On the far side of the hall, a large wooden door creaked open. For what seemed like an age, nothing happened, but then there was movement. A huge, wingless creature with grey skin, a long tail and lizard-like features stalked into the room. It was followed by another, and then another and another; dozen after dozen of the menacing creatures entered through the door until the three companions lost count.

'Relations of yours, Gecks?' asked Ash cheekily, trying to break the growing tension.

'As a matter of fact, yes, they are; these are my people, though they are no friends. I thought they had been wiped out by Legion long ago. It would have been better for this world if they had – these creatures are pure evil.'

'Why have you never mentioned this before?'

'It's not a part of my life that I am proud of. I may be kin to these creatures but I could not be more different. Any of us who were born with sentiment, kindness or any feelings other than pure evil were killed. I managed to escape. My family helped me, but they were destroyed for their compassion. I have lived in this form for both fear of being discovered and a hatred of the people I came from. I ended up finding Arborinium and Valletia took me in. In case you were wondering, all these creatures you see before you have the ability to change. To them it is the most shameful act to crawl on all fours, but to me it was freedom.' Gecks stood on her hind legs and started to grow, slowly changing into a copy of the creatures that stood before them. A deep hiss rumbled through the lizards and they slowly but purposefully advanced as one.

'So that's what you and Valletia were talking about so secretly back in Arborinium – you knew her all along. She sent you to keep an eye on me!'

'She wanted you to be safe; she never really wanted you to be banished, though it sounds like you had it coming. Ash, I'm afraid we don't stand a chance here. For what it's worth, I'm glad you were banished. You're a good friend!'

'You too, Gecks, but we've been close to death before and lived, though I have to admit, last time death did not have teeth and claws.' He reached up a loving hand and patted Gecks on the shoulder, who was now towering over him.

'Romallia, take to the air. These things can leap but they cannot fly. Ash and I will do our best down here.'

A rumbling sound was now coming from behind them in the corridor. 'You must be joking!' said Ash, rolling his eyes. 'We've beaten the shadows – well, Romallia did – and now we're faced with a room full of evil, hate-filled lizards and are about to be battered from behind by something else! This day is just getting better and better!'

The doors behind them shattered. Splintered wood flew past Romallia who was now in the air, missing her by millimetres.

'Hello Ash! I had a feeling you might be needing some help.' A massive, tusky grin beamed at him. 'Gecks, have you put on a little weight?' For once in his life, Ash was speechless.

'It's good to see you too, Snorback!' growled Gecks.

The other Cortuskas piled into the room. 'Finally, an opponent that could make for a worthy fight!' roared

Snorback. Without hesitation, both sides charged directly towards the other and slammed together.

Ash dived below a leaping lizard, feet first, and sliced upwards with his blade, and the creature's innards dropped to the floor. Before he could stand he was leaped upon by another beast; it opened its huge jaws and lunged. Ash desperately slashed his blade and in one slice took the beast's head clean off. Its lifeless body slumped against him, pinning him to the floor; as he struggled free, another creature sprang towards him, mouth and teeth gaping. 'This is it!' thought Ash. But just as he was preparing for the end, the lizard stopped in mid-flight, only a claw's length away from his face, and suddenly flew backwards. It was replaced by a huge furry hand that grabbed his shoulder and pulled him free. It was a Cortuska's hand!

Romallia was nimbly dodging lizards that were climbing the walls and leaping towards her. Each leap was met with an accurately aimed strike of her razor-sharp blade as she picked them off one by one.

Gecks was pushing through the fighting mass of Cortuskas and lizards, breaking necks and dodging claws. At the back of the sprawl stood the lizards' leader who before the fight ended would be dead; Gecks had only one thought in her mind – revenge. This beast would pay for killing her family, for giving life to evil and taking it from everyone else.

The Cortuskas were loving the chance to have a real fight – this is what they were good at. Each warrior in the room was holding its own, and gradually the lizards, though strong and worthy opponents, were falling.

Snorback was surrounded by five vicious lizards. There was a brief stand-off and then they all dived on him as one. He grabbed the neck of one in his hands and crushed hard before swinging the limp body around like a club to fight off the other four.

Ash found himself cornered by two lizards and he was

climbing the wall trying to get away from them. His sword was somewhere on the ground below and he only had his dagger and a blowpipe. The lizards were expert climbers, but Ash had spent what seemed like a lifetime in the mountains and was matching their skill. He placed both hands in a small hole, brought his feet up high and leapt for another small crack in the wall about three metres above his head; he slammed one hand into the crack and looked down. With his free hand he pulled out the blowpipe and took aim.

The dart hit the first lizard in the eye; it fell backwards and crashed into the other, almost knocking it off the wall as well. The second lizard clung on and hissed at Ash, its eyes glinting with fury.

They climbed higher and higher until they reached the ceiling, but Ash did not stop. He made his way along the ceiling using every small crack to gain a hold with his hands and feet; he moved slowly and cautiously across the stone. A slip now would mean falling 60 metres to his death.

Ash reached out for a deep crack wide enough to fit his arm in. Now was his chance to fight back. He pulled out his dagger with his free arm and brought both feet up into the crack. Slowly and carefully, he turned to face the lizard and then let go with his arm. He was now hanging by his feet from the very centre of the ceiling.

The lizard sprang towards him, its only intention to kill Ash. After the leap it would fall to its death, with or without him. Ash swung his body forward, hoping that his feet would hold, caught the lizard by the throat mid-spring and sliced his dagger down its hard, scaly neck. The beast managed one bite before it fell to the floor far below, its jaw crunching into Ash's arm and snapping the bone.

Ash let out a cry of pain. His dagger fell with the lizard and he saw that he was now missing the lower half of his right arm. He was stuck. His right arm was useless, so climbing down was not an option, and neither was hanging from his feet; the blood was rushing to his head and out of his wound. Everything was turning white, consciousness was leaving him, and he felt his feet slip. The lizard had won.

The ground hit him much more quickly and much more softly than he had expected. Romallia's face was the last thing he saw before he passed out.

Gecks had fought her way successfully through the crowd. The leader of the lizards was not aware that she was so close; she was concentrating on the battle and, to her, Gecks was just another lizard.

Gecks crouched low; revenge did not require a fair fight. She leapt at the lizard, grabbed her face and quickly snapped her neck. The leader let out a deep rumbling hiss, and the surviving lizards responded – they knew the fight was over. Their leader was dead and they raised their arms and backed away. Everyone in the room was beginning to realise that this fight was over.

Chapter 31: Darkness

As Legion's warriors flew low over the trees, they realised that they would not have the opportunity to scout the area. They were flying directly for the main force of the Arbitans. The sky above Arborinium was filled with warriors dressed in green. At their front was a familiar face – Krast. He was hovering by the side of Rahmon. Legion's 10,000 warriors stopped in the air and stared at their enemy. Krast raised his sword and the gesture was repeated by tens, then hundreds, and soon thousands across the massed ranks of Legion's army; vast numbers of warriors were leaving his force and gathering together behind it.

Those loyal to Legion were now facing two armies: the Arbitans ahead of them and those loyal to Krast at their rear.

Some distance away, boats landed at the edge of the forest of Arborinium. The warriors aboard were feeling nervous about stepping onto land; they had seen their fellow soldiers battered at the hands of huge beasts and they were worried that they would meet a similar fate.

Slowly and cautiously, they left the boats. So far so good – no beasts. A scout at the front held up a hand and signalled for them all to hide. Large shapes were emerging from the trees ahead; unbeknown to them, the Cortuskas had made it back through the underground tunnels before the ships reached land. Grimbarr, bold and intimidating, approached Legion's exposed and vulnerable warriors.

They began to shrink backwards, expecting the worst, but then he spoke. 'You have seen the demise of your fellow warriors, those loyal to Legion. They were given no chance to surrender. But I am offering you the opportunity. I can tell just by looking at you that you did not originate from Harrashon;

you are all from tribes that were once free – as am I. You have no fight with us, or with the Arbitans; you owe Legion no loyalty. In fact, Legion himself is soon to meet his end at the hands of a child.'

A look of shock and confusion shot across the faces of the troops.

'I am offering you a chance to leave Legion, not to surrender to us, but to once again regain your birthright – your freedom! Reclaim your lands, your pride and your strength. You are no longer bound to the tyrant of Harrashon. I am giving you this one chance to live for yourselves – or to die for Legion. Which will it be?'

Grimbarr waited for an answer. The commander of the ground troops stepped forward hesitatingly. 'I know that I speak for all my men when I say that we will always be loyal to one another. I would die for any man or woman here; we are all brave. But we are not stupid. You are offering a choice of freedom – or death!' He turned to his men. 'Is death for Legion the choice of anyone here?' No one stirred. 'Then I think you have your answer – friend.'

Grimbarr gently took the man's hand and shook it. 'You are a wise leader. What will you do now? This fight is no longer yours.'

'I will take my men and head back to Harrashon. If what you say about Legion is true, we will collect our families and then eventually, I suppose, we can start a new life. However, if Legion does not fall, then an old enemy will become a new enemy. We can never go back to his service. At least now we know that we have strong allies; we – and you – will never fight alone again!'

'It is an odd battle when no sword is drawn, don't you think?' chuckled Grimbarr.

The commander smiled. 'I think I can honestly say that this is now my favourite kind!'

The tension in the sky was growing. Both sides were ready for the fight. Some would relish it, but many others were terrified. The Arbitans were looking the more nervous. They had never been properly tested like this; today they were not in their home city.

The silent moments before the battle could decide if they would live or die. Would doubts consume them, questions of whether they would be strong enough, fast enough? All these distractions needed to disappear if they were to concentrate on the now, to follow their instincts. Some warriors whispered quiet prayers, some played with their swords, some clenched trinkets in their hands to remind them of their families, some were sick, whilst others – those who loved the fight, the danger – just stared unblinkingly at their enemies.

Rahmon looked towards the ground.

'That's our signal. Now!' whispered a hidden voice.

Huge spears flew up through the trees and ripped into Legion's warriors; seconds later, more followed. Warriors were spiralling towards the ground, impaled on huge spikes. Two hundred Cortuskas had remained with the Arbitans and were hidden below.

More spears followed but the element of surprise was now lost, and they were starting to miss as their intended targets flew up and out of range.

Rahmon raised his arm, and the warriors loyal to Krast followed him, and the Arbitans after them, their swords drawn ready and glinting in the sun. Rahmon was at the front, gaining on the enemy. He saw a vague blur to his left and then something hit him hard in the side; he dropped through the thousands of following warriors that were now being led by Krast, and fell away from the battle. Something had taken hold of his wings and he couldn't fly! Desperately, he tried to turn around and loose them, but all he could see was a smoky shadow.

The topmost branches of the tree slammed into his chest,

beginning to break his fall. The impact separated him from his attacker and Rahmon dropped, clattering into branches all the way down. Finally, he hit the floor with a dull thud.

Rahmon slowly picked himself up off the floor and reached for his sword. The shadowy assailant was standing only a metre or two in front of him. 'Who are you?' he asked.

The figure responded by changing, and slowly became more solid.

'Tharik!' Rahmon gasped.

The figure grinned viciously. 'Not any more.'

'Brother, it's you! Tharik, what has happened to you?'

The figure looked at Rahmon with his head to one side. 'My name is Darkness. Your brother is dead.'

Darkness darted forwards. Catching the bewildered Rahmon off guard, his sword sliced into Rahmon's thigh.

Rahmon retaliated and swung his blade, but where there was flesh there was now only a mist that became flesh once more a second later, unscathed, once the sword had passed through it. Darkness punched Rahmon in the stomach, and then smashed his elbow into his head.

Rahmon punched forwards but fell once again through mist. He attacked with his sword but his strikes were either blocked or they sliced through thin air.

Darkness was on the attack now, his strikes fast and accurate. Rahmon blocked most of them, but two cut through his guard. The first sliced his chest and the second cut into his shoulder.

Rahmon knew that if this carried on he would soon be dead. He turned and quickly headed to Arborinium. He had just one chance.

'Coward!' yelled Darkness, and shot after him. They were side by side, flying low through the trees, exchanging blows through the branches as they flew. Ahead was the clearing and then the city. Rahmon flew a little faster to gain some distance on Darkness. His hands fumbled for something in his belt.

Finally he found it. He pulled a small mirror out of his pocket and when he reached the clearing he flashed sunlight at the lookouts.

The huge entrance doors to Arborinium opened. Rahmon screamed through the doors and crashed into the floor, bouncing off the roots. Darkness followed a few seconds later and stood over Rahmon, once again in his misty form.

'Running home, Rahmon? I thought you were a fierce warrior, an unbeaten swordsman. You forget, I know all your moves and now I am faster and stronger. Your skills are suddenly useless.'

'Tharik, if there is any of you left, I am giving you this one chance – quit now or perish.'

'If that was aimed at what you hope could remain of your brother, give up. Tharik cannot hear you; he died when I was born. His fear, hatred, jealousy, guilt and regret created me. I am something new, something better, better even than you. Your brother died crying for forgiveness.'

Rahmon looked at Darkness and smiled. 'Thank you,' he said, as he rose to his feet.

'What was that?' said Darkness with a puzzled look.

'You have made this much easier.' Rahmon thrust his sword into the misty form of Darkness and held it there.

'And what exactly did you expect to achieve by that? If you were aiming for my heart, it would be a little higher. Here, let me help.' He grabbed Rahmon's arm and moved the blade upwards, mockingly.

Rahmon glanced upwards with a smile on his face. Water was starting to rain down inside the city. Darkness screamed in pain as the drops fell, and realised his mistake too late. He suddenly, instinctively, turned back into his solid form, but now a sword was sticking out of his chest as he slumped to his knees with a look of fear etched across his face.

Rahmon grabbed the limp form of Darkness in his arms and embraced the body that had once belonged to his brother.

Tears filled his eyes. 'I always forgave you, brother,' he managed to whisper. The real Tharik had died long before the fight, but his body could now rest in Arborinium. Rahmon collapsed on the cold floor, crushed by grief and weakened by his wounds. His fight was over; the fate of Arborinium now lay in Krast's hands.

Chapter 32: A fair fight

Gid crouched behind a stone pillar near the pool and listened. The room he was about to enter was glowing orange from torchlight and seemed to be alive with the noise of soldiers.

Close by, he could hear a small group whispering; they sounded nervous: 'I don't think things are going too well for us out there, you know...'

'Be careful; make sure you keep your voice down. Legion is only in the next room!'

'When Legion made an enemy of Krast, I think he made a big mistake.'

'You're right on that one; Krast was a good warrior – the best. He also knew how to look after his men. With him on our side, the Arbitans would have fallen by now.'

'Why are we still here, then?'

'We're a backup, of sorts. Legion is expecting a warrior to challenge him. He's never been beaten before, but saying that, has anyone ever seen him fight?'

'I've heard the stories, and if he's anything like as fierce and skilled as they make out, he shouldn't need us as a backup plan – unless, of course, this warrior is more powerful than him. And if that's the case, then we're finished anyway!'

After hearing all this, Gid was feeling a little more confident about facing the soldiers. He rounded the corner and announced his arrival. 'Hello. Look, I really feel that I should probably make a dramatic entrance, but to be honest I don't really know what to say.'

Every soldier in the room was staring at him. He had their attention. 'My name is Gid, and I'm here to fight your boss.' Gid cringed at his own words. But, there, he had said it now, so he might as well continue with the train of thought.

'I am a warrior, and I'm here to rid this world of its biggest enemy. Now I'm going to give you a choice: you can either leave now, or we can do this the hard way.' He felt much happier about the last part of the speech; it definitely sounded more 'warrior-like'.

The soldiers in the room parted without a word, leaving a walkway between Gid and the biggest warrior he had ever seen. The man was wearing nothing but a small leather skirt. He had long, untamed, black hair that covered most of his face, his shoulders were each almost as big as Gid and he had tattoos of skulls covering every visible inch of his skin. One wing was missing from his back, and he also seemed to be missing his right hand, though this had been replaced by a heavy-looking hammer.

The warrior let out a loud roar and ran at Gid. Gid stood completely still; he felt calm, and strangely happy. The warrior raised his hammer and swung it hard at Gid's body.

Gid, who seemed to be seeing the whole thing in slow motion, dodged the hammer, punched it hard and deflected it. It continued its new journey past Gid and slammed into the warrior's left cheek. He dropped instantly to the floor in front of him.

'Does anybody else want to try?' asked Gid, his courage now building.

Every soldier in the room drew a sword. They may have respected Krast, but they remained fiercely loyal to Legion.

'I guess that's a yes, then.' Gid counted around 50 eager opponents.

They charged at him as one group. The first was punched in the face and fell, the second had his legs kicked from underneath him, the third caught an elbow to the back of her head, another was kicked in the stomach. They kept coming and kept falling. Not a single sword was able to get near him. Gid dived forwards and slammed his head into the stomach of the next soldier, the force sending him back into the others behind and knocking them to the ground as well.

Punch after punch was landing on his enemies, and every attack aimed at him seemed to take far too long to arrive as he dodged every strike and successfully landed every elbow, kick or punch that he threw.

The fight had barely begun before it was over, and the room was full of groaning or unconscious bodies. Gid had not even had to use his weapon, which he was pleased about. Killing people was not really his thing. All that now lay between him and Legion was a large wooden door.

Chapter 33: Nearing the end

Rahmon tentatively opened his eyes. He was lying in a bed in a room in Arborinium's hospital wing. He could not feel much of his body but decided that, by the look of things, it was probably a good job. His memory of the fight with the creature that had once been his brother was strange; he could recall every detail, but it did not feel as if he had been involved. He remembered crying but could not understand why.

'They must have given me something strong; my head is spinning,' he commented aloud, to no one in particular.

'Decided to join me, have you?' said a familiar voice from the next bed. Rahmon turned his head to the right. He was met with the large grin of Rowley, the girl he had been 'questioning' earlier. He could feel his face reddening by the second.

'I... I got bored of the fight,' he stammered. 'Why are you still in here?'

Rowley slapped the sides of her legs. 'These things don't seem to be working properly yet. The chemicals in your darts have acted rather strongly in me, for some reason. The doctor says I'll regain the feeling soon, but I'd like to be in the battle. It's your fault I'm like this, you know!'

'Please believe me when I say I'm sorry. If I'd known, I would have, um, I would have either done something else, or maybe I wouldn't have done anything. I mean, I would have done something to help but I wouldn't have hit you with the darts. Am I making any sense?'

'No, not really, but you have just woken up and I think you're on some heavy medication – I heard the doctor talking. He said you'd probably feel confused but in high spirits when you woke up. I know it's not your fault, by the way – I was just teasing, but it's nice that you care. If I could move, I'd come over there and kiss you better, but I can't.'

Rahmon turned from red to scarlet. Then he shocked himself by saying, 'Maybe I should come to you instead!' Rowley didn't say no, so he pulled himself to the edge of his bed, using all the energy he could manage – and then toppled over onto the floor.

For a brief second, Rowley was concerned, but then she burst out laughing. She could not stop herself; she knew she shouldn't be laughing, but it was so funny – at least, now that she could see that he was ok.

At first, Rahmon was embarrassed, but Rowley's laugh was infectious. He forgot his wounded pride and lay back on the floor, crying with laughter, even though something deep inside was telling him that it was inappropriate to do so. A few minutes later, he managed to control himself. 'I don't suppose you could call a doctor, could you?' he asked, and then started to laugh again.

Legion's army in the sky realised that the ground troops were not coming, and neither were the machines. They were suddenly the last and only hope of gaining victory for their master.

Many were beginning to doubt that this was possible; others were wondering if they were on the right side – even one of their own leaders had changed sides, along with a large number of their comrades. If a way out showed itself, there were many who would gladly take it.

Krast had suspected that the Arbitans would fight hardest because they were the only group with a real reason to be in the battle – namely, to save their city and people. He knew that both his own defection and that of his fellow soldiers had had a crippling effect on morale amongst Legion's remaining warriors. They were fighting, but they were concentrating on defending themselves rather than trying to destroy their enemy.

From the city below, the vast number of warriors in both armies had turned the sky black. They were like one enormous dark cloud being blown in all directions, or like the largest and angriest flock of birds fighting to find a place to roost. It was not possible to recognise which army was which, but it was obvious that one side was definitely winning.

Krast knew that Ergerin would be leading the army for Legion. He was a strong commander, an enthusiastic warrior and extremely loyal. Even though they were on separate sides and fighting for different reasons, Krast still respected Ergerin as a fellow soldier. He was an inspiration to all and had a fierce, well-earned authority. If Ergerin fell, his army would follow. There were enough seeds of doubt in their ranks to bring about a surrender if they felt that they were fighting for an unworthy cause.

Ergerin would not be too hard to find: if there was an area in the sky where more warriors were falling than any other, he would be in the middle of it.

It did not take too long to locate him among the masses. When he was close enough, Krast tried to attract Ergerin's attention. 'Ergerin, give up. Call your warriors off!' Krast knew the answer to this before he even spoke.

'You know I will die before that happens!' came the harsh reply from the grey-skinned general.

'You do not have to carry this on. You will lose – you must know that by now.'

'I am loyal to Legion, unlike some others I know! I will not run away like a scared child. I know my place – I am a warrior, a general. I was once your superior and I am now your enemy. My men will fight until their last breath. Can you say the same for yours? By betraying Legion they have already shown, as have you, how fragile their commitment is,' retorted Ergerin, adding derisively, 'Do you honestly think they will stay with you if the going gets a little too rough?'

'The Arbitans are fighting for their lands, their lives, their reedom. My men are fighting for each other and me – you are merely fighting, Ergerin.'

'Krast, though I have always had a great deal of respect for you, you are my enemy, and as an enemy you will die, either by my hand or the hand of one of my warriors.'

Krast could see that the discussion was over. 'Do as you must, Ergerin. I will show no mercy, and I expect none from you.'

They were five metres apart, circling each other, looking for a weakness, waiting for the moment to strike. Krast moved first. He flew directly at his opponent. Ergerin waited. 'Go on, Ergerin, do your worst. I know all your moves,' Krast whispered to himself. 'As I dive towards your stomach, raise your blade high so you can bring it down on my back...'

As if he were under instruction, Ergerin did exactly that: he raised his sword high and brought it down when Krast was in striking distance. Krast dived low at the last second and flew below Ergerin's feet. He turned on to his back and swung his sword across his body. The sword hit its target and sliced cleanly through Ergerin's legs, above the ankles. Ergerin turned around in time to see Krast's sword bury itself in his chest. He looked into Krast's eyes in disbelief, the expression changing as pain took the place of surprise. Ergerin's eyes rolled backwards and he fell from the sky.

The news travelled quickly. It had worked. Those who had no will to fight any more, or the sense to know that they were beaten, surrendered. A few fled, while others carried on until they, too, fell beaten to the ground below.

Legion's overconfidence, his pride and his belief that all his enemies could and would be beaten, had cost him the battle. Fate had stepped in, and even Legion's mighty army could not defeat it.

Chapter 34: Legion

Gid stood in front of the only barrier that was left between him and his reason for being in this new world. His whole time with the Arbitans; his battle with and eventual freeing of the Cortuskas; his many new friends – Snorback, Rahmon, Romallia, Ash, Gecks, and even for a while, Tharik; his entire journey since the fateful night of his arrival – they had all led him to this door and what awaited him on the other side.

Gid placed his hands on the door. 'This is it, then,' he thought. There would be no turning back now. He pushed the huge, heavy wooden door and entered the room to the accompaniment of loud creaking noises.

What he found was not what he had expected; this was no evil villain's lair, or even a majestic throne room. The walls were high and long and filled with colourful, leather-bound books, and there were flaming torches at intervals that seemed to be dangerously close to that amount of paper. In the centre of the stone floor was an open fire, with wooden benches surrounding it. The whole place had a warm glow and was filled with the scent of burning sweet wood. The word that sprang into Gid's mind was 'cosy'!

At the far end of this so far cosy and homely room was a large, dark, wooden chair. Sitting in the chair, dressed in a long, dark, red robe, with his hands on an open book, sat Legion. 'Please, come in. Won't you take a seat by the fire? I will join you,' he invited in a friendly tone.

Gid waited in the doorway for a few moments. He had not expected this. He slowly and cautiously walked towards the fire, expecting the floor to fall away or spears to fly from the walls. But nothing happened.

They took seats on the benches either side of the fire. The flames lit up Legion's features, and to Gid he looked like a ired old man.

Legion looked at Gid. 'We finally get to meet. You have caused me considerable trouble, you know. My army is almost defeated, old enemies are uniting against me, the shadows appear to be wiped out, the city is in chaos and even some of my closest and best warriors have turned against me.'

Gid said nothing.

'You have brought war to this land once again. I strived for many hundreds of years to bring about peace, and now that has ended.'

Gid was shocked; this was not how it was supposed to be. 'I did not bring war to this world – I am here to free it from you,' said Gid, though he sounded less convinced than he had been.

'Do you really believe that, Gid,? Do you really believe that everything that is happening here is for the best? This world was finally at peace; my only real enemy were the Arbitans, and I left them alone to get on with their lives. How am I repaid? They send a warrior to kill me. A warrior who, until meeting them, was an innocent child, but who has since masterminded the bloody slaughter of many of my most loyal soldiers. I know that Valletia has led you to believe that killing me is your destiny, that things have just happened as they should because you arrived in this world. I know you are not from this world. In fact, I know exactly where you are from.'

Gid looked closer and realised that, for some reason, the face opposite him seemed familiar. 'No, no, please, it can't be!' he gasped.

'What?'

Gid did not want to ask the next question. 'Are you going to tell me that you're my father?'

Legion looked surprised. 'What? No, no. I do not have any children'

'Phew! I had this awful feeling for a minute, then. Look, I know it must seem that I'm the one who has brought about the war, and I still feel awful about your soldiers. But I'm not the bad guy here. Valletia told me all about you. You have to be the bad guy; I can't have ended up in this world and have been fighting for the wrong side all this time.'

'Ah, Gid, there are sometimes no right and wrong sides – only sides. You need to ask yourself whether this world seems better now than when you arrived. There may not be good and evil involved, but there are right choices and wrong choices, right actions and wrong actions. Which have you chosen?'

Gid was rubbing his face with his hands; he was feeling confused. It had taken him a long time to believe in himself and his mission, and now to start wondering if it was all wrong, if he had made bad choices, was beginning to overwhelm him. The war had started after his arrival, he thought.

'I don't know. But I can't have got all of this wrong; I'm sure that this will all be for the better, all this fighting – there must be a reason for it. I'm just a kid; I couldn't have made all this happen on my own!'

Legion stood and walked over to where Gid was slouching on the log. 'You are correct, Gid, you are just a child, a child caught up in things that should not be thrown upon shoulders so young. It is not fair to ask any of this of you. Do you really believe that you could take another person's life?'

'I don't know...'

Legion leant forward and placed a hand on Gid's shoulder, looked into his eyes and smiled. 'I could,' he said viciously, and thrust a small and well-hidden sword into Gid's stomach.

Gid looked into Legion's eyes imploringly, and then collapsed on the floor with the sword still embedded in his stomach. Legion straightened and walked back towards his chair. 'That was too easy,' he mused.

'You're right about that. I will definitely have to make it a little harder for you next time. And just so you know, that really hurt!' Gid dropped the sword to the floor. He had pulled the weapon from his abdomen and his stomach had healed.

You're pretty good with words, you know – you really had me confused for a while. The sword in my stomach kind of cleared things up, though. I reckon good and evil *are* involved in this fight, and that move you just made was downright nasty. Oh, and I've remembered who you are. Your name is Brett Johnson, you were on the TV news and you've been in a coma for five years. Now I know why, and now I know where to send you back to!'

These last words seemed to physically hurt Legion. His strongest weapon was lies, and these words of truth had ended that power. Gid realised that what he had said had had an effect. 'Hmm, I guess truth really does hurt, eh old man?'

Legion was furious. All the years that he had been in power now seemed to be coming to an end, but he would not allow this child to beat him. He slammed his enormous wings together in front of him like two giant clapping hands. A powerful gust of air blew through the room, knocking Gid from his feet and back through the doors through which he had entered.

Legion brought his wings back and flapped hard, flying at an incredible speed towards Gid. He grabbed him around the throat and, using his speed and strength, threw him right through the wall into another room.

Gid slid across the floor and stopped at a large pair of furry feet. 'Gid, are you ok?'

He looked up from the floor and smiled, with considerable effort. 'Snorback, good to see you. I'm fine. As you can see I have everything completely under control, though I could use a hand up, if that's ok?'

Snorback crouched down and lifted his little friend to his feet.

'Have you seen the others? Are they ok?' asked Gid.

'They're safe, Gid. Ash is wounded but he will live. He fought well. Romallia caught him when he fell from the ceiling after losing an arm. They walked into a few traps that were meant for you, but they did well. They're being looked after by some of Krast's men. I stayed behind to see if you needed any help!'

'I would love some help, but I think I have to do this alone. If you hear me screaming, though, that will be a good sign that I am ready for a helping hand – or two!'

'As you wish, my friend. I will be close by, just in case.'

Gid dusted himself off, cricked his neck and walked towards a fresh, child-sized hole in the wall. As he walked, long bones were coming from his right hand and slowly forming into a lethal-looking blade.

Legion was waiting on the other side of the wall; he was neither brave enough nor stupid enough to challenge a Cortuska and Gid together.

'That was a sneaky move there, Brett. I'll have to be careful in this fight,' provoked Gid.

'My name is Legion!' boomed the old tyrant.

'No, no, it's definitely Brett. Legion doesn't really suit you. It sounds a bit over the top. You look more like a Brett to me.'

'You will die!'

'One day, but today I'm going to fight.'

Gid swung his blade through the air and sliced Legion's cheek. Blood trickled down his face. Legion wiped it away before slashing in rage with his own sword. Gid slapped it aside with his left hand and then punched Legion hard in the chest, sending him skidding backwards across the floor, doubled over in pain. When he stood up, he coughed, and a small line of blood made its way from his mouth to his chin. He flew directly upwards and smashed through the stone ceiling and out into the air. Gid followed.

Legion flew fast and low across the rooftops of the city, with Gid in hot pursuit. He flew down into alleyways, trying to lose his young opponent, but still the child stayed with him. Legion climbed high into the air once more and headed for the clouds, hoping to shake him off in the mists. He looked over his shoulder; he was no longer being followed. Relieved, he turned back, and a well-aimed knee hit his stomach.

'I cannot let you get away; you will fight me!'

Without answering, Legion attacked. He slashed again and again at Gid, but every slice was blocked with ease. Desperately, he lunged forwards once more and managed to slice Gid's arm, but it started to heal almost immediately.

Legion flew away from Gid and then turned, folded his wings back, pointed his sword and threw himself back through the sky towards his enemy.

Gid was too fast; he grabbed Legion's wing and flew towards the ground, dragging the tyrant behind him. When he was within ten metres of the earth, he stopped suddenly and sent his opponent smashing hard into the dirt.

A crowd was forming in the city, as civilians and warriors from both sides gathered to watch the spectacle unfolding in the sky above them.

Legion slowly and shakily got to his feet. Something caught his eye. He flew into the crowd and came out holding Romallia by the neck. 'Give in, Gid, or I will kill your friend; I can easily snap her fragile neck. One way or another I am going to beat you.'

Romallia slammed her elbow hard into Legion's nose. He let go. 'You will not win that way – and I am not that fragile,' she snapped.

Gid landed and walked towards Legion. 'You are going to lose today; you will no longer hurt my friends or this world. Your time is up.'

Legion let out a frustrated scream and ran at Gid. Lifting off at the last second, he grabbed Gid's upper arm and stabbed forward with his sword. Gid used his own blade to slap it away, and then pulled himself free of Legion's grip before being attacked again. They matched each other blow for blow. Legion was fighting for his life; he was a powerful warrior and until this day he had had no equal. If his reign was to end, he would not go easily, and he would take Gid with him.

Legion managed to punch Gid in the jaw. For a split second he was stunned, and that second was all that Legion needed; he stabbed again with his sword at Gid's stomach, but missed as a warrior in the crowd threw their weapon to deflect it. It seemed that the onlookers knew who they wanted to win. Gid took his chance: he spun around and kicked his foot into Legion's back and sliced with his bony blade, cutting his right wing clean off. Legion yelled in pain. Gid held him in the air with one hand and then reluctantly drove his blade into Legion's chest.

The bones left Gid's arm as they had entered and quickly disappeared into Legion's body.

The beaten ruler of Harrashon suddenly felt the pain of every person who had ever been killed by his own sword or by the sword of one of his warriors. All the deaths he had ever caused were now ending his own life.

Legion's eyes showed both pain and terror and he lashed out, knocking himself free of Gid's grip. The once mighty leader fell, spinning out of control, towards the ground. As he hit the floor, a large cloud of dust flew into the air.

Gid landed softly next to his crumpled opponent.

Legion was dead. Gid's job was done. The young boy sat next to Legion's lifeless body with his face in his hands and began to cry. A large, furry hand picked him up and carried the sobbing figure away from the crowd.

Chapter 35: A new era

For Gid, the few days following his fight passed in a blur. He had been brought back to Arborinium but was not yet ready to see the inhabitants of the city, so he had stayed in his room. Snorback had been with him constantly, only leaving to fetch food.

Gid's many, regular visitors were keeping him informed of events. Rahmon was the first to see him. His news was the hardest to deliver and the hardest for Gid to hear, but they both understood how important it was for him to know. Gid and Tharik had become friends; even though Tharik had betrayed him, Gid had been hoping that Tharik would eventually realise what he had done and come to his senses. He wanted the chance to be angry at Tharik but also to be able to forgive him. Now he would find it harder to remember the good bits. As for Rahmon, he seemed much smaller than before the fighting, and looked very tired. His eyes were red from tears and circled by dark rings, and his skin was a little paler.

Valletia had been in a few times to check that Gid was ok and to let him know that Ash, Romallia and Gecks were still in Harrashon but would be coming back as soon as Ash was well enough. She told him all about the trials that the trio had faced in the palace that had made it possible for Gid to fight Legion on his own. Romallia had made it very clear that Valletia was to tell Gid that she had saved Ash's life, though she had not been able to save his arm. Gecks had once again turned back into her normal, smaller lizard form after the fight and was desperate to see Ash – and apparently he was still annoyed that he had lost yet another limb, and was now very concerned about which of his remaining ones he would lose next!

Borrea was the next to visit, bringing Gid a plant that gave off a scent to make him feel more relaxed and help to lift his spirits. It seemed to be working quite well. He told Gid all about the new accommodation that was being provided for the Cortuskas, who were now permanent residents and citizens of Arborinium. He had decided that it would be better to spread the rooms out across the city to make it easier for everyone to mix. So far this had been met with a number of reactions, ranging from delight to fury. Even after their decisive part in securing a victory for the Arbitans, it seemed it would take a while before the Cortuskas were properly accepted by all.

'I think it's about time you and I went for a walk; you've been in here for long enough now,' said Snorback one morning, mainly because he wanted to get outside himself, but he would not leave Gid on his own.

'I think you're right,' replied Gid. Without Snorback, Gid would have fallen to pieces over the last few days. Gid had talked a lot about what had happened and how he felt, and he knew he could trust Snorback. What made it easier was the fact that Snorback had just sat and listened; he had not tried to give Gid any advice or offer an opinion, making Gid feel that Snorback both understood and agreed with him.

Snorback left the room and headed to the ground floor. Gid opened the door to the outside, took a deep breath and flew towards the trees. He met Snorback by the pool.

'Snorback…'

'Yes, Gid?'

'I saw a lot of mounds of dirt by the edge of the trees – hundreds of them.'

'The fighting here was pretty fierce, apparently. The mounds are fresh graves, mainly belonging to Legion's warriors.'

'This war hasn't been easy for anyone, has it?'

Snorback grinned. 'I know this will probably sound pretty

bad, but, well, it has kind of worked out alright for my kind. We are finally free; we are peaceful, but we love a good fight. I know we lost a few, but for what we have gained, it was worth it. I for one am happy that the battles happened. You know, I have a feeling that most people would agree with me. I can feel it in the air. Though some things have been and will be hard, only good stuff can come from it all now.'

'I think perhaps I'm a little too young to understand everything that my arrival has meant to this world. I just can't seem to see past the fighting and killing. I killed someone, didn't I?'

'What you did was to free this world. Legion is dead, but I think Brett might be alive. I'm not sure why, but I have a feeling that his soul has been sent back to where it belongs.'

'I never really thought of it like that. I hope you're right...' said Gid pensively. Then he continued, 'Snorback...'

'Yes, Gid!'

'You know I told you about God and my prayer? Well, I've been thinking. I really think – no, I really believe – that I was listened to and that my prayer was answered.'

'Well, from what you have told me already, it seems that maybe this God sent you here in the first place, and if he sent you, he was probably just waiting for you to ask him for help – though I'm sure he would have helped anyway!'

'Hmm, but why me? I still don't get it. I've never been that special; I'm pretty average at everything back at home!'

'Well, maybe – just maybe – this God could see in you what I see, and there's nothing average about that, I can tell you! Maybe you should see yourself the same way.'

'Do you mean it? Do you really see me like that?'

'I do, and I'm sure your God does, too,' said Snorback with meaning, looking Gid in the eyes. 'If you want a minute alone with him, just let me know.'

Gid was quiet for a while.

'I do want to talk to him, but will you stay?'

Snorback smiled and nodded.

'Well, God,' Gid began, 'I just want to say thanks, really – thank you for looking out for me and my friends. Thank you for the people you put around me and thank you for freeing this world and trusting me to be good enough. Thank you for listening – though I suppose you always do – it's just me who needs to do a bit more talking. Anyway, just thank you. I also just want to pray for Tharik; it was hard for us all, you know, with him leaving us and all the other stuff. I just want to believe that he was sorry, and I hope he made his way to you.'

Gid wiped a tear from his eye. 'Err… Amen.'

Snorback closed his eyes and cleared his throat. 'I want to thank you too, for keeping my little friend safe and for letting me meet him. And you'd better keep keeping him safe too!'

Gid picked up a stone and tried to skim it. The stone bounced across the pool, though he was not paying attention. But Snorback was. 'Gid, what comes after seven?' he asked.

'Eight.'

'Ok, and after that?'

'Nine.'

'You just bounced the stone nine times then!'

Gid jumped up and down and threw his arms in the air in victory. 'Yes! I've never done that before!' he shouted, forgetting all their concerns.

'Right, my turn,' said Snorback, as he picked up a thin stone the size of a large plate and threw it hard. The stone bounced once and then disappeared into the trees on the other side of the pool. It was followed shortly after by the high-pitched cry of an animal.

'Oops, well that's dinner sorted, at least!'

Gid smiled and then started to laugh. He had felt so sad and tense that this sudden release was unstoppable and contagious. Snorback's laughter boomed through the forest. A flock of birds flew from their branches, small animals scuttled away into their holes, and a small group of farmers stopped building a fence and looked at one another, puzzled.

A victory celebration was planned for the following day. There would be lots of parties, food, dancing, singing and drinking going on in both Arborinium and Harrashon. A prestigious ceremony was to be held to hand back land to the rightful owners. The tribes were once again going to separate, but this time they would have a common interest in keeping the peace.

Harrashon was going to be given to Krast to govern, though the city was going to be open to all tribes. Most of its inhabitants had lived in the city for their entire lives, so to them it was home, even if their ancestors had different origins.

Representatives of the many tribes would meet in the city daily to try to work out the best possible futures for all their peoples. The years to come would no doubt be hard; peace would not be easy, but this time it would come with freedom and tolerance rather than fear and hatred.

The following morning, Gid was woken up by a lot of noise and a sudden weight on his chest. He opened his eyes and came face to face with six other eyes staring back at him. Ash, Romallia and Gecks had all piled onto his bed. Thankfully, Snorback had not joined them!

'It's so good to see you! I was so worried about you; I didn't even know if you were in the palace. Normally I would have just "known", but I had a bit too much on my plate – or mind! – destroying those shadows. I was pretty fierce, you know.' Romallia leaned forwards to give him a huge kiss on the forehead. Gid blushed; he could feel the redness fill his cheeks.

Ash had his upper right arm strapped to his chest and was trying very hard not to lie on it. 'Whoa there, you may be a big hero and all, but she's still my girl!' interjected Ash. 'Only joking! Boy, am I glad to see you. You did it, Gid, you really did it. I missed the fight, but Snorback's men told me you were awesome. We were pretty good as well, you know. I ended up hanging from my feet about 60 metres from the ceiling, battling hundreds of lizard-beast things – or at least that's how I'm going to tell it! Romallia saved me, Gid. I blacked out, and when I woke up I had an itchy nose but nothing to itch it with!' Ash pointed to where his arm should have been. 'I can't believe I lost another bit of me! The doctor in Harrashon is working on a fake arm with claw bits on it, and little bits of metal of different sizes, so I can still climb. So it's not all bad, eh?' Ash smiled unconvincingly.

'Shush now, Ash,' said Gecks soothingly but sternly. Turning to Gid, she said, 'I don't know what the doctors gave him for the pain, but he simply won't shut up; actually, he was always like that, wasn't he? I knew you'd be ok, Gid. From the moment I met you, I knew you were special; I could sense it. And, of course, Valletia told me who you were, so I suppose it might not really have been intuition. The lizard beasts, as Ash referred to them, were my people. I killed their queen, which kind of makes me queen, but they disappeared after the fight so I don't think I've really been accepted. Could you imagine it – "Queen Gecks!" – sounds awful, doesn't it?'

Gid had never felt happier than at that moment. He was with a group of people who, in such a short space of time, had become close friends, all of them willing to put their lives in danger for him. He would never forget it.

'So, it seems your God was listening then, Gid,' said Gecks.

'Yeah, I really think he was,' said Gid with a relaxed smile. 'I don't think we could have done this on our own, but then again, I don't think we ever were on our own, were we?'

Gecks winked. 'No, I don't think we were!'

Gid was given new clothes to wear for the day. He had a dark blue slip-on shirt that came to below his waist. Over the shirt he had a wide, white belt, and on his legs white, baggy, cotton trousers that were tied at his shins by black ribbons that led down to sandalled feet.

'Trousers! And I was just getting used to the skirt,' he laughed to himself.

He joined his friends, including Grimbarr, on a large, open carriage; they were to be flown to Harrashon at the head of a huge procession of warriors. Grimbarr was wearing his smart cloak, and Snorback had washed and combed his hair – it was looking shiny and clean, tied back on his head with black ribbons. He looked very smart and very proud.

The sky was filled with people throwing flowers and cheering. Gid felt like a star, and he could tell that his friends were feeling the same.

When they reached Harrashon, they were carried along the streets and were bombarded with more flowers and gifts. Many of the warriors in the procession were talking and laughing with the people, accepting flower necklaces and carrying children on their shoulders. Music was playing loudly and the city was full of people dancing.

All along the road, people were being entertained by fire breathers, magicians, dancers, acrobats and singers – all the kinds of people who suddenly arrive whenever a festival takes place. The air was full of smells and sounds coming from traders who were selling food, drinks and gifts and shouting offers to the crowds.

The carriage stopped in the main city square where Gid had seen people playing board games the last time he came to the city. A large raised area had been constructed in the middle. The friends jumped off the carriage and made their way onto the platform and into seats that were waiting for them. Valletia, Rahmon, Rowley, Krast and many other tribal leaders were waiting for them.

The warriors who had travelled in the procession stood around the platform. The square was now packed with people waiting in expectant silence for someone to speak. For the first time, Krast stood in front of his people as their governor.

'Thank you all for coming out today, this first day of

freedom!' The crowd cheered. 'We are here, all of us, to thank our brave warriors.' More cheers. 'The fighting has ended; there are no longer any enemies; we are all once again Friends, Brothers, Sisters. All that went before today will never be forgotten. A tyrant once ruled this world, and we must never let it happen again. We must learn and move on. Legion is no more, and we owe it all to one who is younger, braver and wiser than any other here. Gid, we want to thank you. Please stand!'

Gid stood up and the crowds went crazy, cheering his name; they all wanted him to hear their own personal thanks.

'Gid, would you like to say something to the people?' asked Krast quietly.

'I'll give it a go, but I'm not sure what to say,' he whispered back. He cleared his throat and the crowd quietened once more. 'Thank you, everyone. I don't really know what to say.'

'Say you'll marry me!' shouted a young girl from the crowd.

Gid went red, again. 'There is so much I could say, but not a lot that would make sense or that would be very interesting. What I would like to say, though, is this: I have found that, no matter how hard things can seem, no matter how impossible a task may be, even if you don't believe in yourself, there will always be people there for you, great friends who will stand by you when you think that everything is too much. If you know of people who have no one to turn to, be there for them. I could not have beaten Legion on my own, mighty warrior or not. These people here with me and, more importantly, every brave warrior here among you, beat Legion. They won back your freedom, not me. I might have finished him off, but on my own I would not have had the chance; on my own I'm just an 11-year-old kid.

'Legion thought that one person could rule this world, and that's why he is dead. It was never his world, and it is not mine now. This world belongs to every one of you, and though this may all sound corny, I think that together you are all going to

226

make it a better place.'

Once again the crowd cheered wildly.

'Well done, Gid,' said Valletia, coming up to him. 'That was the speech of a true hero.'

The festivities carried on throughout the day, and would continue for several more. Gid went back to Arborinium; the day had flown by in a glorious dream and the city was now having its own party outside, beneath the stars. Snorback was dancing with a group of Arbitan girls; Rowley and Rahmon were sat staring at each other, laughing like children at one another's jokes; Romallia and Ash were dancing, spinning around in their own world. Valletia and Grimbarr were deep in conversation.

'Gid, come over here; there's someone who would like to meet you,' said Snorback with a wry smile.

Rather nervously, Gid walked over and joined his hairy friend. A bright, young Arbitan girl grabbed him by the hand and started dancing. 'I'm not very good at dancing,' he mumbled.

'Nonsense! I watch you when you fly – you are very graceful. Not that I always watch you or anything...' the girl blushed.

'What's your name?' asked Gid.

'I am called Lostallia, but my friends call me Tallia.'

Gid said the name over and over in his head and stared at her. She had long, dark purple hair and bright green eyes that seemed to sparkle. He thought it might have been because everything in this world had been so tense and dangerous until now. Or maybe it was because of the beautiful stars and moonlight. Whatever the reason, one thing was for sure – he had instantly fallen in love. Tallia and Gid danced for hours. He did not want the night to end. Eventually, though, it had to, and it was Tallia's mother who did it.

'Come on now, Tallia, put the boy down. Pleased to meet

you, Gid, by the way. You can say a quick goodbye and then it's time to call it a night.'

Tallia leaned forward and kissed him on the cheek. 'Goodnight!' she said, and ran away, looking back over her shoulder.

'Goodnight…' stammered Gid as he stood watching her go, with a huge grin on his face.

'I reckon I'm going to call it a night too, my little friend!' Snorback gave Gid a rib-crushing hug. 'See you in the morning.'

'Goodnight, Snorback,' choked the young hero.

One by one, people started to leave the party. Romallia and Ash walked towards Gid. 'You off to bed, lover boy?' asked Ash cheekily.

'Shut up! And yes, I am kind of sleepy. Where are the others?'

'They're all sat at a table, chatting. Goodnight, Gid. It's been a great evening – one to remember,' said Romallia, kissing him on the head.

'Two kisses in one night – it has been a good evening!' thought Gid as he walked over to the table.

'Goodnight everyone,' he said.

Rahmon took Gid by the hand. 'Gid, I am so glad to have been able to fight for you. I see you as a brother, a true brother; I hope you don't mind – I miss my real one, you know.'

'I know you do, and I do too. I would be proud to be your brother. I really am honoured!'

Gecks crawled onto Gid's shoulder. 'You're an amazing person, Gid. I'm happy to be your friend. We make a good team, don't we?'

'The best!'

Valletia seemed to appear from nowhere. 'I am going to bed now myself. I have a busy day tomorrow. Do you mind if I walk back with you, Gid?'

'Please do,' replied Gid. 'Goodnight, Rowley. I know I

didn't get to meet you properly today but I'm sure I will soon.'

'I'm looking forward to it,' she said shyly.

'Night everyone!'

As they walked, Valletia and Gid chatted about the fight, the prophecy and the future, until he reached his room. 'Well, that's me. Goodnight, Valletia.'

'Goodnight, Gid. Pleasant dreams.'

Gid walked into his room, closed his door and lay down on the bed. He thought about Tallia and smiled, yawned, closed his eyes and drifted off.

A few hours later he awoke feeling hot and restless and in need of some fresh air. He fumbled for the door handle but could not find it in the dark so he opened his window, climbed outside and leaned forwards. It was at this point that he realised that he no longer had wings – he was no longer in Arborinium!

'Oh no!' he said, and fell from his bedroom window ledge. He landed with a bump on his slightly frosty front lawn.

'Ouch,' he wheezed, winded. He did some initial checks: he moved his right leg – it seemed fine. His left leg... 'AAArgh,' he yelled – it was definitely not fine. Neither was his right arm, two of his ribs or his head.

Behind him he heard a door open. 'Gid, what happened? Are you ok? Why are you out here? Did you sleepwalk?'

'Not exactly, Mum,' he grimaced.

'You're hurt. Oh my, don't panic. I'll call an ambulance,' his mum said, trying to stay calm.

'Thank you,' he replied quietly as he lay face down on the ground. For a second everything went white, and then he passed out.

Chapter 36: Home

A figure concealed in a long, dark, woollen cloak walked along the hospital corridor, checking the ward numbers. He walked to where Gid was lying.

Gid was watching television. He glimpsed the hooded, cloaked figure walking towards his bed and turned in fear, only to see it pull back its hood to reveal an old friend. 'Ash, what are you doing here?'

Ash gave a signal for Gid to be quiet. 'Gid, I may have been followed. Some of Legion's faithful have found a way to your world. They want revenge; they want you dead.'

'What can I do? I'm only a normal kid now,' Gid said with trepidation.

Ash was about to speak when he silently dropped to the floor; behind him stood a tall, grey-skinned figure, cleaning its sword.

Gid gasped and sat up. He opened his eyes. 'Son, are you ok? Did you have a bad dream?'

'You could say that!' Gid's arm and leg were in plaster and his head had been stitched above his left eye.

'The doctors want to keep you in for observation. I have to go now, but I've got you a TV. You should be ok, but the doctors are going to call me if anything happens. See you later, my little soldier.' His mum stroked his hair and left the hospital to go to work.

Gid flicked through the television stations and stopped as an item on the news caught his attention. 'In the early hours of this morning, the American coma patient, Brett Johnson, made a brief and remarkable recovery. He awoke and started shouting out something that sounded either like 'Gid' or 'God'. Shortly after, the teenager ran to a window and dived out. One of the nurses on duty stated that he had dived out as f he thought he could fly, our own Mary Jacks reports.'

Gid was stunned and relieved at the same time; he had not killed Legion, after all. Snorback was right. But Legion, or Brett Johnson, was still dead, and he seemed to have been seeking revenge.

Gid carefully crawled out of bed and limped his way to a window. He looked out over a car park; it was midday and people were busy either arriving or leaving. A nurse was putting on a coat and walking towards a car. A man was hobbling on crutches towards a taxi. Some people were smoking cigarettes near the entrance, and a figure in a dark grey cloak was standing near a lamp post staring towards his window...

Gid quickly moved back against the wall. 'Surely I can't have been followed; it can only have been another dream. Please let me be imagining it,' he said, and slowly peered out of the window once more.

The nurse was driving away in her car, the man on crutches was climbing into the taxi, the smokers were still there, but there was no one near the lamp post.

Gid climbed back into bed, his hands shaking. 'I'm a bit on edge. Get a grip, lad,' he said to himself.

He figured that things would take some getting used to; he had to remember that flying was no longer an option. School was going to feel a bit dull for a while, but things would get back to normal eventually.

He was going to miss his friends, especially Snorback, and he was devastated that he would never again see the girl who had given him his first ever kiss, though he would get over it. He was happy to be home but he would always remember Arborinium. Gid lay on his bed and slowly drifted into a deep sleep. Finally it was all over.

Outside the hospital, a taxi driver was helping a man on crutches into a cab, one member of the group of smokers was stubbing a cigarette into an overflowing cigarette stub-troff, and a figure in a hooded grey cloak was walking through the hospital doors.